"The series is f[...]cleverly plotted, combining elements of hard-boiled true-grit crime with the best aspects of speculative fiction."—*Fiend* (Australia)

Crash Deluxe

"Forget Lara Croft or Aeon Flux—from Australia comes the most kick-ass heroine ever. Parrish Plessis is the postmodernist woman to end all cyborgs . . . Emma Peel cool and Uma Thurman capable. But she's Stephanie Plum funny and totally unpredictable. . . . [A] fitting finale to the Plessis trilogy; a darkly humorous, dizzyingly fast, and technologically dazzling series which had readers clamoring for each installment."
—Queensland Books

"*Crash Deluxe* will find a place with its fellows on my 'first-rate cyberpunk' shelf."   —SF Crowsnest

Code Noir

"Just another day in a city where magic and high technology meet . . . de Pierres continues to play fast and loose with post-cyberpunk sensibilities while fleshing out the slums and characters she set up in *Nylon Angel*."
—Jon Courtenay Grimwood, *The Guardian* (UK)

"Refreshingly unpredictable . . . *Code Noir* delivers fast-paced tension and futuristic cool by the bucket-load. . . . [A] high-tech, fancy-free world . . . the writing is vivacious."   —SF Crowsnest

continued . . .

"The pace is breakneck and there is never a dull moment. . . . A great read . . . and a fantastic first novel. Can't wait for *Code Noir*."   —*Scene Magazine*

"Violently independent, game for a go. As tough as the titanium in her boots, but with a rich vein of compassion for the underdog and the oppressed, [Parrish is] the Aussie action hero."
    —*The Courier-Mail* (Queensland, Australia)

"Parrish is one of the most vivid characters science fiction has produced in years: brazen, intense, and unstoppable."   —Warpcore SF

"[An] action-packed and brutal style."   —*Time Out*

"A well-written cliff-hanger ending makes it abundantly clear there is going to be a second book in the series and if it is as good as the first there could be a bright future ahead of Marianne de Pierres."
    —SF Crowsnest

"Gang warfare in a world with clear lines of wealth and poverty but less clear lines of what is and isn't human demands a well defined, confidently drawn character to lead us through it. . . . In Parrish we get that. And like Lara Croft, she's damn sexy, too!"
    —*LadsMag*

Crash Deluxe

THE THIRD PARRISH PLESSIS NOVEL

Marianne de Pierres

A ROC BOOK

ROC

Published by New American Library, a division of
Penguin Group (USA) Inc., 375 Hudson Street,
New York, New York 10014, USA
Penguin Group (Canada), 90 Eglinton Avenue East, Suite 700, Toronto,
Ontario M4P 2Y3, Canada (a division of Pearson Penguin Canada Inc.)
Penguin Books Ltd., 80 Strand, London WC2R 0RL, England
Penguin Ireland, 25 St. Stephen's Green, Dublin 2,
Ireland (a division of Penguin Books Ltd.)
Penguin Group (Australia), 250 Camberwell Road, Camberwell, Victoria 3124,
Australia (a division of Pearson Australia Group Pty. Ltd.)
Penguin Books India Pvt. Ltd., 11 Community Centre, Panchsheel Park,
New Delhi - 110 017, India
Penguin Group (NZ), 67 Apollo Drive, Rosedale, North Shore 0745,
Auckland, New Zealand (a division of Pearson New Zealand Ltd.)
Penguin Books (South Africa) (Pty.) Ltd., 24 Sturdee Avenue,
Rosebank, Johannesburg 2196, South Africa

Penguin Books Ltd., Registered Offices:
80 Strand, London WC2R 0RL, England

Published by Roc, an imprint of New American Library, a division of Penguin
Group (USA) Inc. This is an authorized reprint of an edition published
by Orbit. For information address: Orbit; Time Warner Book Group UK;
Brettenham House; Lancaster Place; London WC2E 7EN

First Roc Printing, October 2007
10 9 8 7 6 5 4 3 2 1

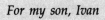

For my son, Ivan

Acknowledgments

I would like to complete this series by acknowledging Eidolon editors Jeremy Byrne and Jonathon Strahan. Jeremy gave Parrish her first outing as Loretta in issue 28 of Eidolon. He let her strut her stuff when no one else in the world would have dared.

The original Parrish's Patchers, Amy, Cj and Mouse, thanks for digging The Tert enough to create your own community.

Crash Deluxe was written in a period of considerable personal difficulty. I wish to thank our loving families who sustained us through it and some special friends who supported me as I wrote: Helen Smith, the RORettes (Maxine, Rowena, Margo, Trent and Tansy), Kate Eltham, Julie Walsh, Pam Haling, Debbie Phillips, Desiree Johnson, Kath Holliday, and Vicky Heiwari.

Many thanks also to Darren, my new editor—how impossibly lucky have I been—Ben Sharpe and now Darren Nash. Sheesh! Darren embraced Parrish's quirkiness without batting an eyelid and she's better for it.

Lastly, to Tara Wynne, my lovely agent, who never fails to look out for me.

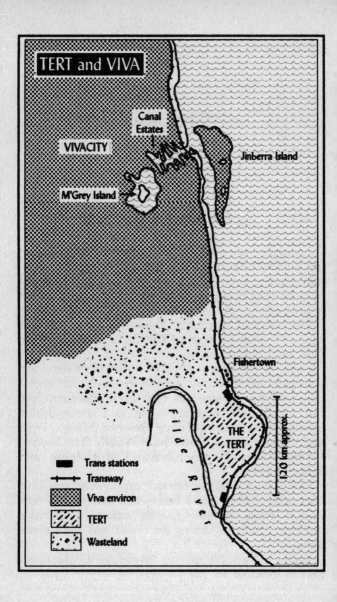

TERT and VIVA

VIVACITY

Canal Estates

M'Grey Island

Jinberra Island

Fishertown

THE TERT

Filder River

120 km approx.

■ Trans stations
┼ Transway
▨ Viva environ
▧ TERT
∴ Wasteland

Prologue

Networld Live Feed 5 a.m.

*N*etworlders, a truly shocking scenario is unfolding in front of us this morning as we get set to enjoy the opening of the Pan-Sat games.

The stolen copter on the right of your screen is being used in an attempt by notorious gang lord Parrish Plessis to abduct one of our principal media personalities.

As we leave the Viva environs and head southward, you can see that Plessis is being tracked by a welter of heavily armed Militia.

Implicated in the murder of Razz Retribution, Plessis is thought to be the instigator of the recent war in the Tertiary Sector and is currently the Southern Hem's most wanted criminal.

Her brazen approach seems to be the key to why she has eluded arrest previously, but there is no way out for the intriguing character this time.

Rumors and questions about this woman abound. Did she kill infamous gangster Jamon Mondo? Does she have unnatural healing powers? Is she the reincarnation of a voodoo deity? Is she trying to build a superrace?

Sounds absurd, viewers, I know, but these are just some of the outrageous myths surrounding Parrish Plessis.

More reliable sources say that she was born in the sub-urbs of the Outer Gyro and developed sociopathic tenden-cies in her teens. Unable to fit into society, she opted for life in the slum town known to the locals as "The Tert"— which according to the Militia is where she is heading now.

Stay tuned as we go to a short break. . . .

. . . Viewers, as we return to our coverage of this unprece-dented abduction, an astounding phenomenon is taking place. Hundreds of ultralights have taken to the sky above the Tertiary Sector.

Not only that, but Plessis appears to have made her move. Her copter is hovering low above the very heart of the slum city, a place thought to be uninhabited. As I speak, she is forcing her captive to sit out at the very edge of the copter's cabin.

What will this woman do next?

Word is coming through. Yes . . . yes . . . we have visual confirmation. Oh, my goodness. Plessis's captive appears to be none other than—

transmission interrupted transmission interrupted transmission interrupted trans—

Chapter One

I went looking and found my best friend, Teece, in Hein's bar, smashing up an invisible opponent by using a set of vreal gloves. My other best friend, Ibis, was lounging in a tactile nearby, drunk. The two had gotten real friendly since working together on restoring the barracks.

I tore the cheap game-set off Teece's face without warning.

His pupils dilated at the reality shift. When he saw who it was he slipped the gloves off as well and tucked his hands under his armpits in a stubborn, defensive gesture.

"What?"

"I need to crack the Viva prison data banks. Can you get me in there?"

His jaw set hard. "There's a few places even you can't go, Parrish. That's one of 'em."

"You won't help me?"

He shook his head. "Nope."

Pretending to be annoyed, I stamped over to Ibis and grabbed him by his collarless shirt. "Get up. We're going to call Gigi. You'll have to be my rider."

Gigi, the Tert's banker, had the best net-vreal in The Tert. I'd have to deal to get use of it. But when didn't I have to deal?

Ibis jerked like a drunk puppet. "Your what?"

"My rider—my backup. Some places you don't net-vreal without a partner," I explained.

Ibis rolled his eyes and looked helplessly at Teece, but Teece wasn't buying in.

"Just go along with me," I urged in Ibis's ear. "Please."

I didn't say "please" much.

The amazement factor got him out of Hein's and back to my place without an argument.

My place was a large bed, brown ceiling marks, a couch, no kitchen, a den and too many bad memories. Luxury for The Tert—but then, this had been Jamon Mondo's pad. I'd claimed salvage on it when Mondo took a Cabal spear in the back.

The living room was big enough to host a dinner party. Now there's a joke. The Parrish Plessis dinner party—half a dozen meat shawarmas, beers and sugar dough, sitting on the floor in between the bloodstains and making polite dinner convo:

"So who tried to nail your arse today, Parrish?"

"Three 'goboys, one shape-changer and a canrat up a gum tree."

I sat Ibis on the couch and made him a triple-strength mockoff.

After he drank it, his wits sharpened.

"What are you up to, Parrish? I retail retro fashion and dabble in interior decorating, darling. *I'm no freaking back-room cracker.*" The last he said in a perfect imitation of my drawl.

"I know that. You know that. Teece knows that."

I was banking on Teece's protective instinct. Net-vreal for someone as uninitiated as Ibis was likely to be lethal.

"Ah-hah," he said, sipping. "To use your turn of phrase, dear, clear as mud."

"Remember those kids I bought back from Dis? The ones who look more animal than human? A guy called Ike Del Morte did that to them."

Ibis nodded. "I've heard his name around."

My mind skidded back a week or so. The Cabal Coomera—the truly scaries—had lured me into pursuing a dangerous shaman named Leesa Tulu. The chase had taken me to a place called Mo-Vay in the inner Tert, where I'd discovered Del Morte busy manufacturing a whole generation of twisted punters and then infecting them with the Eskaalim parasite.

I knew all about the Eskaalim: I was infected with it myself and pretty soon it would turn me into a monster as well.

If it hadn't already. Killing was sure getting easier.

I left Mo-Vay with one clue as to who was behind this lab-designed slavery. It had been given to me by a secret ally in the media in the form of Ike Del Morte's eyelids—shriveled, dried and stamped with a prison brand.

Someone powerful had sprung him from a Viva quod to do his weird work.

"He was a lunatic—a *smart* lunatic. But someone gave him the cred, the backup to do terrible things. I want that person, Ibis."

He shivered—maybe from the look on my face.

"Pity them," he whispered.

"I don't," I said.

I got up, kicked the couch and paced a bit. Where was Teece? Maybe my ploy hadn't worked. Maybe I *would* have to do this by myself.

"Merry, get me Gigi," I said at last.

My fashion-conscious p-diary pretended to count money and eat it until Gigi answered—her little joke.

"Plessis?" The fat banker's face filled Merry's projection.

"I want to use your net-vreal."

Gigi gave a slow smile. "Just like that? No 'please'?"

"How much?" I didn't have time for shit.

The femme rubbed her lips together. "Shares."

My eyes bulged. "In what, for chrissakes?"

"Plessis Ventures."

"There is no such thing."

"Haven't you been watching your accounts?"

I shrugged, embarrassed. Teece had been looking after that. "Been kinda busy."

"Remarkably, Parrish Plessis, you've engendered a confidence climate. All your debtors are paying up because they think they should keep faith with you. Some small holders have even been asking to put their cred into your funds. Seems they think it might be safer with you than with me." She sniffed. "You want to use my vreal, you give me five percent of your profits."

Sweet—a jealous banker.

"FIVE PERCENT?" Teece's bellow at my elbow made me jump. He planted his head between my face and the holo. "That's loony even for you, Gee."

I shoved him back out of the way. "One percent but I get access to it any time I want. And we review the deal in three months."

"Done," Gigi said.

"We'll be straight over." I snuffed the link.

Teece grabbed my arm. "What are you thinking?"

"What are you doing here?"

He scowled in a way that made me proud. "You want to get yourself killed in there—fine. But I won't let you do that to Ibis."

I shrugged as though the idea had never occurred to me, my mind skating to the next thing. "We can quit the agreement with Gigi later."

"What are you looking for?"

"The terms of Ike Del Morte's sentence."

He clenched his jaw but stayed silent.

I was already on my way out the door. If I didn't get out of The Tert soon I'd end up in a face-off with someone. Everyone wanted a piece of me for one reason or another, and I had more urgent things to do than play Parrish, War Queen of the Urban Dump.

Gigi was waiting for us behind more security than Raul Minoj, my favorite armament dealer, could muster. She also had worse body odor.

"Teece will sort out the details with you later," I said.

"No details," Gigi laughed. "Cred comes in, I take my slice."

The pair glowered at each other. Entrepreneur and banker. A tradition.

"Save the bone-tugging, you two. I'm kinda in a rush, Gigi."

She nodded toward a corner of the room that was half curtained off. "Don't sweat up my gloves."

Two body-sized sheaths hung in there, looking like humans with the flesh sucked out of them. Neither of them had resuscitators or bio-monitors.

"No safety," Teece whispered. "If you lose me in there, you'll be relying on Gigi to unplug you in time. You still want to do it?"

I threw Gigi a look. She was gorging on a carton of warm dough and licking the sugar off her fingers.

"Gee, you better come get me out of this if I get into trouble. Or I'll be haunting you."

"Sure," she burped.

I wasn't keen on the quality of her reassuring smile.

"Let's get on with it," I said.

* * *

The Gigi-stench of the first glove was so bad that I handed it over to Teece.

"Too big for me," I lied.

He frowned and swallowed hard a couple of times before he stripped off and got into it.

I followed his lead with the other, ignoring his stare. It smelled better than the first one but stuck to my skin in patches like a cheap Band-Aid.

"Should I turn down my olfaugs?"

Teece shook his head. "Gigi's set is visual with only some basic auditory. Two-Gen vreal."

He didn't waste time on an orientation, plunging us straight into full immersion before I had a chance to blink—his revenge for my bossy antics. I hadn't done proper vreal since net-school, and that had been to all the tourist spots, so the plunge sent my brain shrieking at the sensory rush.

I vomited into the mask and heard it drain down the spit-sucker.

So much for giving Teece the stinking glove.

He maneuvered us to the top of the launch pad queue.

I stared into the vastness. My net-school's visual representation had been a rain forest—intertwined organics and nutrient-seeking roots. In between, among the roots, was the debris. A system that simultaneously lived and died. Replicated and ruined.

Gigi's metaphors fitted more with the cityscape of the original virtuals. Hi-ways and caches of dwellings. Streets and business fronts.

I caught the reflection of the avatar Teece'd rented me—a Viking woman with oversized helmet horns.

Funny.

His was an enduro bike that pinged like a hammer on a nail. I climbed aboard him and held on.

We dropped straight into a traffic stream, my horns tangling with other avatars as I craned to stare at the passing sights. A tenet appeared from nowhere and screamed warnings at me for corrupting other travelers' boundaries, forcing me to keep my horns still and my eyes on the road.

"Lose these frigging tusks, will you?" I muttered.

I got a snort of exhaust noise and a burst of neck-snapping speed for my trouble.

The ride through the Hi-ways was slick and blurred but missing the thrill of wind tear.

When we finally took an exit, it felt as if the world narrowed and the sky got low. I told myself it was just a ploy to keep wanderers out of certain environs. Even so, I felt claustrophobia in me.

Relax, Teece thought-instructed.

I glanced behind and noticed that he'd constructed a giant muffler to quiet himself/the Gerda.

We slowed and nosed quietly in and out of side streets, winding our way toward a set of huge buildings near the docks. I saw feral animals on the streets that bore no resemblance to anything familiar. Plain people avatars—some in full-color jackets, others in just the cheap outlines of bodies, some deliberately wafting about in spirit form. Gambling. Fighting. Buying, selling, cruising. It was the thing I hated most about net-vreal. Human imagination. There was no accounting for their weirdness and opportunism.

Prison's the gray one. The blue one is Militia data-corps, Teece thought-said.

I stared at the imposing shininess of the Militia façades, each with their coat of arms. *Why are there three of them?*

Dunno. I've often wondered about tha—

As if Teece had tripped an alarm, gunfire started up on both sides of the street.

He accelerated, weaving between bursts. I hunched low on the seat—the Gerda's faring molding over me for protection. I heard the projectiles glancing off it.

What are you doing?

I've got my own virus defense.

How long can you keep it up?

Teece didn't answer, swerving straight into the side of a small building. I braced against the crash but it didn't come. Instead a narrow passage opened up, closing again behind us as we rode. It brought us out into the last street before the docks.

Drain hole, he told me before I could ask.

No gunfire now.

I sat up.

The sudden quiet stung my mind; the tang of salt stung my nose.

I shouldn't be able . . . T-Teece? My teeth chattered. *I can s-smell . . . salt. I got a b-bad feeling.*

He pressed stubbornly on along the street, ignoring me. The prison building grew, blotting out the skyline. A monstrous, shimmering wall that I knew contained the information I wanted.

So close and yet . . . so much freaking security.

A faint thrum was the only warning we got. Then it came for us.

An olfactory firewall reeking of sulfur. The stench liquefied the Gerda underneath me.

I held my breath . . .

And woke up with Gigi giving me mouth-to-mouth. The taste of her foul breath and the feel of her lips on mine panicked me more than the realization that I'd flatlined.

I knocked her on her arse and struggled out of the glove, sucking air like an asthmatic.

Teece was still gloved and twitching.

"Is he OK?" I shouted, spitting Gigi taste and sour vomit away.

Gigi hauled herself off the floor and rubbed her arse sulkily. "He knows what he's doing. They came after you anyway."

I stared at her suspiciously. "How do you know that?"

She tapped a polymer-capped stent behind her ear. "Gigi don't need that primitive shit."

I looked at the fat banker with new respect. Not many people could handle a full-time net-vreal feed *and* realtime. No wonder she spoke slow.

I was also mad at her. She'd given us her crappiest vreal tackle. She could have hosted us in something much smoother.

Despite her reassurances I dressed myself and hovered over Teece until he dropped out.

I helped him strip himself out of the glove. His skin was slick with sweat. He dashed tears from his eyes.

"I lost you. I thought you'd—"

I stepped back, angry and relieved, not wanting to hear what he thought. Not wanting Gigi to hear. I handed Teece his clothes.

"Let's get out of here."

Chapter Two

"I thought you said it was just visual. Traditional. No surprises," I yelled at Teece. "You could have gotten us killed for nothing."

He prowled around my living room. Ibis had wisely hightailed it back to the bar, leaving us alone to have it out. "I didn't know. Gigi must have bridged her old set to a Three-Gen. She just didn't think to tell us."

"Gigi never stops thinking," I retorted.

"I guess that means you don't want to hear what I found?" he said.

I stopped dead. "You got in?"

"Some of the way." He nodded. "I didn't think you'd want me to mention it in front of Gigi."

"Mention what?"

"I saw the terms of Del Morte's sentence. He was serving life for murdering and dissecting a bunch of cadet Prier pilots. Seems he had a thing for their bio-interfaces. His term was bought out."

"Who?" I held my breath.

"I couldn't access that." Teece hesitated, as if there was something he didn't want to tell me.

I crossed my arms and waited.

"There is a record of it, though. I followed the signature as far as I could. The name you want is kept on an impartial."

"Where?"

"Jinberra Island Detention."

Jinberra. My heart plunged. Jinberra wasn't just quod—it was another dimension in prisons. "Cool."

He ceased prowling and stared suspiciously at me. "*You* can't crack in there."

"No," I agreed. "But there'll be someone who can. I just have to find them."

I expected Teece to argue. To tell me it was impossible. When he didn't, I knew he had someone in mind.

I grabbed him. "Teece, you must help me if you can," I said fiercely.

He stiffened.

He was right to be careful of me. I'd come back from Mo-Vay with more preoccupations than scars— only to develop a bad case of sour grapes over his new love life.

I forced myself to back off and reached out an appeasing hand to him instead. "*Please . . .* help me."

He took my fingers hesitantly. Then he squeezed them together, hard.

A Teece-size bear hug would have been nice, but I settled for a crushing handshake.

I smiled.

He smiled.

Things were better again. Not the same—but better.

"I need that name, Teece. Whoever paid to have Ike freed also paid him to infect the whole of The Tert with the parasite and form those . . . those . . . creatures. If the canal hadn't been saturated with copper sulfate we'd be overrun by freak knows what right now. As it is, some of them may be loose on this side already."

Teece groaned.

"What?"

"I owe you an apology, Parrish."

I dropped my fists, surprised. "You . . . me?"

"When you came back from there, I thought you were going to run out on me . . . on us. I should have known you better than that," he said.

I sighed. "You *do* know me, Teece. The truth is . . . I *was* going to. But not for the reasons you thought."

I hesitated. I hadn't told him this—should I now? The chances of coming back from my next jaunt rated in the minus minuses. Somehow it was important that he knew everything if I was going to wind up dead or in quod for life.

His stare drilled me. Faded blue eyes—slightly aggrieved, always concerned.

I sank down onto the couch.

"In Mo-Vay . . . I lost consciousness at the end of it all—when I was with Tulu. I woke up and Loyl was waiting for me. He told me I'd changed—sh-shape-changed. And I believed him, because . . . well . . . I tried to. I stopped fighting the parasite and let it take over."

Teece's expression got incredulous and I rushed on, justifying myself.

"It was all I had left to fight with, Teece. I was dying and I wanted to buy the Cabal some time so they could defeat Ike. I thought that if the parasite took me over totally, I'd have the strength to hang on a bit longer."

"And . . ."

"Loyl said I'd gone all scaly monster and then healed. I believed him. But I wanted to come back and see you, put things in order before I went away. And I *had* to go away, Teece. No one else was going to put a bullet in me but me . . . you understand?"

He nodded slowly, processing all the nuances and implications of my confession.

"But now you believe that you didn't shape-change?"

I nodded slowly. "I've got an . . . ally. A Prier pilot. She's contacted me a couple of times. The last time was to say that she had taken Wombebe, one of the Mo-Vay ferals."

"You call someone like that an ally?"

"She wants me to stop whoever is playing God with us. She said she scoped me unconscious back there in Mo-Vay. Swears I didn't change, and that Loyl is lying."

"You believe her?"

"Yes." I tried to sound confident.

"And you expect me to believe you, regardless of how crazy it sounds, don't you?"

I shrugged. "I just want you to trust me, Teece, the way I trust you."

He took a step over to the bed and grabbed my wrist, pulling me into his arms. His hug was better than I remembered. It forged our bones together.

"You never tell me the whole story when you should," Teece muttered into my ear.

"Yeah, probably."

He gave me a resigned look and stepped away. "Meet me at Hein's tonight. I should have something that will help you."

"Thanks." I gave him my best smile.

He gave *me* the once-over. "Meantime, if you want to go anywhere without ending up in prison, you'll need to do something about the way you look."

Teece was being practical, so I stopped short of punching him.

Chapter Three

"Larry. Tequila."

Every person on a bar stool turned to look at me.

When I'd gotten over the insult, I'd seen the sense in Teece's suggestion and had used the time to work up a different image. In my normal clobber I'd be arrested in double-quick time for looking suspicious.

So here I stood: waist-long, bloodred tresses, hip-smooth leather mini (long enough to hide the knife sheaths strapped to my thighs), high heels and a sleeved corset thingy to hide my armored-up leather crop.

Teece swiveled right off his stool to gape.

"Shut it," I growled before he could say anything.

He didn't. His tongue was too busy sweeping wetly across the floor. In fact, the whole of Hein's bar assumed a kind of bewildered silence.

For a tough-arsed drinking establishment that boasted holocaust decor and a sticky excess of back-room smut, it was more than vaguely unsettling. Even the phlegmatic proprietor, Larry Hein, retired behind his cred-comm partition to sniff something calming.

Maybe this hadn't been such a great idea—trying out a new look on the locals. Parrish Plessis, warlord and all-round-tough femme, had transformed into a legs-and-hair princess . . . and the sky *had* fallen.

One sliver of grrl consolation. Tingle Honeybee— Teece's girl—looked like she might faint.

I stared along the bar at Ibis. He was back again, drinking. Shot glasses littered the space between us. He propped his head up with his hands and looked me over in slack-mouthed awe. "Freaking miracles."

My face flamed. If I'd been an average sort I'd have wished for the ground to open up and swallow me—instead, I wished them all a new kind of plague.

I took a seat next to Ibis, annoyed that I had to fiddle around and tuck the skirt underneath my thighs.

"You know, the pishtol gives you away a bit," he slurred.

I looked down at my holster—only one instead of two: my concession to the whole grrlie thing.

"Trial run," I croaked in my own defense. "Larry, where's my drink?"

I wet my throat and tried to ignore the prickle of confusion around me.

Teece was the worst. His stare didn't prickle—it burned. But he didn't come to me with news, despite his promise. Instead, he stamped over to a Res-booth and began smashing a set of gloves around, leaving Honey by herself at the bar.

I sighed and turned back to Ibis. *Now what?*

"So you got your way with Teece," said Ibis.

"I usually do." I noticed his mottled skin. "How are *you?*"

Ibis had arrived in The Tert enthusiastic and cheeky. Now he was drained, discontent and more than a lot wasted. I felt pretty guilty about that. He was my mate and I hadn't looked after him too well.

He cleared his throat and puffed his cheeks in a

way that told me he had something to get off his
chest. I swallowed my tequila while he worked up
to it.

"I knew it would be rough here, Parrish. I knew I
wouldn't like the filth and the poverty. But I was
naive enough to think it wouldn't touch me. Well, it
has." He sighed. "People shouldn't have to live the
way they do in this place. And the trouble is, now I
can't go back and forget. The smell, the dirt, the
abuses—they won't go away."

I kept my expression neutral. I'd never heard Ibis
impassioned about anything before. That was usually
my corner of the ring. Where had my flirtatious, friv-
olous friend gone?

Alcohol had turned his mood maudlin and I
needed to shake him out of it. The Tert was all the
things he said and more, but you couldn't let it get
to you—bleed your heart.

"People make choices, Ibis. Most of them wouldn't
change things if they could. Face it—they're content
living on the limits."

"If you believe that, then why are you helping
the children?"

I thought about the ferals. "Kids are different. They
need to know they can change if they want."

"I think you're wrong. Not about the children, but
about the rest. I think they all want something better
than this."

"You're being romantic," I argued flatly.

"Better romantic than indifferent," Ibis retorted.

I shifted irritably on the tactile stool. It jigged a bit
and muttered a breathy complaint. I thumped on its
sensor pad.

"I'm not indifferent. I wish I was," I said.

Instead of any further argument he sighed in resig-
nation. "I know." He shrugged and downed another
shot. "You'll get killed this time, you know."

Ibis's warning, delivered so matter-of-factly, sent an involuntary tremor through my body.

Two large, silent tears squeezed from his eyes. Pity for me? Or for himself? I didn't get a chance to ask because he slumped forward onto the bar and fell into a noisy doze.

I made a cut-throat signal at Larry Hein. No more booze.

Larry nodded and gave me Ibis's beer.

I watched Larry smoothing his lacy apron. Underneath it he wore a latex jumpsuit—like he might have a hot date after closing. The idea of Larry even having a libido distracted me momentarily from my disappointment that Teece wasn't keeping his promise. Men were always yanking my chain.

Take Loyl-me-Daac. When did he ever tell me the truth? I so *wanted* him but I couldn't cop the personality disorder that came with the package. He and I were like an old-fashioned coin—two sides of the same creation. Permanently connected but from a different angle.

He wanted a better world for his chosen few. I wanted a better world for anyone that wanted a better world. Believe it or not, there's a big difference.

I hadn't seen him now for a week or so and I ached for it already.

Eyes on the road, Parrish.

I reminded myself that I hated Daac at the moment.

"M-Ms. P-Plessis. May I speak with you?"

Ms. Plessis? Teece's grrl, Honey, was sweet and feminine and polite. The sort of grrl that guys wanted to crush tenderly to their chest while they put their other hand up her skirt.

I was jealous about her and Teece, but I cogged it as well. I'd given Teece nothing but grief and aggravation. He ran my business, loved me too well despite my shortcomings. Now he'd found someone who could love him back and who might be alive tomorrow.

"It's Parrish. And make it quick." I fingered the pistol and plucked irritably at the bar mat with my other hand.

She bit her pretty pink lip and her eyes grew large and nervous.

Crap. I hated that.

"T-Teece said you were looking for a bio-hack. I m-might be able to help."

Ah. I glanced over at Teece. He had the vreal-gloves on but he wasn't punching anymore.

I understood what he'd just gifted me. I had to get inside Jinberra and he'd maybe found a way for me—at the risk of involving his new grrl.

My gaze met his with gratitude. His slid away in pain and guilt.

"Where does this bio-hack live?"

"Inner Gyro."

Viva. I'd figured Honey for a city grrl. For one thing she kept her fingernails clean.

She took a deep breath. "If I tell you about him . . . they mustn't find out . . . about me. . . ." She slipped her thumb in her mouth like a kid.

It reminded me of Mei Sheong, the crazy pink-haired Chino shaman who drove me nuts. The Loyl-me-Daac addict.

My curiosity stirred. "Who mustn't find out?"

Thumb out. A nervous swallow. "Delly. He o-owns a pleasure club called Luxoria on Brightbeach. His clients are top tier. Media, Royals, athletes."

"Why is he after you?"

"He doesn't like his employees vanishing. Teece said if I explained that, you'd be sure to look after me," she said.

My fingers spasmed so hard on my holster that I

nearly shot my high-heeled toes off. "Sure. What about the hack?"

"There's a guy who works for him called Merv. He's the bio-hack. A g-genius, in my opinion."

"How so?"

"He can crack anything." Honey lowered her voice. "Whatever you want to find out, he's the one."

"Lots of people say that," I said dryly.

"He cracked Militia to get me out of Viva."

My interest increased. Militia had as much ice as Prisons. "I'm impressed."

Her thumb went in and out several times, nervous again. "One thing you should know about him . . . he's got a thing. . . . He thinks shadows are taking over the world. He's fighting a war against them. Sees them when he's jacked in."

Brain-fry. Most bio-hacks get it. It wasn't the popular, glamorous pastime it had once been. The attrition rate was high—it messed with your brain's electrical impulses after a while. Most hacks still preferred to work off voice and touch pad and to avoid vreal. Slow but safe. I squashed a sigh. *At least it isn't parasitic aliens.*

She hurried on. "He used to work for the media. Then something happened. Brain-fry is my guess. Most of the best hacks end up with it. Delly found him DJing the screens at a meathouse and offered him a job. He's harmless, just weird. If you can convince him to help you . . ."

What are the chances of that? "Let's talk more," I said as sweetly as I could.

Turned out that Honey's ex-boss Delly was a prominent flesh operator in the Inner Gyro. She said he had some rules that she didn't go for, like insisting that all his people should mainline *rough.* So she got out.

According to her he was a grudge bearer, didn't

like his employees doing runners. He sent bounty after her. Teece had "disposed" of them.

Honey showed me her stent. It was an exxy number: fine polymer tubes flush with the surface of her skin in the pattern of a star. *Très chic.*

"The star shape was Merv's idea. It's a protective charm. He's big on superstition, says it's the twin of intuition. He says we don't give the psychic thing enough cred."

"So how do I get close to Merv?"

She tongued the bow of her top lip. "That's the hard thing. Delly keeps him close so nobody poaches him. Merv's job is to watch over the grrls and keep the hackers out of the club's system. He doesn't go out much. Doesn't like people."

Honey's face fell into an arrangement of pretty thought-creases. I got the feeling the process was hard for her. I'd give her about seventy percent lucidity; the rest was probably mulch.

Bitchy? Moi?

"Once a week Delly trolls the lobby of the Globe for new clients. It's the one regular time he leaves the club. Maybe, if you were there, somehow you could convince him to hire you. He'd rather buy the opposition than have any."

I followed the threads of her idea.

"How would I do that?"

Honey set her feet and crossed her arms as though she'd suddenly got comfortable. "The pleasure industry's different in Viva than it is here. It's illegal for anyone in the burbs to procure *Amoratos* or pay for physical pleasure. The law says they have to use NS if they don't have a partner. Delly said the laws changed when the media took over from politicians. Part of the safe-city campaigns. I think they just wanted to keep the whole thing exclusive."

I flashed on to Irene. There was no doubt where

my mum got her bliss, and it wasn't from my step-dad, Kevin.

"So this guy—Delly—his flesh business is only for the wealthy: media and bankers and such?" I asked.

"Yes. His workers are called *Amoratos* and are trained to give pleasure."

"And?" I could feel the impatience coming back.

"*Amoratos* have to be working for someone like Delly—otherwise they are breaking the law."

I digested that for a moment or two. I could see a crack in the door I wanted so desperately to open. "So if he thought I was an *Amorato*, he might want to hire me? That way I could get to meet your friend?"

Honey's eyes glazed with remembered fear. "Yes. Delly loves anyone exotic. He loves new blood. But he's smart too. If he found out you weren't who you said you were . . ."

"Too dangerous, Parrish." Ibis had woken up, and his eyes were red-ringed with sadness and alcohol immersion. "I've heard of him. He expects his people to do . . . unhealthy things."

I ignored him.

"You say his clientele is the media?"

Honey nodded. "He's obsessed with them. Especially the ones he hasn't been able to attract as clients."

I pinned her with a stare. "Like who?"

"James Monk is one," she whispered.

"Monk owns the sport media," Ibis piped up again. "His sports stream takes a huge chunk out of the ratings pie."

The Big Country was crazed over sports, so Monk had to be a big fish. I knew nothing about the media power divisions in Viva. Maybe it was time I did.

"Delly wants James Monk as a client, desperately. He's obsessed by him."

I tucked that info somewhere tight. "Tell me more about Merv the bio-hack and this place, the Luxoria. Who works there?"

"It's in a big-rise on Brightbeach called Cone Central. One of the best on Liberty Crescent." I heard the tiny sigh in Honey's voice, as if she missed it. "All the rises along Liberty are connected by the Glass Bridge."

The Glass Bridge—a spectacular glass esplanade running from the middle of one building to the next and on like a see-through belt. "I know it."

Who didn't? The exxiest piece of architectural whimsy in the Southern Hem.

"The Luxoria is on the one hundred forty-ninth floor, just one story below the bridge. Delly's people pretty much live between the club and the bridge." Her voice quivered. "He won't let them go anywhere else." She flushed up both sides of her neck. "Merv got me a job as a bar hostess. But I got to help him out as well. We met when I worked for Heads Up." The flush worsened.

Heads Up was a liveware company.

"What did you do there?"

She looked away from me, embarrassed. "I was a pig."

I understood the flush now and her often-vacant expression. Guinea pigs made a lot of cred and spent it mostly on their health.

"It was OK for a while, until Delly started pushing me to work with clients." Her voice changed, catching in her throat. "I got scared. Merv helped me get out."

Grudgingly, my opinion of Honey shifted. Coming to The Tert must have been a last resort.

"An *Amorato*." Ibis smirked. "You couldn't do that, Parrish. You'd likely garrote the first person who put their pinkies on you."

Teece loomed up over my shoulder. "Yeah, stupid idea. You'd never pull it off," he agreed.

I eyeballed them both. "Why not?"

"Face it, Parrish, you're an acquired taste," Teece said.

Ibis stifled an embarrassed laugh.

Even Honey looked away.

Perversity reared in me. "Is that right?"

Teece shuffled and stared fixedly at my drink, knowing that he'd said the wrong thing.

I whirled around to Larry. "Let the babes know I want to talk to them. And set me up an appointment with Dr. Drastic."

Larry looked as though he might faint, but disappeared behind his p-comm to contact Torley's resident plastics-butcher.

Satisfied that would shut them all up, I turned back to Teece and caught him wiping away a smile.

I froze. Had he just played me?

Did it matter if he had?

What did *I* want to do?

The short answer was that I wanted to find out the truths behind Dis so bad that nothing else mattered. Roo had died. Punters had died. My life had been reduced to the status of a rat in a cage.

I wanted my life back.

And to make it worse, thanks to the Eskaalim mucking about with my libido the thought of posing as an *Amorato* wasn't *entirely* repulsive. But I wasn't telling *anyone* that.

Let Teece think he'd had a win.

"Jeez, grrl, you get a sex change or something? Why you wearing a skirt?" a voice behind me inquired.

I cogged the voice instantly so I didn't draw my pistol.

Maybe I should have.

Instead I swiveled, beer in hand. Casual. "What do you want, Mei?" I didn't waste pleasantries on her— we had too much history.

She stood with hands on hips, breasts peeking out of a halter top. Tight pants and tottery high heels completed the look. Loyl Daac's loyal shaman and part-time . . . whatever.

I resisted the urge to bare my teeth and snap.

Due to a "spiritual" experience, Mei Sheong and I had wound up with some type of mind bond. Along with everything else that was weighing on me, I now needed an exorcism from that.

She eyed off my skirt and heels. "Miracles."

I couldn't help myself—her second taunt had me clenching my fingers just short of my piece.

A rifle bolt clicked across the other side of the room.

His Majesty, Loyl-me-Daac.

I heard it because Hein's had gotten dangerously quiet. The locals knew the deal with Loyl and me.

"Easy." Teece took one step and was breathing in my ear.

"Leave Mei alone, Parrish," ordered Loyl.

"Do as he says," Teece urged me from the side.

Surely by now these boys knew better than to *tell* me?

"Why?" I growled.

"There's something you don't know," Teece said.

Mei heard our whispered interchange, winked at me and twirled confidently on her heel. She sauntered over to the door and stood next to the man with the rifle, slipping her hand possessively onto his hip.

With extreme difficulty I unclenched my fist and moved my beer along the bar, trying to ignore how Daac's lean physique and unnaturally handsome face sent loudspeaker messages of desire to my brain. His hair had grown and I liked it. Dead straight, black water-silk falling in his eyes. This man had lied to me and used me and my heart still did cartwheels on demand. His demand.

I forced myself to speak coldly, icing down my

stupid, long-suffering admiration. "You should teach your pets some manners, Loyl," I said.

Daac lowered the rifle and frowned. "What are you wearing? You look ridiculous."

I felt like he'd punched me in the stomach.

I didn't *like* my new look either, but I didn't want him agreeing with me.

What *was* his problem?

And as for his tone . . . he seemed more annoyed with me than usual.

"What do you want?" I sighed.

"I brought you a present," he said, staring uncomfortably hard.

"Hand delivered?"

"It's that sort of thing."

He had me then.

I nodded to Larry. "Drink for the guests."

Loyl threw me a mocking smile and stalked to the bar. "How kind."

Hein's clientele relaxed collectively and the murmur of normal conversations reignited.

I soaked it in for a second. That sound was the sound of home.

Loyl leaned on the bar next to me and looked around.

"Tomas." He nodded at Teece on my other side. Teece and Loyl had a family connection but no good mutual sentiment.

"And . . . who's this?" His stare slid way too appreciatively over Honey tucked under Teece's arm.

She stared back, lips parted, awestruck by Mr. Brave-and-Beautiful. Not quite panting, but nearly.

I couldn't tell who was more annoyed by it—Mei, Teece or me.

Mei, I decided.

The Chino shaman wedged herself between Honey and Loyl with a fierce look on her face. I should have laughed.

We sucked down our drinks as if it might ease the tension.

Nup.

Loyl banged his down and reached into his pocket. He brought out a sheath and slid it along the bar to me.

I twisted the catch on the sheath and touched the handle. The dagger inside it came easily into my hand. Not any dagger—the Cabal Coomera dagger, polished iron ore with an astonishing ability to cut through anything. It had to be charmed or voodooed or something.

Not that I believe in all that spirit shit.

Loyl stepped around Mei, touched his fingers to Honey's golden hair and came to stand in front of me.

This close he was half a head taller. I hated having to look up to anyone so I stared at his mouth.

Bad move. Now I wanted to finger the curve of his lip.

What's wrong with me? He's just made a pass at Teece's grrl.

I held up the dagger. "This belongs to the Cabal. I returned it to them," I said.

"I know."

"What are you doing with it?"

"Let's say it's mine to give now. You can have it, Parrish. In return for something you have that belongs to me."

I risked a glance into his eyes. They were black with unfathomable thoughts and emotions. If I'd been a "Loyl" believer I would have said he cared. But these days I actively resisted standing in his devotional queue.

I knew what Daac wanted: Ike's wetware—a piece of grisly alloy memory that contained all the research notes of his genetic fooling.

What good will that do him now? He has no media

money backing his pet project. His cash cow, Razz Retribution, is dead.

"Things are moving ahead again. I have some potential investors." He answered my unasked question in the softest of whispers—more a touch than a spoken word.

I swallowed hard. What was worse? Someone deliberately infecting Tert citizens with the Eskaalim parasite or Daac hell-bent on genocide by default?

"You're *still* going to do this?" I hissed. "You saw what I saw. You know what your gene splicing has let loose. How can you ignore it? How can you just get on with your crazy business?"

Daac showed only a tiny flicker of irresolution, moving closer to me, turning his head at an angle so that no one could lip-read our conversation.

"I've taken steps to destroy the original infected trial group. That only leaves you." He leaned down, his breath fanning my cheek. Threatening and intimate at once. "Why haven't you come to me? You said you would."

I hesitated, appalled and relieved. He'd killed a bunch of people. People who would have become— might have already become—the thing I so dreaded. He was playing God again.

And yet . . . at least he'd had the guts to try to tidy up the mess he'd made.

There was only me left now.

And I didn't want his help.

I also didn't want to know that I'd seen through his lie that I had shape-changed.

Anger came quick and hard in me. My thoughts flew in all directions.

Daac had said the dagger was his *to give now.* That meant a change in Cabal Coomera politics. He was no longer an outsider. Somehow he was back in favor.

No mean feat. The Cabal had ostracized him be-

cause of his obsessions—seemed they weren't in line
with Cabal law and beliefs. No matter how crummy
and toxic the place where you lived was, there was
always someone in charge of the show. The Cabal
was at the top of the Tert pile. They ran the hits,
scared the crap out of most of us and had the monop-
oly on the last word. If Daac was back in favor, then
his power had increased exponentially.

I shifted my glance to Teece, who'd shouldered his
way in, blocking Mei and Honey out altogether.

What a sad lot we were—raw with suspicions and
jealousies. Flick a Zippo between us and we'd blow.

Teece's steady expression told me that Daac's news
was no surprise to him.

Why didn't he tell me?

Mei squeezed out from behind Teece and tugged
Daac's arm.

"Your pet needs a leash," I said.

Mei raised her long fingernails toward my face in
a scratching gesture. Daac pushed her hands down.

"My people are merely loyal to me," he replied.
"I honor that."

I honor that. Phew.

How was it possible that I had any feeling left for
this guy? He was so cunning. So *deluded*. And now
so powerful.

"The Cabal saw fit to give that dagger to me,"
I said.

"I've told you. Things have changed. They made
a mistake. Come to me with the wetware and I will
help you."

I pretended to consider his proposal. "Leave me
the dagger and I'll come today," I said.

Daac shook his head.

I persisted. "I want this to look like some sort of
trade, otherwise the rumors will be wild. I don't want
anyone to know what's happening. Give it to me and

I will give you my pistol. You have my word that I will come to you tonight."

He stared at me so hard that I thought the glue on my hair extensions would melt.

"Break your word this time, Parrish, and I will come after you."

I handed Daac my holster and pistol. In return I took the dagger and slipped it down into the front of my hip band. It set my skin tingling.

Too late, baby. I'll be gone.

I stepped away and spoke loud enough for the eavesdroppers. "Nice of you to think of me—now get out."

I watched him leave Hein's, my pulse racing for more than one reason. I didn't lie very often but when I did it was usually a big one.

I had to get out of Torley's before Daac realized that I'd gone. But there were a few things I had to check out first.

Like—Wombat help me—some sex toys.

Chapter Four

The babes on the strip were more than happy to impart their wistful knowledge about their rich sisters, the *Amoratos*. I got the feeling that if I came back from a stint in a Viva pleasure house, my reputation among them would be golden.

As it was I struggled back to my place laden with gear. Most of the clothes I discarded as cheap, nasty and used. Most of the *stuff* I kept because it *was* nasty. Some needed a talk-manual to operate it and some of it just looked like torture instruments. I appreciated their donations but didn't plan on using any of it for pleasure.

Merry 3# observed my unpacking with interest.

"Stop gawking and find me anything you can on the media's Information Owners."

She bounced three names back at me in no time: James Monk, Sera Bau and an ex-muso, Esky Laud.

"Transfer everything you found to screen."

I sat down and read through it.

James Monk was homegrown from the marriage of some grave Australian media pedigree—the remnants of the Packer-Murdoch dynasty, mainly. Sera Bau boasted mottled but powerful religious connections. And Esky Laud, from what I could see, was short on talent, long on ambition. There was a lot of public-domain knowledge about these three media heavyweights, but when I asked Merry 3# to find me a current whereabouts, the connection threw up errors.

"Useless pile of . . .," I said.

"Well, they're not exactly going to advertise," Teece sniped over my shoulder. "What did you expect?"

"Can't you ever knock?" I stood up and stalked past him to my bedroom.

"You gave me the key code." He followed me in. "What's crawling up your leg?"

"You knew about Loyl taking over the Cabal and you didn't tell me."

"It was just rumors."

"Rumors are more reliable than the truth round here," I countered, stuffing spare knickers into a borrowed case. I'd given up G-strings for something altogether more practical: skinny-band hipsters with a flared leg. They didn't interfere with you running or give you bite marks.

While I remembered, I slipped Ike's wetware into a pocket in my leather crop.

"I'm trying to keep you alive," Teece said.

"Then you're doing it wrong. I need to know and hear everything. *Everything*. Keeping things from me will get me killed."

He grabbed my arms and spun me around. "No, *you* will get you killed."

Instead of thumping him, like I wanted to, I softened.

Teece felt it. He wound his hands into the strands of my new red hair and kissed it. "Why can't I get you out of my head, Parrish?" he groaned. "It's like my every breath is tainted with you."

I leaned into his shoulder, trying to will away the rush of desire building at his touch.

"Teece . . . please . . . go . . . now," I panted.

He knew why, could feel the tremble spreading across me. Another moment and I'd be clawing him.

He grabbed my shoulders and forced me to look into his eyes. My desire was more than palpable—it was intoxicating.

I saw his control slip, felt his hand move to my waist, tug at my clothes.

"Get on top of me," I said.

Teece sprawled with me sideways onto the bed. In one movement he wrenched my skirt up around my waist. Maybe dresses *were* good for some things.

Heedless of regret or consequences—and of the knife sheaths strapped to my thighs—he was inside me with thrusts of fierce possession, bruising my body, riding me across the edge.

My moan turned into a scream of pleasure. Orgasms piled over each other, saturating my body with waves of release and pleasure.

Inside me, though, something far darker was drinking them in.

My response left Teece panting, trying to stay with me.

We tumbled on to the floor, a mess of limbs and bedsheets, to the sound of Merry 3# screeching a message.

"*Parrish. Message for Teeeeeece. It's Honeeeey.*"

I swear that p-diary was possessed.

Teece rolled away from me almost immediately. He stood, pulling his shirt down, zipping his pants guiltily. The look on his face wasn't exactly afterglow.

"You're an addiction, Parrish, and I want the cure," he said harshly. He stalked out of the room.

I lay on my back, momentarily sated, and contemplated the shape of the damp stains on the ceiling. I wasn't hurt and angry like Teece. I was probably going to die soon and everything I did felt good in comparison to that.

Why why why . . .

The parasite echoed its frustrations in my mind. It strained for release. If it found it—I might as well be dead.

"Paaarrr-iiisshh."

Merry 3# again. I hauled myself up and my skirt down, and went to see what the fuss was about. She shimmered in the corner next to the comm screen, dressed up in clothes identical to mine.

It wasn't meant to be flattery—more like ridicule.

"What do you want?"

She put a translucent finger to her head and stuck her tongue in her cheek as if trying to remember.

"Oh, yeah. Teece left the door open."

"And?" I spun on my heel.

"Bad company," she trilled.

I swung around. A stranger with an ugly expression was framed in the doorway. I sized him up in the time it took me to drop my hands to my thighs. Competitor. Probably here on his own whim, though maybe on a cheap contract.

He was my size: scarred fingers, boxer's stance, unarmed. This scud liked to do it with his hands.

That gave me an advantage despite my pistol—a replacement for the one I'd traded with Daac—being in my kitbag. I lifted my skirt and went for a knife.

His eyes widened in interest for a second.

Damn, no knickers.

It bought me a precious second of edge, though, and I threw. My aim was straight but the stranger was no longer there. A blur of movement to one side, and everything had changed. Including him.

The boxer had disappeared and a beast came at me instead—a shadowy thing hunched onto massive thighs.

I dived sideways and fell heavily against the comm. The beast leaped over me to the other side of the room. As I scrambled to my feet, he repeated the action, this time raking me with long-clawed feet. Blood spurted from a graze along my arm.

Why is it playing with me?

Merry 3# fizzed and spluttered over my shoulder, then came back screaming a grrlie war cry and flashing guns.

Cut the show, Merry. How about just shooting the bastard? "Get me some help," I shouted at her.

The beast edged in front of my bedroom, cutting off access to my guns. I eased more upright and calculated whether I could make the front door. As I willed the distance to shrink, it filled with shapes.

That's why it was playing. More of 'em. Growling and howling.

I felt at the waist of my skirt. The Cabal dagger was still there. Luckily Teece hadn't ruined his manhood on it. I launched myself at them without ceremony.

They fought each other to get through the doorway, giving me a chance to pick them off.

One, slit throat. Punctured adrenals.

Two, slit throat. Punctured adrenals.

Three, straight into the heart. Punctured adrenals.

Then the first one jumped me from behind. It tore my skirt right off and took a chunk out of my neck.

Blood in a fountain—high. My blood. The world hazed.

Jeez, I'm gonna die with no knickers on.

. . . The Angel swooped furiously past my eyes, its sword cauterizing-hot . . .

"Boss?"

I blinked. I hadn't passed out exactly, more like hovered between two realities. Link, Glida and some of the feral children I'd helped in the past crowded through the door. They liked to follow me around to keep an eye on things. I used to think it was cute. Right now I was just damn grateful. Calmly, they sprayed acid in the last shape-changer's face. His screaming banished the last of my hallucinations.

He toppled on to me. Which was bad . . . and good—at least I was covered.

The ferals tugged at the body, trying to move it.

. . . The Angel seared my neck wound until it closed . . .

"Leave the body," I grunted. "Get Teece."

. . . Stupid human. Why . . . why . . .

"I'm here, Parrish. Merry called me," he answered. I couldn't see him but at least he'd come, and he'd been running.

"Get . . . everyone . . . out. Don't let them touch the blood." My ribs felt broken with the shape-changer's weight. I concentrated on just getting air in until I heard the door clunk shut. Then the weight shifted.

Teece stared down at me. His expression shifted from shock to amusement to disappointment. The room looked like a serial killer's debut. Dead shape-changers lay around and I was seminaked and awash in blood.

"I left too early—as usual," he said, shaking his head sadly.

I tried to laugh but my chest burned and ached at the same time and it came out like a gurgle.

"Who were they?"

I craned my neck up. The beasts had reassumed their human shapes in death.

"Nobody," I lied. *Loyl was wrong. I'm not the only one left.* "That's the problem. Even *nobodies* want to kill me."

He nodded in resigned agreement. "I know how they feel."

"Teece," I whispered as I lay there. "I'm sorry about before."

"Yeah, I know. So am I."

"Paaarrrrr-ish."

Merry again. "What?" I growled.

"Message from Laaa-rrrry."

I was on up my knees in a second. "What?"

"Loyl Daac and a bunch of his men are looking for yoo-oou."

Teece moved to the door. "I'll stall him."

I nodded. "Buy me ten minutes and I'll be polite and sweet for the rest of my life."

We didn't smile. Or say good-bye.

I took a quick shower to wash away the shape-changers' blood.

My ribs felt like they were broken and the mark on my neck resembled an overcooked love bite. They wouldn't take long to fix, though. The only constructive thing the parasite had done for me—accelerated my healing.

But what had it done to the rest of The Tert? Loyl obviously hadn't dealt with the problem. The parasite must be spreading of its own accord. Those shape-changers were just the beginning. Not all of them would choose to transform into beasts, either. They could just as easily come after me in the shape of Teece or Ibis.

That thought got me worried enough to make one last, quick call—to Lize, a bounty hunter who owed me.

"Parrish Plessis?" She squinted into the comm like she hoped she was seeing things.

"Nice trip down the coast?" I asked. A casual reminder that I'd let her live when she'd tried to kidnap me—a contract put up by Leesa Tulu.

She looked embarrassed.

"I need you to watch someone's back," I said.

"Who?"

"Actually"—I grinned—"there are a few of them."

I gave her names and a short version of what she was watching out for.

She looked more scared than I liked. "I've heard stuff, but I didn't believe it. What you're telling me—shape-changers—it could be anyone any time."

"You got it."

"I can't promise nothing on a deal like that."

"Do your best. And I'll do my best to forget you ran a contract on me."

She frowned and sighed. "You gonna use this forever? I'm just a grrl trying to earn a living. Can't you dig that?"

"You keep these people safe while I'm outta town and I'm off your case for good. Deal?"

She held the back of her hand to the screen, Tert-style.

I returned the gesture and cut the line before she could ask, "How long?"

I ran my checklist one last time. I wouldn't be coming back to get something with Daac dogging me. Reluctantly I locked the Cabal dagger into my gun safe. Then I slipped Ike's wetware onto a chain alongside a good-luck charm Honey had told me would convince Merv that I was kosher.

Knickers, some dress-ups and the address for my net repository with my fake identity. On impulse I snapped the lid on Merry 3# and bundled her into my pocket as well. She wasn't gonna do me much good here and her scream was damn near a nuclear weapon.

I velcroed the strap on my borrowed luggage closed, slung it over my shoulder and spared a glance in the reflect.

New clothes.

New hair.

Same old grudges.

Time to move.

Chapter Five

I wiggled my toes to stop myself squirming as the laser sculpted my face, and I wondered about the ridge of scale along my cheekbone.

Dr. Yan Drastic, Plastique's best cosmetic man, told me flat out he couldn't do anything about it—it wouldn't come off. He didn't even know what it was. When he tested the edges my reaction became violent.

We compromised on a paint job. He said he'd make it look like a beauty spot.

After the face sculpt came an iris tint—all done in a quickie package. Money really could buy almost anything in Plastique.

As I waited for fake skin to set over my scars and the nanos to gobble my blemishes, it occurred to me how ironic it was to be having a physical makeover when all I had to do was stop fighting the parasite and I'd be able to shape-change.

When the face-over was finished, I bought a language infusion from Leong Shu's Smart Shit stall. He hit me up with it right then and there. When I asked him about the warranty, he threw in an extended dictionary to shut me up.

"How long?"

"Three months if you don't overuse it," he said in his perfectly snobby way.

Breaking my own rules, I flagged a Pet to get me to the Trans station. If Loyl Daac was out looking for me, I wasn't going to make it easy for him.

My mind ran another list as the Pet trundled me out to the Pomme de Tuyeau depot.

Get a job in the flesh industry.

Use it to get close to Merv.

Convince him to crack the Jinberra impartial.

Track down who was Ike Del Morte's sponsor.

Deal with them.

Find Wombebe.

Leave.

Easy.

I slipped Ike's wetware out and fingered the delicate webbing. Maybe along the way I would finally learn what the Eskaalim was.

Most of the time I believed it to be alien. But occasionally I got a reality shift, especially when people like Loyl Daac practiced their mind games on me.

I mean, if anyone had told me that they were infected with an alien parasite who lived off the epinephrine in their body, I'd have thought they were nuts.

On the other hand, I was the one living with hallucinations and a voice in my head. Although the hallucinations had lessened since Dis, the inner voice was there like breathing.

I wanted to believe it was a parasite, and that was the dangerous thing. There's no tragic glamour in being just stone-cold crazy.

Or paranoid.

And I was having a tankload of trouble trusting anyone.

Teece had fallen in love with someone else, and Daac . . . well, his treachery was worthy of Judas.

I sighed and returned to my mental list as the Pet ploughed a path past brawling Fishertown slummers.

Look up Bras.

Bras was a kid who'd helped me once and had wound up adopted by the banking royalty of Viva and head of her own company—the new face of prosthetics.

And Gwynn.

Gywnn was an amputee who lived in a drain on the Tert–Viva border. He'd been a onetime Pan-Sat athlete, a weightlifter who'd been reduced to minding an opening to the old sewer labyrinth. I'd promised him I'd get some turk called Trunk off his back, and I hadn't been keeping my promises as well as I'd have liked.

I decided to call the last two items on the list my before-someone-puts-a-bullet-in-me resolutions and went back to the top . . .

I was still recapping the order in my head when I caught the Trans up to Fishertown and dropped past Teece's bike biz.

Mama was minding shop for Teece while he was minding shop for me.

"You got a nerve, turning up here," the ex-sumo said with a glower.

I still owed Teece for the damage to the last bike I'd hired from them. Mama looked as if he wanted nothing more than to suffocate me between his huge thighs in settlement.

"So they tell me," I said. "If Loyl-me-Daac comes looking for me, Mama, you send him south, OK?"

Mama grimaced. At least, I think that's what it was. The fat folds on his face and neck made it hard to tell. "You got it coming, grrl," he added.

I had to be content with that.

I caught the Trans north, changing connections until it brought me to a huge, badly air-conditioned puff-ball dome full of comings and goings.

Trains, Aeros and Cruisers all docked at Viva's Eastern Interchange, which made the place busier than most of the supercity's checkpoints and the best point of entry to slip through cracks.

I paid for a luggage drone and walked to the Viva Visitors lattice to dodge the Militia with body scanners positioned along the ped-ways. When I got there it was bottlenecked, with everybody being physically searched.

"What's the go?" I asked the p-diary salesman lined up in front of me.

"Someone heard that Garter Thin and the VBs are coming to town to play at some big, rich party for the Pan-Sats. Seems like everyone on the east coast's come to Viva thinking they might catch a glimpse of 'em."

Thin and the VBs were a big deal in the Southern Hem. I'd heard their music. OK if you liked that old-style hard-grrl-rocker image. Personally I thought they looked like they wouldn't last a round with Mama.

Or me, come to think of it.

The doors to the celeb lounge seemed a helluva lot quieter than the cattle grid so I headed for the nearest san, slipped off my coat and reemerged in full borrowed *Amorato* regalia. Translucent high-collared shirt and floaty skirt, high heels and pliable snake bracelets up to my armpits. I'd left my leather crop in my case.

I passed through the weapons scanner without a problem and the doors popped open.

Four stoned-out bodies and one luggage-burdened Intimate occupied the perfume-aired, satin-decorated lounge. A couple of ornately uniformed Militia sat in a booth near the exit.

I threaded between the bodies, giving the Militia boys time to look at me.

And me time to look at the bodies.

I recognized Garter Thin, the singer from the VBs,

by the tattoos on her voice supplemental and her cosmetically adjusted lip sneer. The rest of them could have been any dregs from the street.

Maybe they were.

"Go round the other way," the singer rasped.

I ignored her, stabbing my heel into her leg as I stepped over it.

She swore and kicked out at me.

I caught her foot in both hands and twisted it, dumping her on the floor.

Without breaking stride I walked on to the booth. The soldiers hadn't seen my antics. Too busy watching porn.

I tapped on the booth to attract their attention and slid my fake visa under the glass.

"Jales Belliere. *Amorato,*" read the one with the vreal implants and a svelte muscle-conditioning suit.

The other, wearing the logo of a runner on his uniform and prettily plaited hair, opened the door and stepped out to make a more personal survey. He began to feel me over, his tongue busy in the corner of his lips as though he might like to taste me.

"Haven't had one of your . . . kind through in a while," he said.

I stood rigid in his grip and slapped his hand away when it reached my waist. If he was hoping that I might jump his bones for free, then he was way, way, waa-aay south of wrong.

"Hands off," I growled and stepped back.

Mr. Pretty Plaits looked affronted and confused.

The one with the suit stiffened at my reaction. I saw his head shake as he ran a more thorough check of my details through his oculars.

"Bend over," he ordered me through a monotone larynx.

Plaits smilingly held up a tissue probe.

Do something, Parrish, I told myself. Anything to

avoid breaking their heads and ending up arrested before I'd even begun my business in Viva.

I thought back quickly to the lecture that Ibis had given me about *Amoratos* before I left.

"They have class, Parrish. And they're comfortable with what they do. Sex is like breathing to them. They have all sorts of tricks and artistry that no one outside their profession understands. They've turned it into an art form. A reputation like that builds expectations. You can make a little work a lot for you, depending on how smart you are."

Amoratos certainly didn't bare their teeth and growl at potential customers. And now these two were suspicious of me.

Honey had assured me that *Amoratos* never got body searched on account of the booby traps they used to keep themselves safe—part of their immunity to the normal laws.

Plaits here hadn't read the same rule book.

I needed to distract them and allay their suspicions.

On instinct I sought out the Eskaalim presence and found it crouched inside me like a prisoner down a dark hole awaiting release.

What would happen, I wondered, if I carefully—soooo carefully—loosened my mental control?

The answer came in a surge of black, raging anger. I seized the sensation and tried to focus it all into one image.

Loyl Daac between my thighs.

Instantly the aggression turned to lust. Warmth seeped through my limbs, building into a torrent of urge. Heat blazed off my skin. I could almost smell the thick scent of sex rolling from me. My hips tilted forward of their own accord.

"What I mean is . . . my business is urgent. But . . ." I wet my dry lips. "Perhaps I could find time. . . ."

Crap. Who the hell is that talking? Another freaking stranger in my skin.

My body invaded my mind and tossed out its inhibitions. I found my hands sliding down to cup my breasts and rubbing my nipples erect under the gauze of my top. I shivered down the length of my body and leaned over to the svelte suit, breathing raggedly in his ear.

The effect was electric, as if the Eskaalim reached out of me and into him.

A small part of me watched and hated what I was doing. Parrish Plessis did *not* put out.

But as usual when I got into these situations, I was on a one-way road to no good place. And the alternative to flirtation was the probe that Plaits was waving around like a weapon.

Surely I could coquette a second or two longer.

Suit abandoned his search on me. Plaits stared openly at my fingers as if they were capable of great things.

". . . for a little extra pleasure," I finished.

One of my hands had left my breast and was finding its way up under my skirt.

Plaits's eyes glazed over.

Suit's thin, tek-dependent body jerked and shivered in his chair. Through the glass I saw dampness stain his crotch. He crossed his hands over his lap in humiliation and wheeled out of the booth toward the san.

Involuntary orgasm.

Well, at least it wasn't me for once.

I signaled my luggage drone and headed for the "Welcome to Viva" doors.

Plaits didn't even notice me go—his private fantasy had him with one hand down his own pants and a distant expression on his face.

As the bombproof doors sucked shut, I found myself in a long corridor.

Right about then my control wavered.

Lust claimed me. I wanted to grind my hips against something. I wanted to moan and climb onto a large—

Jeez, Parrish. Get a grip.

I scrambled on to a table and knocked the security cam from its mount. Then I kicked over a singing-frogs terrarium and punched a hole in a glass tapestry. I stamped and swore and punched until my hands bled and sweat ran and the desire, finally, waned.

When I'd finished the corridor looked like a demolition site and the security sirens had started to waah-waah.

A single punter cowered at one end, clutching a wad of complimentary map holo-shells like a shield.

"Who do you think you are?" he squeaked, outraged.

"Garter Thin, of course." I smiled, took a map from him and stalked past to the exit.

As soon as I was out of the building, I ran.

Outside, Viva shone. Literally. The latest craze for chrome gutters, downpipes and window trims, as well as for rainbow glass, created a radiance of its own. When I figured I'd put enough distance between Puffball Central and me, I stopped to marvel for the millionth time at the supercity's fragrant air, law-abiding cits and immaculate streets.

I'd grown up in the burbs, where the shine had tarnished some. Central Viva still awed me. I inhaled the cleanliness, moving automatically to find a public san, where I washed my hands and used the free medi-kit next to the sperm-kill dispenser to patch them. While I waited for them to stop bleeding, I gave myself a lecture.

Trashing the corridor—stupid.

I extracted some gloves (courtesy of the babes on

the strip—one of them had even given me a royal
blue cheongsam with slits to my armpits: a bit frayed
but not as tacky as the lamé one that she'd tried to
offload as well) from my suitcase and headed for an
Interchange café and a table where I could see the
door and study my free map.

My fake ident worked fine for the tea I ordered
and I began, at last, to settle. Ibis—with Honey's
input—had worked me up a fake performance history. The pair of them had argued over the details
of my profile as if I hadn't been there. Ibis wanted
me to have an imaginary customer base in Eurasia.

Honey thought that was posey and unrealistic.

Teece added that if I were introduced as a newbie
it would explain my rough edges and perverse
nature. . . .

Me—rough edges? Perverse? Must have had the
wrong grrl.

"More importantly, though," they had all ha-
rangued me, "don't attract unnecessary attention."

"*Amoratos* get it anyway—without trying," added
Honey.

"There's attention. And then there's *Attention*,"
warned Ibis. "No violence, Parrish. No headlines.
Your cover won't stand up to close scrutiny."

I guessed that included trashing corridors.

I slipped Merry 3# out of my bag and fixed her
processor to my wrist. Then I switched her settings.
The tiny, discreet 2D display scrolled through the
story they'd concocted.

*Jales Belliere was born in Katchemite, a descendant of
the famous Interior family. . . .*

I flicked on to the last section, vaguely suspicious
of the final touches that had been added while I was
collecting accoutrements from the babes.

Jales Belliere is a second-position Amorato *from the
Yo-Rakine school. Included in her specialized repertoire
are advanced autoerotica, transcendental-energy sex, pro-*

longed orgasm and related stamina, group work, and chic oral storytelling.

I got a choking sensation in my throat.

What was Ibis thinking? Wait till I get hold of him.

I put the p-diary back in my pocket and went over the map of the Inner Gyro until I found the location of the Hi-tel that Honey's ex-boss visited.

I sighed. What would her involvement mean in the end? You'd probably never do anything if you knew how it would affect other people's lives.

I savored the tea leaves in the bottom of my beaker and the precious minutes of calm. I was getting a whole lot better at enjoying the little things.

I got up and queued for a slot on the café's public net-access. When my turn came I requested recent images of James Monk and the infamous "Delly."

I took care to spread my searches so that none of the watchdog programs were triggered. The "Delly" search came up with nothing, which meant that I only had Honey's description to go on.

On James Monk, though, there was a foto smorgasbord of a heavily built older man and a public address to direct mail to. I mulled over Honey's comment that her ex-boss was obsessed by Monk.

It had to be the perfect bait.

I noted Monk's call address and began to plan my trap.

Chapter Six

The InterGlobe lobby was on the seventieth floor. I wafted in past the human doorman, trying to do the gloved and sinewy thing. He followed my trajectory with limpet eyes and twitching fingers. His eyes were explained by an ID scanner, his fingers . . . well, I guessed, maybe I was still exuding some of that crude sex scent. Or he was using some old-fashioned sign language.

I marched up to the desk. "I'm expecting a message from James Monk. My name is Jales Belliere."

The desk clerk checked his messages.

"I'm sorry, Ms. Belliere. There is nothing. Do you have a reservation?"

I sniffed, as if annoyed. "That was not up to me. I shall call him."

I flounced over to one of the plush comm booths and sank into the armchair, leaving the screen ajar. A pad automatically slipped up under my hand.

I thought about the "private" booths I'd frequented in The Tert and Mo-Vay. In this one you couldn't catch your breath for perfumed velvet. In The Tert you could catch anything.

After the comm had ascertained my gender, a

cache in the velvet wall opened and shot out a complimentary lip tattoo, cover-all cream and a hairbrush. I snaffled the cover-up and pushed the cache shut.

I recited the address loudly and began my charade. Honey said Delly knew all the comings and goings at the Globe. If she was right, then attracting his attention was just a matter of time.

The comm welcomed me to the Interchange Globe, listed locations of the other luxury Hi-tels in the chain and asked me to confirm the name of the person I wished to speak to at that address.

"James Monk."

The connection hummed for a few seconds before it asked me to give more details.

I requested an F-T-F, knowing it would never happen, and waited for the request to be processed. The answer came back soon enough.

"Mr. Monk is unavailable. Please insert your ident if you wish to leave a message."

I dropped the fake ident spike into the slot and worked hard at summoning a breathy softness to my voice.

"Jales Belliere, Mr. Monk. I'm at the Globe and I'll call again."

I thought about saying other things but my ident told the story—and, anyway, my call would never make it past his first layer of security screening. It wasn't James Monk I was after.

I retrieved my spike and wondered why I felt so exhausted.

Because you can't act for shite, Parrish, and here you are pretending to be a professional of the arts of desire.

It was so ludicrous that it brought a hiccup of laughter to my lips.

Parrish Plessis, warlord *and* lust-bunny.

It just got better and better . . . didn't it?

*　　*　　*

I ordered a drink from the bar and made as if I was waiting for someone. Everyone from the lobby's human sculptures to a courier in a tuxedo tried to hit on me, and I wondered how long I could put up with the masquerade. The pseudo-submissive slash pseudo-predatory manner I was practicing was giving me pains in my chest—though the hair extensions were kinda cool.

I flipped them around and affected an air of purpose, scanning the comings and goings in the lobby until I noticed a man whose stare had locked fast on me. From where I sat his face looked sharp and immature, his expression sulky.

He studied me from the plush drop couches behind the faux waterfall and his eyes weren't exactly glowing with appreciation. In fact they burned with raw anger.

After a few moments he got up and stalked over, a young, self-important predator, on the balls of his feet.

"This 'Tel is spoken for. Staked. Off-limits," he said. "Savvy?"

I froze him off with an almost-Parrish stare. "Whose stake is it?" I asked bluntly.

He held his ground despite being smaller. I glanced appreciatively over his slim physique: either a gymnast, or he'd had a shitload of fine muscle sculpting.

"Mine."

"And you are . . . ?" I slipped into the more snooty tone of my *Amorato* persona and stared down my nose in a way that really got shorter guys jumping.

He blinked in disbelief. Then his lip curled. "Lavish Deluxe—*Delly.* And freelancers *never* tread on local tours. *Who* are *you?*" he demanded.

I put my hand out, careful to handshake in the traditional way. "Jales Belliere. I'm from . . . out of town. I don't know anything about stakes and I have no desire to work on your patch. I'm meeting someone . . . important," I said.

"Important, eh?" He curled his lip again, this time in disbelief. "Just keep out of my way."

He spun on his heel and resumed his pose under the waterfall as if I didn't exist.

Not quite to plan.

I swore a bit.

Then a commotion started up behind me and I watched a red-haired woman of perfectly paid-for proportions enter the lobby, circled by Militia. I tried not to gawk at the radiant perfection of her skin and the dangerous stilettos that lent her a high power-saturation rating.

My observations were interrupted by a discreetly veiled Intimate with the emblem of a runner on his gold lapels tapping me on the shoulder. He passed me a palm p-diary and inflated a privacy fedora to slip over my head.

Seeing my hesitation, he said, "Mr. Monk does not converse over public comm."

I opened my mouth in astonishment and closed it again as quickly as I could, lowering my head so that he could put the fedora in place.

Underneath it the mature, heavily jowled face I'd been studying on the net floated into view before my eyes as though we were underwater.

"Jales Belliere, I assume you are looking for a secondment."

"Er . . . yes. M-my . . . acquaintances tell me your secondments are among the best," I stammered.

"And your acquaintances are?"

I reeled off some of the names I'd just been reading on the media profile lists and mumbled something about being new to town and having a gap in my tour calendar.

Monk's mouth spread into a smile that lent some charm to the heavy face. "Then perhaps we should let you have the opportunity to be able to say that a secondment with James Monk *is* the best. When are you free?"

I gulped in shock.

"Er . . . soon."

Lame, but his invitation had caught me by surprise. I didn't want to shut the door on this unexpected turn of events, but I had other immediate plans.

"I shall leave Derek to make the arrangements," he said.

Monk terminated the exchange and I shrugged out of the bubble.

The Intimate blinked his live vid-feed off. Seemed I was being cammed while I commed.

Between the Hi-tel's doormen and Monk's servant my skin itched from the bombardment of photons.

How the hell had I got an interview with James Monk? What should I do now? My *Amarato* guise would never stand up to real scrutiny.

From the corner of my eye I could see that everyone seemed to be staring at me.

Delly.

The desk staff.

The doormen.

Even the security-clad redhead frowned as though she was trying to place me. She gestured to two of her muscle boys, who detached themselves from her entourage and headed over.

"We should leave now," said Derek.

I ran my options. Go with Derek now—and risk losing a chance with Delly. Or stay and play wrestlemania with the red-haired woman's muscle who didn't look like they wanted to just chat—and risk losing Delly.

When would I ever get a freaking even break on a choice?

"Sure," I said. I called up my luggage drone. "Where to?"

"Our transport is on the helipad."

I headed at an indecent pace for the express lift, dragging Derek with me.

In the whoosh-time it took to get to the hundred and thirtieth floor, I remembered how much I disliked flying and how much I liked my feet on the ground—the absolutely best place for them. The last time I'd been in the air had been a mad-brained escape from M'Grey Island. Someone had chopped the damn rotors off the copter I was flying and dumped me in the moat in a cheesecloth skirt.

Very inconsiderate.

Outside, the Hi-tel roof was divided into large helipads by the square outlines of the control booth, the lift hutch and some portable, blinking-light barricades.

Monk's transport sat on one of them. I knew it was his because his initials lit the tail like sequins on a cheap bustier.

Other than two air-traffic staff there was no one else around.

Derek opened the door. "Please get in."

I shook my head. "Tell Mr. Monk I appreciate his offer. I'll call him later."

His hand locked onto my elbow, crushing the joint. "I have no wish to use force, Ms. Belliere, but I have instructions to do so if necessary. Please get in."

I jerked away but couldn't shake him. My elbow went numb.

He pulled me around and opened the palm of his other hand to reveal a derm big enough to knock a nightclub full of speed freaks on their collective arse.

"Please get in or I shall be forced to sedate you."

Stunned by his change of tactics, I let him push me into a seat.

He climbed in next to me and began takeoff protocol straight away as if he was expecting trouble.

Indecision gripped me. What to do?

I glanced around the cabin, desperate, and spotted emergency flares stacked alongside my seat. I whacked Derek with my best backhander, hoping to disrupt a sensor or two. The skin casing ruptured on one side of his face but he ignored me and the copter began to lift.

Across the tarmac the express lift opened. Delly walked out and around behind the control room to the helipad on the other side.

Two sensations coincided. Relief—that it wasn't the redhead's muscle. Panic—my chance to snare Delly was about to slip away.

Adrenaline took over. I grabbed two flares, popped the door and jumped the few meters down onto the tarmac, rolling about as neatly as an overripe melon dropped from a Hi-tel penthouse.

I dropped the flares as every bone in my body jarred. I tried to get up and crawl after them. At least, my mind told my body to do it but my body refused.

Lie still and recover, it ordered. *Take a sauna. Get a life.*

Then I heard the distinctive whine of gun turrets aligning. Over the copter's shoulder I saw a broadbacked Troop Float rising from a channel alongside the building. This one was unmarked and utterly businesslike, front-mounted .50-cal. machine guns cooking and ready to fire.

Whenever I got close to death—which was getting too damn frequent to be thrilling—it was never how I wanted it.

Never the right way to die.

Suddenly my mind and body were in complete agreement again.

Move.

I rolled toward the scattered flares as the copter

nosed forward, altering the angle of its landing struts to try to scoop me up.

It pummeled into me and somehow snagged the strap of my chic little top. For a second I became airborne—until my weight tore the fabric and I dropped to the tarmac again.

I kept rolling this time despite the pain.

The copter corrected its lurch and came for me again.

The Troop Float sent a warning spray of fire along the tarmac. I wasn't sure if it was aimed at me or at Monk's copter but I wasn't going to raise my hand to ask.

Instead, I scrambled the last couple of meters to the flares and set them off.

The Troop Float fired another warning burst as Derek made his move. In the smoky confusion the gunfire caught his aircraft by chance on the tail.

The copter crashed down within meters of me, exploding. The sky rained fractured plastic, hot metal and tiny bits of Derek's jelly tissue-replica.

A chunk of rotor cartwheeled straight toward me, slicing into my leg as it bounced on over the edge of the building.

While the smoke continued to plume, I rolled like crazy toward the gutter covering along the edge of the building and forced myself underneath it.

I heard excited shouts as the Hi-tel's own security burst from the lift, spraying semiauto fire. I peered out from underneath the corrugated plas to see the Troop Float peel off.

Much as I appreciated the rescue, I didn't want to be caught up in the postmortem, and Delly was about to leave the building, so I squirmed on along under the gutter shield, dragging myself through a cushion of rat dung.

As I crawled past the control room and behind a set of tall barricades, I squeezed out from under the cover and scrambled unsteadily to my knees. Not only was the chic top in tatters but my pants looked like shit-crumbed shredded paper.

I was bleeding all over the place, especially from the leg. The fleck of burns on my back throbbed.

"You *are* popular." Lavish Deluxe was leaning against a flimsy UL, waiting for me.

"What will it cost for you to get me out of here?" I couldn't see any point in wasting time.

He didn't even have to consider. "An introduction to James Monk."

Yes.

"Sure thing. Wrapped in a bow if you like."

The smile that spread across Delly's face was almost indecent. He hopped in and powered up the tiny engine, maneuvering it for a short, tight takeoff across the tarmac. *Right off the edge of the building.*

"You can't take off there. There's not enough room." My words were lost in more explosions, and my heart leaped across the abyss to the next building then back into my chest.

Jail and failure had to be better than flying in an ultralight off the edge of this building. Didn't it?

Delly hopped out again and nudged the lightweight craft backward until the tail touched the back of the lift housing.

I glanced over my shoulder. The control room was empty—deserted. The only audience we had was the Hi-tel security, and they were fighting the blaze engulfing Monk's crashed copter.

I ran to the tail and climbed into the wire basket built into it. Not exactly how I'd planned to leave one of Viva's classiest Hi-tels. I really had to do something about my lifestyle.

We came off the building and fell—a nauseating, ear-popping drop. I kept my eyes shut and gripped the sides of the basket, wondering how long before we smacked a hole in the ground.

Fierce pain constricted my chest and breathing. It didn't matter how long it took, I realized. I was going to have a heart attack long before we hit.

I tried to remember what I wanted my last thoughts to be. There was something, I was sure. Something I'd made a pact with myself that I would think—something that would counteract all the bad karma and mistakes. Something that would gain me entrance to a bar where I could sit and get drunk without watching my back.

Nope. Gone.

The world spun. Literally. The UL, Deluxe and I were in a death twirl.

I heard him scream in exultation as I vomited. The spin of the UL slapped the mess back into my own face.

I felt all my muscles slacken toward unconsciousness. Not good. My grip slipped. I pitched out of the basket, tethered by one hand only.

Another Deluxe scream. And words that I couldn't savvy.

The fingers on my grip hand began to uncurl. I couldn't do anything to stop them.

His scream went on, long and hard and exultant. I focused on the sound and used it as a reason to stay alive, forcing my fingers to close again around the steel.

Try, you fool.

The Angel shot me up with renewed adrenaline that tightened my muscles and penetrated enough into my consciousness to piss me off.

I'm no fool, I'm—

Woof.

The UL came out of the spin and leveled off without warning. There was a sharp, bone-cracking encounter between me and the steel basket.

Deluxe's scream turned into laughter as we straightened and slowed.

I craned a look through vomit-encrusted eyelashes. The maniac pilot had his head thrust back and tears streaming down his face.

I was pleased that I was going to live a bit longer. It would give me enough time to wring his neck.

Chapter Seven

By evening the city's advertibles and One-World overflowed with headlines about the whole thing.

Amorato *missing in desperate kidnap attempt.*

Duel over femme is fatal.

Globe's air-traffic regulators abandon their post in crisis.

Rooftop carnage.

Who is the mysterious missing woman?

Virgin Brides singer fined for trashing Interchange corridor during band frenzy. "It wasn't me," pleads Garter Thin.

I smothered a laugh at the last one.

⁻ The rest, though . . . what was it that Teece and Ibis had said? *"There's attention. And then there's Attention."*

I was watching it all from the bar of the Luxoria, where Lavish was paying for the drinks. The violet downlights barely lit our corner of the bar, making it easy for me to observe the decor and the company without being obvious.

The company was . . . stunning.

Even though it was off-hours, Lavish's club buzzed as *Amoratos* drifted in and out, some wearing portable NS, others simply stoned or drunk—all in underwear or casual track gear. But it was they, not their taste in entertainment or fashion, that staggered me. I'd never seen so much beauty in one place—all types and tastes.

Actually, it was more than just beauty. It was as though a . . . residue of sex lingered on them. A syrup-thick come-and-do-it-with-me aura.

I felt the lust rising again. Not surprising—I had the most desirable pieces of flesh in the city strutting about in their knickers right under my nose.

I told myself it was a reaction to the adrenaline rush of the UL ride and that this was *not* the sort of place to be feeling those sorts of urges. I forced myself to checkout the security instead.

Mr. Muscle Massive, squashed onto a seat barely big enough to contain his bulk, made Plastique's boys look soft and small.

Flesh parlors were the same anywhere: you had to have some visible bulk. But I suspected that Mr. Massive was mainly for show. Strong, sure, but slow and awkward. And from the way the *Amoratos* were teasing him, I figured he was probably altogether too nice.

Over by one of the doors, though, were two Koreans dressed like hired help and playing holo-cards in a restless kinda way.

I figured them for the real deal.

Them, and the antibeserker screens, and the restraint gear not quite out of sight behind the bar.

I shivered. Paralysis tek scared the Jeez out of me.

Behind the section of the bar where Lavish and I sat, a withered guy who could have climbed straight out of one of Ike Del Morte's petri dishes mixed more drinks. I didn't think they allowed punters that ugly to live in Viva—let alone in a place like this.

Around his collar I saw the telltale orange stains of a wethead.

"Hurry up with those drinks, Merv," ordered Lavish.

Merv frowned and slopped tequila over my hand.

I could've gotten pissed off—but this was the guy I'd come to find.

I gave him a friendly wink. If he was half as smart as Honey had said, I didn't care if he tipped the whole damn bottle over me. At the very least I could get him to fix Merry 3#.

Muted tribal music pulsed around us. Some of the *Amoratos* danced to it. One perched on Mr. Massive's knee and massaged his temples.

His grin spoke bliss.

Lavish swallowed his drink and demanded another. He seemed to be getting in a mood to talk as he came down from his own high, so I put on a listening face while I kept an eye on Merv's movements.

The club was his, Lavish said. Used to be in the lower fifty levels of the Cone. The move above a hundred floors meant he'd made it in the flesh-parlor business. Especially in a building attached to the Glass Bridge right near the Old Mall and Casino Central.

I had to agree with him there.

Apart from the Globe, Lavish's club was the most luxurious place I'd ever set foot in. A mix of sensuous furnishings and pica-cleanliness. The air con filtered fresh eucalyptus scents, and the jade syn-marble bar where we sat flickered with sequenced inbuilt lights. Inside the circle of the glittery bar, mirrors ran perfectly concentrically, ceiling to floor.

"I hate the smell of that shit," Lavish complained. "It's giving me hay fever. Change the fucking thing."

Merv turned and opened a door camouflaged by rows of glasses. Beyond the door I glimpsed a jumble of hardware.

Lavish saw me looking.

"That's his room. He lives in there when the club's open. Merv doesn't like people. He just likes to watch them."

A sip or two later, Merv returned and I could smell wafts of sandalwood instead. It reminded me of Pat and Ibis's shop.

I took in the large dimensions of the bar and the various doors exiting into the spiral of corridors that led to the 'doirs.

The 'doirs were so different from the tawdry back rooms of Torley's that it was hard to believe they performed essentially the same services. *Essentially.* I'd have bet some things happened in this place that the babes on the strip had never even REM-ed about.

I'd seen inside them after I'd washed up, salved my burns and dressed in some borrowed clothes. An *Amorato* with an amber tan and a stunning spill of unnaturally white-gold hair that fell to her hips showed me around. She told me that her name was Glorious.

"Our clients are top-end," Glorious said.

"There must be a lot of your type of services around?"

"Ours isn't a service. It's a way of life. Delly only employs people who enjoy what they do." She tilted her head and scraped the tip of her fingernail over one of the bruises on my bare forearm. "What do *you* like?"

I tried not to flinch: she was more than a little beautiful and she was coming on to me. It had been a relief to get away from her when Lavish called me into the bar for a drink and a confab.

And Lavish was still talking in his sharp voice. I turned my attention back to him, cutting across his monologue with a direct question.

"Do you know who blew up the copter at the Globe?" I asked.

He clinked ice in his drink and sidestepped my question. "I thought they were friends of yours."

I pulled an innocent face. My ident said I was from the other side of the continent: I reminded myself that I could afford to be politically stupid—to a point.

"James Monk made contact with you. Anyone he wants, everyone wants. The IOs are like squabbling gods." He fingered the rim of his glass, giving me the feeling that there was a whole lot more he wasn't telling me.

"So why did you agree to help me?" It seemed like the logical question to ask, even though I'd gone there looking for him. Everything had gotten kinda crazy and mixed up. I had no idea why Monk had responded to my call but I couldn't tell Lavish that.

Maybe, for once, I'd had a little luck? It had certainly forced Lavish's hand.

Luck? Me? Nah.

Lavish leaned toward me, his sharp features softened by the gloom. Desire still lingered in me, even after my fourth drink. The guided tour with the amber goddess had been arousing in its way and the general vibe of the place was altogether sexy. I could feel my heightened state like new clothes and for some reason even this skinny, arrogant flesh seller was turning me on.

"I want Monk's patronage," he said.

"And?" I asked, knowing that there was more.

He slid forward on his stool so that his legs hugged either side of mine.

I wasn't sure if I was feeling *that* mellow, but I gave him the benefit. I needed to know what was going on.

"I'm also curious why he would allow a Series Seven Intimate to be destroyed *for you*," he said.

Does he mean Derek? Obviously a Series 7 was worth more than a human being to Lavish Deluxe. I sat back to consider the question and to get the scent of him out of my nostrils. Casual sex wasn't on my list of things to do while I was here, yet it was pretty much all that was on my mind.

"Maybe it wasn't in his plan. What else?" I stalled.

He slid his hand along my thigh and cupped my crotch.

The brash move got me pushing off the bar, dumping us both on the floor. I rolled quickly so that I was astride him, one hand gripping his throat and the other in a fist above his face.

He smiled up at me with the keen lasciviousness of someone who would welcome the right sort of pain.

"And why would an *Amorato*, even a raw one, react like a street fighter to a mild flirtation? Unless, of course, she wasn't who she said she was. . . ."

I smacked him in the mouth anyway. It probably proved his point but I couldn't help myself. I had a head of steam to let off—and he was so . . . so . . .

Blood trickled from where I had split his lip. I wanted to lean down and taste it.

Yes . . .

The Eskaalim was in my head again. The building strength of its presence got me up and putting some distance between Delly and me.

I knew my self-control was slipping. Since I'd used it to help me with the guards at the Interchange, it had found a new way around to get at me. If I stayed in this place too long . . .

I paced a little, keeping an eye on the Koreans who had closed in.

"OK. Let's just say I'm new to your business. My . . . er . . . speciality . . . is violence. You saved my life back there. Let's work on an deal that's acceptable to both of us," I said.

Lavish got to his feet and waved the Koreans away. He climbed back up onto his stool and sucked his bleeding lip. "I'm sure we can work something out."

I joined him at the bar and swallowed my drink in one gulp. A tremor seemed to have been with me since we'd climbed alive from the UL. It wasn't getting any better. Lust? Shock? Anger? Whatever, I couldn't find a way to release it.

"What do you know about James Monk?" I asked.

Lavish's expression got cagey. "Media are our main clientele. I've tried to secure Monk's business before but he's got a consort and doesn't usually hire out for himself. When you contacted him I thought you were just another opportunist. When *he* contacted *you* . . . well, that was a different matter."

I pretended to be astounded. "How could you have known who I was contacting?"

"There isn't anywhere less private than a Hi-tel lobby, Belliere. In every sense of the word."

"You hacked the comm line?"

"Let's just say I have a very good technician."

So I hear.

"So how can we both get to Monk now?" It seemed the logical question I would ask under the circumstances. "Or should I say, what do you want me to do?"

"You must contact him and insist on servicing him here."

"What do you get for that—the kudos?"

He smiled, his lips compressing in a narrow line. "If you like. Once he's patronized my club, my profile will grow exponentially and I'll call things square between us."

"He may not want to come here," I said.

"Well, that depends on how persuasive you can be."

I immediately thought of my guns and my pins and my knives—none of which I had with me. "How do you mean—persuasive?"

He laughed—until he saw that I was serious.

Putting his glass down, he slid off the stool and came around to my side, locking his arms around my waist. Tilting his head back, he stood on his toes and ran his tongue along my jawline, up to my ear lobe.

Despite the sensations trickling into my crotch, I found myself reaching for an absent knife with one hand and wiping his saliva away with the other.

Instead of persisting, he withdrew, levering himself on to the bar.

He tapped his cheek with a forefinger. "I don't know who you are, but James Monk wanted you. If I set this up, you must learn enough to pass as what you pretend to be. My reputation is at stake."

"How long will that take?" I complained, faking impatience.

"Glorious will coach you. A few days should be enough." He nodded toward the amber goddess.

Shite, no.

Before I could protest aloud he'd beckoned her over.

"Glorious, Jales is from the other side of the world."

"Country," I corrected.

"Whatever." He sniffed at my interruption. "Her skills are . . . raw. If you were to teach her some basic sophistications, enough to pass as a local artisan, how long would it take?"

Glorious looked me over critically. "Depends on how quickly she learns—a few days, a week at the most for the rudiments. Years if you want her to be good at it."

Lavish nodded. "Days will be enough. When Glorious thinks you're ready I'll set up another contact with James Monk. Not before. My reputation is everything."

I got a stubborn look on. "What if I don't want to play your game?"

He shot a glance at Glorious and she moved off out of earshot, eyeing me curiously.

"I'll throw you out on the street and blow your cover. You are no *Amorato*, Jales Belliere. People want to kill you," he whispered.

"What about if I kill you first?" I whispered, only half joking.

He didn't smile. "Now that would be stupid. You're almost untouchable while you're in the Luxoria. You have what we call . . . *Corpus Immunity*. As long as the sanitation and health laws are obeyed I can employ anybody I want, make them *do* anything I want. No interference. Set foot on the street and I'll see that you are snatched up by the nearest Militia patrol as an illegal alien at the very least. I'm sure that once they start digging they'll find other things about you they want to know."

Oh, yes.

"If you're after James Monk, then it's my way or . . ." He trailed off.

I didn't like blackmail but it was buying me the time I needed with Merv. I let myself look annoyed.

A small guy dressed only in a disposable nappy burst into the bar. His low-pitched wail cut across the background tribal beat.

"Delly, Brigitte's got a spinner."

Lavish nodded to Muscle Massive and the Koreans and they all disappeared into the corridor. Glorious and the other girls ran out after them.

It left me alone with Merv. I forced myself to smile at him again. He squirmed so nervously that I figured it was a new experience for him.

"What's happening?" I asked.

"S-spinner's a b-bad client." He backed away, dropping a glass so that it smashed on the bar. "I got to go back to my i-bugs. Shouldn't be doing t-this s-stupid j-job anyway. . . ."

"Can I come?" My smile got wider. I stopped short of batting my eyelids.

He glanced around at the empty bar.

"I g-guess so," he said doubtfully. "Seeing as you'll be working here t-too."

I vaulted over the bar and followed Merv through a narrow door into the cylinder of mirrors.

Inside was a small, dark, circular room that could have been running the universe. The walls and ceiling were one large screen, or hundreds of small ones. They flicked up images from every cranny of the 'doirs and ran panoramas on the outside of the building from ground to penthouse level and into the city.

Two full-body, coffin-shaped sensoriums took up half of the floor space.

What was left was a bedroom complete with a deep recliner chair/bed and armrests wide enough to set up shop on. One of them winked and hummed with a variety of command controls: an old keyboard, pick-ups, touch pads. The other could have been the back room of a pharmacy—tabs, derms, a portable drip—everything that frizzed, popped and kicked.

Merv pulled out a tray of brown globs from a slot under his right armrest that looked and smelled like meatballs in sauce. He slapped one on his neck. Ooze dribbled down onto his collar.

Meatware. *Ugh.* I had the same abhorrence to it as I did to NS. It all worked on the same principle though NS was tidier, more straightforward. As far as I could see, invisible implants were one thing. Having stuff sucking at your neurologics through your skin was quite another.

I had enough of that sort of thing going on inside me.

Aside from the mayhem of tek, good-luck charms crammed every spare mill of space. Rabbits' feet, Lady Lucks, horseshoes, shamrocks, Samadhi and mojo bags. Every shape, size and incarnation. Some more obscure than others. Necklaces, brooches, tie-pins, ornaments, rings, bracelets, mobiles.

I felt for the chain under my shirt and wondered

if Merv would even recognize the charm on it as one of his own.

He moved confident as a canrat among the clutter and sank in his chair. The sandalwood scents didn't disguise the scent of stale body fluids. A tiny portable san had been rigged in the corner. By the smell of it the nanos needed renewing.

I swallowed a couple of times and switched my olfaugs down to minimum.

"I-impressive," I said.

I tried to memorize the hardware—just to piss off Teece—but the range of gear was over my head.

I noticed a circle burned into the floor around the chair. I went to step over it and got stung by something.

"What the freak was that?" I swatted at my ankle.

'To-oo close," Merv yelled. "Y-you're too close to me."

I stepped back from the circle.

"This is *my* place. N-no one comes in h-here." He made a circular motion with his hands.

I spread mine wide, placating him. "Sure, I understand." I wasn't sure I did, though. I liked my own space too but Merv was . . . twitchy.

"I don't usually have people in here when I'm working, so keep still."

Before I could reply, he spasmed and his jaw went slack.

The screens flicked alive with images of one particular 'doir. Every different angle you could imagine. I stared at it for a minute or two, trying to make sense of what I saw.

"Aura bugs," Merv said. He was back with me again, eyes alert, jaw tight. The meatware squirmed like a leech on his neck. "B-better than CCUs, 'cepting that they die."

He made a garbled noise in the back of his throat and the bugs arranged their view to one composite.

"Y-you need anything, Delly?" He spoke into a pickup shaped like a cross.

Lavish was bent over a body of a grrl. Her blood pooled around his feet. In another corner of the room the Koreans restrained a naked man. Muscle Massive was crying.

"Get me the cleaners and a taxi 'pede. Mr. Pregora understands not to leave his top-ups so long next time. Please deduct fifty thousand Hems from his account," said Lavish.

Merv sucked his lip in, chewing at it. "What about Brigitte? Sh-shall I call the medic, Delly?"

"Not the medic, you fucking moron—get the body bus," Lavish hissed.

With another curt noise, Merv cut the pictures dead and replaced them with other images of the Luxoria. The audio stayed live, though, with Lavish screaming about the blood staining his clothes.

After a few moments Merv killed that too.

I sat, numb, while he went through the official protocol of reporting the death to the Militia. When the body bus had been ordered and the death logged through the correct channels, he peeled the meatware from his neck and stood up. His skin was blotchy with distress.

I felt an impulse to squeeze his shoulder, to comfort him—or myself—but I suppressed it. Merv didn't like to be touched.

"Happen much?" I asked.

"Once is too much, isn't it?" he said hoarsely.

Emotional answer, but he was being evasive, I knew.

"No Militia inquiry?"

Merv paced the two steps that his circle would allow. "Our clients are mainly media. M-Militia can only touch us if we breach licensing regs. S-stupid stuff. Hygiene and fire. Everything else that happens here is . . . well . . . untouchable. Besides, the media own the Militia. If the client had been a R-Royal, then maybe . . ."

Suddenly the sandalwood scent cloyed my airways. We sat in silence while I digested what he'd said. No wonder Honey had done a runner.

"How do you work in a place like this?" I said quietly.

Merv licked his lips a few times, deliberating over his answer.

"It's w-worth it, see?" With shaking hands he picked up and caressed a small black dog-shaped object from his console. I'd assumed it was another charm.

"See this? She's a QI mole. Her name is Snout. Keeps Brilliance from knowing where I am. Where I'm looking."

I knew I had that stupid look on my face again, but I couldn't seem to find anything else to replace it.

Strange world. Strange people. Strange rules.

"What is a QI mole and who the freak is *Brilliance?*" I snapped, losing patience with myself more than with Merv.

He flinched and clasped the dog defensively against his body.

I took a breath. "I'm sorry, Merv. There's a lot I don't understand and what just happened . . . Well, it shocked me."

He nodded, relaxing his grip.

I felt the teeniest bit guilty at the lie. I sure as hell didn't like what I'd seen. But had it shocked me? Sadly, no.

"You're going to get yourself into trouble round here if you don't know," he said.

I squirmed a bit. True. But I didn't need to hear it quite so plainly from a superstitious nerd in a flesh joint.

Still, that realization was beginning to sink in. I'd been born in the burbs and thought I had a handle on the city. But this place was as dangerous as The Tert, only it was dressed up in air-fresh and high heels. If I was going to survive long enough to accomplish anything, I needed to bum a ride up a steep learning curve. A week, Lavish had said, until he'd contact Monk again. Looked like I had that long to learn enough to survive.

Time to play my trump. "Honey sent her love."

Merv froze for a second, then mumbled a command into an interface pick-up. Around us the screens dimmed as though everything had gone to sleep.

"D-Delly likes to see records of everything," he said. "We got about a minute before I have to do some explaining."

I nodded.

"You've seen h-her?" His eagerness was pathetic.

"She said to tell you that she was fine. That she'd found the guy who'd take care of her. Just how you planned it."

I made the last bit up. But Merv seemed to buy it. Probably because it was close enough to the real story. I didn't tell him that the guy used to be mine.

Tears misted his eyes. "Delly mustn't know where she is. He'll s-send someone after her."

I touched my fist to my chest in a gesture of honor. "Trust me."

He nodded, jiggling and biting his lip again. The flush rising in his cheeks told me that the news had given him more pleasure than a day in a sensorium.

So I hit him up. "She said you'd be able to help me?"

Merv's face closed over as soon as I said it. "H-how do I know this is for real? H-how do I know you've seen her?"

I flipped out the mystic star and looped it over my head, dangling it in front of him. Ike's wetware hung on the same chain, a grotesque twin.

His expression now was a mixture of relief and pleasure. He tried to snatch the star but I held it out of his reach.

For a terrible moment I thought he might cry. I got a rash when people cried.

"What do you w-want for it?" he said.

"Information," I said. "I want to know who is behind a project called Code Noir. Cross-reference it with a name, Ike Del Morte."

Merv stroked a tiny empty space between St. Christopher and a blood doll. I figured the space belonged to the mystic star. "And you'll give me my s-star back?"

"*When* I have the information."

His whole body jerked in agreement. "The *Amoratos* eat in a c-café called Breeza's that Delly owns. We c-can talk more there at breakfast. You better g-go now.

I took my cue from him, slipping the star around my neck. Then I headed back out to the bar.

Chapter Eight

I was helping myself to another drink as Glorious and the Koreans reappeared at the door. She made straight for me, pale and distraught. Her hands dabbed at the blood spatters on her underwear as she blurted her message straight out.

"Delly said I should show you where your room is. He said you can eat with us at Breeza's Café on one fifty one, or you can stay in the club—otherwise the deal's off. Either Lam"—she nodded at the Korean with a shaved head—"or Tae will . . . be with you."

I gave the small, tightly muscled men my best grimace.

Their return smiles were uncomfortably bland.

I switched my attention back to Glorious. "Everything all right?"

She trembled violently. "Brigitte was new. She didn't have a spotter." She blinked at me through frightened eyes. "I know it's selfish. But all I can think of is . . . one day it might be me."

Suddenly she bent over, hair spilling around her face, looking like she might get sick.

"You should . . . er . . . lie down," I said awkwardly. I wasn't used to comforting beautiful women about murder. Actually, I wasn't used to comforting anyone. And the gloom of the low-lit bar was getting to me. I wanted out of the place.

Glorious straightened up and swallowed a couple of times, composing herself. "I'll show you your room. It's right next to mine."

Lam trailed us out into the corridor and onto the lift.

"We live on the floor below the club," Glorious explained, pressing the button.

We were there in a blink. Lam stepped out first and held his hand to the sensor to make sure the door stayed open. Just in case.

I followed him and Glorious out into another plush corridor decorated with native plants and squirming fish murals.

Glorious caught me eyeballing the fish and managed a laugh. "Used to make me seasick at first. It's supposed to be relaxing."

A sleek black-and-silver-tailed fish swam alongside me for a few paces before it flicked its tail and retraced its path toward the lift. I thought of Kiora Bass, one of Daac's Fishertown devotees, and wondered if she was still alive.

Lam showed me the code to my door lock and watched me go inside. Then he settled himself outside, cross-legged by the door.

The room was more than luxurious by my standards. The bed was the real deal and so were the 'drobe, san and entertainment unit. A weird module hunkered down at one side.

"What's that?"

Glorious had followed me in. Color had seeped back into her cheeks and her crafted turquoise eyes had regained some shine.

"That's the Alkem. And those clothes in the wardrobe belong to the Luxoria. You're free to wear any of them if they fit but if you damage anything Delly takes it out of your pay. Merv keeps account of all that side of things. Don't you, Merv?"

I glanced behind me for the nerdy boy but came up empty.

"Every room in the Luxoria and our apartments contain i-bugs for our protection. Merv monitors them all the time," she explained.

"Doesn't he ever sleep?" I asked, wondering what would happen if I inhaled a bug.

"Only the hours when clients aren't in." She saw my expression and tried to reassure me. "Merv's very discreet. You'll get used to it. It's kind of comforting."

I knew a few voyeurs—all of them would have murdered to get a gig like this. No wonder Merv hung around.

I pointed to the Alkem again. "What does it do?"

"Put your things away and tap me here when you're ready." Glorious pointed to a number on the comm. "We'll start right away."

Start what? I didn't want to start anything. "Don't you wanna take some time to . . . um . . . recover?"

Something about Glorious made me trip over my words.

Maybe because she was cultured. Maybe because she was inordinately beautiful—I'd always maintained that beauty fucked with people's minds. Or maybe it was that she was soft and feminine and polite and I didn't know how to deal with that.

She shook her head. "Thanks, but I need to think about something else." She smiled shyly.

I tried hard to tell if it was practiced or real and came up with nothing.

"So when you're ready . . ." she finished.

Try never.

She left me and I paced the room in agitation.

I badly wanted to have a wash but not with an audience. I was allergic to strangers watching me naked.

"Merv," I called.

"Yes, Jales?" A thin disembodied voice came back.

"I'm going to wash. You eyeball me and I'll flush Snout down the san. Understand?"

I took his silence to mean clear-as-Viva-water.

It would have to do.

Before I thought about it any more, I stripped, dumped my clothes in the separate cleaner and jumped into the san. When I'd finished, I repacked my kit and sat it by the door. I wanted out of here the moment I could. I certainly wasn't settling things neatly in drawers.

Hell, I *never* put things in drawers.

I paced again until the indecision of what I should do next made my limbs heavy with fatigue. The entertainment unit told me it was late afternoon of what already seemed like a very long day.

Now I was here, I had to wait for Merv to find the information I needed. Frustration sandpapered away under my skin. I hated having to do anything slowly. Impatience was my virtue—my curse. I wanted to tear the fabric of Viva apart and make someone answer for Mo-Vay.

And Roo.

And Wombebe.

But I couldn't do that with my fists. I had to be smart for a while. I had to learn.

Calmed a little by that thought, I lay down.

Not meaning to, I slept. Dreams crowded in, worse than ever before, semi-waking dreams full of blood and the deep ache of unfulfilled orgasm.

Sometime later the bed got too soft and I woke, finally, on the floor, twisted up in the sheet in a corner of the room. The sky through the window polar-

iser looked like morning. The entertainment unit said
5 a.m. when I asked it. I stretched and disentangled
myself.

"What time is breakfast, Merv?"

"Morning, Jales. Were you comfortable on the
floor? I didn't like to wake you." He sounded weary,
like he'd been up all night.

"Fine," I lied.

"Lam will show you the way to Breeza's for breakfast when you're ready."

"Thanks."

"They often run out of bacon by seven," he added
casually. "I always like to be there before that."

I took his hint and nodded at nothing in particular.
I-bugs made it odd to have a conversation with him.
Not even a camera lens to look into.

"Where can I exercise?"

"Delly doesn't allow the *Amoratos* to leave the
building. But three doors up from Glorious there's
an aerobics glove."

Aerobics glove. Ugh. The memory of Gigi's vreal set
was fresh in my mind and this sounded like something you might get buried in.

"I think I'll settle for bacon," I replied.

Lam was waiting in exactly the same position that
I'd left him, cross-legged and chewing something
that looked like last-century biltong.

"Don't you get a cramp?" I sniped.

He gave me the benefit of his perfectly bland smile
again and sprang up, immediately limber and agile.

Obviously not.

"Lead me to the bacon," I said.

He turned on his heel toward the lift.

I tried a couple of times to lure him into conversation as we whizzed up two floors and made our way
through some heavily glazed security doors and an
ID check.

The Korean wasn't biting.

We stepped through into an abyss. The transparent walkway gave me instant vertigo as though I was flying without an engine or wings. Annoyingly, Lam didn't even seem to notice the drop of thousands of feet to the pavement.

My thoughts of a hearty breakfast faded.

How on earth did people eat up here?

Others walked behind us, emerging from other floors. They were suits, mainly, with a smattering of clergy dressed in their brocade robes and snazzy sandals.

We marched a step ahead of them until we reached the middle of the bridge where the sides curved outward into a bowl shape. Lam waved me into the entrance of a jungle-decor café, complete with animal noises and a bio-robotic python slithering among the fake tusk stools.

Merv sat in the corner under the jungle vines, drinking coffee through a straw and stroking Snout. Caked orange dribble on his collar told me he was dry, but only just.

I ordered tea and something that resembled sugar dough.

Lam nodded at the waiter to confirm that my request was on the house. Then he sat himself at the counter.

I picked up my order casually and made for a table under the vines. I sat with my back to Lam, blocking his direct vision of Merv.

"C-can't talk for long," Merv muttered. He fingered the chocolate roll in front of him.

"Have you found anything?"

"Not yet. Snout's been digging b-but there's a quiver. I had to bring her in." His hand shook as it lifted the roll to his mouth. "Y-you go out in a quiver, y-you don't come back. No matter how good you are."

I sighed. A quiver was a hack's equivalent of an

earthquake—major shake. It spooked them all. The paranoid ones believed that it was a rogue surveillance program. But nobody knew who wrote it and nobody knew who sent it. Maybe that was what Honey meant about Merv being scared of shadows.

"How long does a quiver last?"

Merv shrugged. "Not long. M-maybe."

I swallowed a surge of impatience and tried another tack. "What is Brilliance?"

The fear put there by the thought of the quiver didn't fade from his voice. "An AI."

"How does it work?"

"*Sh-she* edits everything we see on the screen. I mean everything that is supplied to her."

"How do you mean?"

He tapped the bitten end of his roll into his plate as though he was stubbing out a cig. "She relies on r-raw feed from the Priers. All the Priers are owned by the big three."

"Monk, Bau and Laud?"

He nodded. "M-Monk feeds her sport. S.K. Laud feeds her lifestyle. And Sera Bau c-cams everything she needs for DramaNet. Brilliance edits and p-programs, depending on her gauging of the v-viewers' response."

I stared down through the transparent floor. Breeza's. Good name. You could almost feel the wind licking between your toes.

"Sounds like Brilliance has a lot of say."

"Her original program was designed just for multimedia editing. Programming selection is something that seems to have evolved."

Merv hunched his shoulders in a way that told me there was more.

Behind me I heard Lam clank his plate on the cafébar. I stretched and looked around. He was staring at me with an empty expression that made me nervous.

I turned back to Merv and spoke quickly. "Who else figures in the big-time stakes around here?"

"The b-banking royalty, I guess. They m-manage the money still but they don't have much p-personal wealth. Information is p-power and they don't own it."

He looked away from me suddenly—just before Lam slapped me across the ear.

I jerked upright, fists clenched.

"What's so interesting?" Lam said in perfect Australian.

The surprise of hearing him finally speak stalled my gut reaction to hammer him. I used the moment to tell myself that a full-scale brawl probably wouldn't further my cause.

"Well, you're not exactly scintillating conversation," I snapped, rubbing my ear.

He laughed. A breathy snort.

Before I had a chance to reconsider my passive line, *Amoratos* from the Luxoria spilled in, chattering and laughing, as beautiful in the daylight as they were in the dimness of the club. Glorious was among them.

Merv got up and left as they approached. They ignored him as though he was invisible.

Glorious came over to me, glowing with beauty— a combination of effects created by her incredible hair, her amber-tinged skin and some early-morning exercise.

"You look better," I said spontaneously.

"We have to keep in shape for our profession. But then, you'd know that. You have an exceptional body."

The others giggled and made rude noises at her. They settled at tables around me, calling for food and coffee. Lam resumed his bland expression and withdrew to the counter.

Glorious's compliment made me squirm. I didn't like social chat, and I didn't like the direction of the conversation. She was flirting.

She sat on the stool next to me, leaning in close as if we were good friends.

"I'm glad you're here," she said. "When you didn't call me last night I thought something might have happened. That you'd left."

I grunted. Noncommittal. My heart accelerated, though, disturbed by her easy manner.

"Look at your bruises. I'll put something on them when we go back." She reached up and stroked my face.

"What are you doing?" I growled, glancing around.

The others didn't seem to notice—only Lam, who watched from a distance over the lip of his cup.

Glorious stared at me, eyes wide with innocent interest. "There's something about you, Jales. I've never met anyone who . . . Delly said you are an *Amorato*. I can sense desire in you but there's resistance too. It's not usual for someone of our trade to be divided."

Divided? It described exactly how I was feeling. She'd forgotten to add *confused, crazy and infected by a lustful, violent parasite.* What else would explain this femme turning my stomach to liquid and my legs to purée? Doll Feast was the only woman I'd been with before but that had been more about survival and need.

Women weren't to my taste in that way—they got competitive about all the wrong things when sex came into it. This . . . attraction was something I'd never experienced before and it was freaking untimely.

I pushed her hand away. "You got a degree in mind reading?"

Glorious looked puzzled. "Applied endocrinology, sexual alchemy and bio-communication, actually. But you must have similar qualifications?"

"Er . . . yes, though things are different in the west. We train on the . . . er . . . job."

She brought her face closer to mine. "I can work out most people within a few minutes of meeting them. After that, their inhibitions are easily overcome. But I cannot find the beginning of the thread with you." She whispered the last, her sweet breath fanning my lips. "You frighten me."

This was not the sort of conversation I was used to having at breakfast—sophisticated and loaded with sexual undertones. I was usually too busy stuffing in hot dough and cursing Teece.

I turned my mouth to Glorious's ear, careful not to touch her flesh. "Be frightened," I whispered, hoping to put her off.

She gave me a wicked smile. "Fear is exciting."

Without warning she locked her arms around my neck and slipped her tongue straight into my mouth. An explosion of taste hit me—sweeter than jam, tangier than lemon.

Desire sprang loose like a wild thing. I wanted to reach under her clothes and feel the texture of her skin.

"I still haven't shown you my room," she breathed.

"You should," I said.

We left with Lam trailing behind, smirking discreetly. Whatever his instructions from Lavish, they didn't prevent me *fraternizing*.

As we walked back across the bridge Glorious wound and unwound her fingers through mine, tickling and pinching the flesh of my hand.

By the time we got to her room my self-restraint had failed completely. A haze fell across my vision. I wanted her so badly that it hurt.

Or maybe it wasn't *her*. Maybe I just wanted *it*.

My hands trembled on her shoulders as she keyed in her door code.

We stumbled inside and I snatched Glorious against me, forcing a leg up between hers. Our kiss wasn't tender or loving. It was something far cruder.

I rolled her onto the bed and tore her shirt open. My mouth covered her nipple. I sucked roughly, without any expertise, only need.

Glorious seemed to like it. She freed the other nipple from her opened shirt so that I could squeeze it between my fingers.

Then she reached down to my pants and slid her fingers inside the waistband. I loosened them and wriggled them down over my hips.

She trailed her fingers from my navel downward, so lightly that I thought I might die from the teasing agony of it.

"Please," I groaned. "Hurry."

In the back of my brain I registered that she'd barely touched me and yet I was out of my mind with desire for her. No one had ever done this to me before—not even Loyl. The flesh hunger denied the existence of anything else.

Glorious's fingers probed and stroked, finding the entrance to the moist slit where she could slip inside me. I arched, ready for it, but she suddenly pulled away, climbing off the bed to put some distance between us.

Confused, dizzyingly so, I watched as she picked up a small spray from her Alkem module and doused herself with it. She returned and sprayed it on me as well.

I went to touch her but her flesh felt different, almost repellent. Somehow, in a few seconds, the heat had gone from my lust. The sight of her breasts was no longer erotic. My near-orgasm faded back to a troubled urge.

Glorious read my reaction and smiled. "I think the mélange I made was strong enough to disarm your defenses. Don't you?"

I opened my mouth and shut it again three times. Even then I couldn't form a word.

She smiled again, almost smug in her sincerity. "I love what I do, Jales. But to me it's science, you understand?"

Glorious stripped and stepped straight into the san, calling out some instructions to the Alkem module.

I turned away from her nakedness and forced myself over toward the window to think. I'd been dosed with an aphrodisiac without even knowing it.

Embarrassment left me hot in a different kind of way.

Lesson numero uno in the art.

I tried to clear my mind by staring at the view from Glorious's room.

One hundred and fifty floors up and not a vestige of smoke in the sky. I didn't know if Viva had climate and pollution controls—but it sure seemed like it.

To the east Jinberra Island floated on a glinting sea, taunting me. In a data collection, somewhere on that island, was the name I desperately wanted—the reason I was here acting as sport for a bored sex worker.

To the south, the grayish line of The Tert was the only blemish between the expanse of glittering chrome-edged city and the horizon.

I had a colossal desire to go home where I understood the rules. Where I wasn't at the mercy of Glorious's beauty and my overactive glands.

Thinking about The Tert soothed me some and my libido slid back under my control, leaving behind the usual restless frustration. I didn't want or have time for these distractions and yet without Merv's help I couldn't get the name I needed.

Patience.

"What did you think of my blend?"

I risked turning to look at Glorious. With relief I found that the intoxicating effects had waned. Behind me stood a clean, naked grrl with beautiful, intelligent eyes and a well-toned figure. The question she was asking was purely professional, one colleague to another.

I tucked my embarrassment away and tried to look casual. "Sure. Fun stuff."

She bent over in the doorway of a large built-in 'drobe crammed with clothes, wig kits and other trimmings. "You're not a standard size—we'll have to order in," she muttered, bending down to rifle through some low shelves.

"I don't need new clothes," I said automatically, wishing she would stand up and put some clothes on.

"You're right. Let's start with the important things." She sat down in front of her Alkem and tapped the side of her seat. "Come here, there's room."

A lesson in theory had to be safer than the hands-on variety even if the tutor was stark naked—so I did as she asked.

"How much do you know about blending?" she asked.

"Just give me the quick and dirty version." The unfortunate words were out of my mouth before I could stop them.

Glorious gave me a searching look, to see if I was joking.

I took a deep breath. The heat in my cheeks annoyed me. This kind of talk was not something I did with flair. "Er . . . I mean, give me the short version. I'll ask if I need to know more."

She nodded and leaned forward, flicking her wet

hair back, blowing onto a sensor. The Alkem's cover opened to reveal rows of multicolored vials with exotic stoppers: angel's wings, mermaids, birds of prey, naked statuettes . . . one even featured a tiny solar system with rotating planets.

"Our range of aphrodisiacs is extensive." She ran a hand lovingly along the rows. "And most clients still prefer to think that the effect on them is entirely natural. You can administer a blend in a number of subtle ways—stroking, kissing, biting, scratching if you aren't geno-fixed; sweating if you are."

Glorious pointed to an object shaped like a hollow finger. "If you place a finger into it, it will coat the tip in a blend. When you touch your client's skin, their body heat dissolves the coating in a few seconds. This is safer than a direct spray inhalation or a sweat exposure for new clients."

She saw the question in my expression.

"At the Luxoria we manufacture our own dizzies internally and our tolerances are naturally high. The receptivity of each client's vomeronasal receptors varies so much that it's very easy to overdose them."

"What do you mean, *internally*?"

She didn't hide her surprise. "I suppose you must use primitive means, Jales."

The heat rose in my face again. *Primitive* was a pretty good description of everything in my life. "We . . . er . . . spent more time on actual techniques."

Glorious didn't look convinced but she continued anyway. "My sex glands have been geno-fixed to produce pheromones on conscious demand. I don't need the right environment or the right partner." She grinned. "The alchemy side of things is purely for the clients. Once I know someone well I can use my own perspiration to stimulate them. It's slower to take effect but ultimately more powerful."

"Fascinating," I said, despite myself. "I'm surprised I've never heard of it before." I thought you could get anything done in The Tert.

"The procedure is expensive and only one genetic chemist in the Southern Hem performs it. It's irreversible, you see."

"What's the payback on that?"

Glorious thought about it for a moment, giving me a chance to study her. I figured her makeup was either permanent or geno-fixed as well: full, shaped lips, balanced bone structure and seductively sloping eyebrows—more than her share of beauty. The whole package was a freaking lot more effective than the quick-sculpt I'd had to straighten my face and cover my more obvious scars.

Even her hair had been tampered with so that it fell about her face like combed silk. The artifice ran so deep that the line of distinction between real and unreal had vanished. She could have been born ugly and deformed—you would never know.

"I guess it changes you fundamentally. Pleasure becomes so simple, and so necessary. My libido is constant if I want it to be." Another smile: a dirty one this time. "And sometimes I do—if I think my partner can handle it."

The conversation was taking a turn for the worse and I tried to steer it. "You used the finger coating on me?"

She nodded. "On your face."

I remembered her stroking my cheek in Breeza's.

"I've never seen a skin work quite like that before, Jales. It must be something to do with your different training." She paused. "I'd like to hear more about where you come from and what you've learned."

"Er . . . sure, later," I mumbled.

Glorious shrugged and went on methodically describing her formulas and their specific effects. "This one prolongs orgasm. This heightens its intensity but the muscle contractions can be severe. This sensitizes the body to pain. This does the opposite. This combined with this is called Elusive. It's the one I used on you. You rarely have to touch the person's genitals to bring them to orgasm. It can be quite useful if you find your client distasteful or potentially diseased. Of course, here we screen for the latter."

I stared at her, not sure whether to be insulted or relieved.

"One thing to remember." She tapped each elaborate stopper lightly with her tattooed fingernails, making a clicking noise. "Unnecessary amounts of any of these can either kill or inflict permanent damage. And overuse is addictive."

"What about you?"

"Oh, I'm addicted in a different way. We all are. If anyone attempted to alter the hyper-functioning of our glands, we'd die. But it's not like I'll ever have to stop."

She threw me a questioning look.

"Delly wants me to dizzie you up for your interview with Monk. But when you meet him in person he might be difficult. Jaded."

"Oh?"

"If you get in a tight spot, these can be . . . useful."

Glorious handed me a small, flexible ring.

"We call them lifesavers," she said. "Just lick it if you need to use it. The acid in your saliva breaks the seal, then the blend is released into your mouth. If you kiss your partner, the chemicals are shared. This one is called"—she squinted at the colored stripes—"Castles in the Sky. Whoever you use it on will have the experience of their life."

I wanted to laugh. But this was her practical way of helping me, so I took the ring and slipped it on my little finger.

"We make all our blends here but we buy in the base ingredients like synthesized androstenol and androstenone. Then we mix it with a few of Delly's specialities."

She pointed to a vial with a lable that read *5-a-androst-16en-3a-on*.

"It occurs naturally in male sweat but we don't advertise the fact." Glorious grinned as I wrinkled my nose. "I do the alchemy for some of the others as a trade-off for learning other skills. Each of us has a domain. I help Dazzle with his dizzies. He's taught me how to tie knots." Her eyes widened a little. "You can't believe how particular some of my clients are. Placement and style are everything."

I blinked, knowing that I was all out of that kind of chat. If she didn't stop, I was either going to roar or damage something.

The door clicked open and a small, fragile guy in an outfit made of rope came in. He stopped when he saw me.

"*You're* the new grrl?"

Glorious got off her seat to put her arms around him. "Dazzle, meet Jales."

The top of his head was level with her breasts. He seemed the type who might like to burrow in between them for comfort.

Who am I to talk? I'd been trying to do something similar a short while before.

I managed to maintain an affable face. "Yeah, I'm here on work experience."

Dazzle's curiosity turned immediately to boredom and he pirouetted out of Glorious's grasp. "Pity. You look like you might know what you're doing. I'm going for a swim. Buzz me when your next client is in. I'll come down." He addressed his last remarks to Glorious.

The door clicked again behind him.

"Must take him a while to get dressed."

She shot me another puzzled look and sat down again.

Shut up, Parrish.

"Dazzle and I sort of . . . mind each other. Delly has things in place to keep us safe—the i-bugs and Lam and Tae—but it's comforting to have a spotter," she said.

"Brigitte didn't have one?"

For an instant, I saw her fear. Despite her insistence that she loved her job, it was there, lurking.

Sympathy ignited in me but I blew it out. I didn't want to have any connections to this place. I wanted to find out—and *get* out.

I couldn't help one question, though. "How did you come to work here?"

Glorious's beautiful face went taut. I'd seen that happen so many times before with so many people. Closing off. Hiding the truth.

"I told you before: It's a choice. A way of life. Better than the one I had before I came here," she said. "In a few days, you'll understand why."

Chapter Nine

Glorious was right.
And she was the consummate teacher.

Worse, though, I soon became the consummate student, ambushed by the Eskaalim.

Every minute I practiced the art it grew fat and bloated, and I was powerless to fight the pleasure in the way I had fought the violence.

The visions started again and in a matter of days I became lost. Concerned only with prolonging the euphoria.

She taught me to prepare blends, crudely but effectively. I learned how and where and when to administer them and she'd let me overdose so I knew the side effects.

"You recover so quickly," she marveled.

But Glorious was wrong. I wasn't recovering. I was deeply hooked and reaping the consequences. The parasite that I'd struggled so hard to control was shaking free again, feeding off the sex just as it fed off the violence—adaptable and resilient.

I might have resisted the shape-change before, but it was coming for me this time. Gaining ground every time I used the dizzies.

And yet I couldn't stop.

The chemical addiction was worse than anything I'd ever tried—worse than Lark and NS. Now I understood what happened to the spinners like the one who'd killed Brigitte. And why Glorious stayed with the job. And why scum like Lavish Deluxe could make a living from it.

I'd become consumed, like them.

Worse. I'd become obsessed with Glorious, not wanting to share her with anyone. In fact, I wanted to kill anyone who touched her. I wanted her every minute, without exclusion, without conscience or restraint.

Glorious seemed fascinated by the intensity of my response.

"We have one last experience," she said, not looking at me as she spoke. "So you understand how deep it can go."

Her half-closed eyes and swollen lips told me that her proposed teaching *experience* wasn't just for me. Glorious was enjoying herself.

Strangely, that made me glad.

It was early evening. At least I think it was—Delly had given her several days off work to tutor me and we'd only been out to eat.

"I don't know if that's such a good idea." But my protest was brittle. In truth, I'd become ridiculously compliant. I just wanted her to dizzie me up and touch me. Nothing else mattered.

"Don't you want to take a little risk, Jales?"

She closed her eyes and concentrated for a few moments. When she opened them she ran her finger along the sweat that had appeared under her armpit.

Before I realized what she was doing, she had covered my mouth and forced her finger into my nostril.

I inhaled her geno-fixed sweat deeply.

Glorious took my hands and cupped her breasts with them. I watched her eyes roll back in her head as if she was fitting. Then something exploded in me, obliterating all other experiences.

She climbed my body, legs clutching tight around my waist. The weight of her toppled us on to her bed. Her tongue in my mouth, she undressed me while I lay shivering and jerking with the shock of mounting sensations.

The Eskaalim presence, already bloated by my hormones, erupted. Coherent thought deserted me entirely. My skin caught fire.

I rolled her over and mounted her, my hands around her neck.

Who was I? Should I kill?

"Jales. Relax. It's like tripping. If you fight it you'll become psychotic," she said.

I battled the desire to strangle Glorious and closed my eyes. Images rushed me. The past. Mo-Vay. Roo—flesh dissolving in the copper canal. Jamon Mondo. Kevin. Everything terrible.

Somebody was screaming.

I opened my eyes.

Me. I was screaming.

Glorious pulled me down on her. "Suckle," she ordered. "Take comfort."

I put my lips to her nipple, tugging and sucking it like a baby.

She petted and soothed me until the bloodlust subsided. Her legs wrapped around me, tight and secure.

The position seemed to give her pleasure and I felt her back arch.

I slipped my hands underneath the hollow, drawing her in to me, and suddenly everything changed.

The fire on my skin was back but now it blazed *for* her.

We slammed from one thing to another as we joined.

I had her in every way I could dream of until she cried out from fatigue.

Then I wanted more.

"Stop now," she gasped.

"No." I grabbed her and began kissing her body.

"Stop, Jales." She tried to push me away. "Merv!"

"Jales?" Merv's voice cut into our privacy. "Glorious's vital signs show that she's suffering from exhaustion. You must stop now or you'll have to be restrained."

"No," I whispered. "I need more."

I didn't even hear the door open as Lam and Muscle Massive burst into the room.

Massive tried to pull me away from Glorious but I elbowed him in the mouth, knocking him backward. The gentle giant touched the blood on his lip with surprise.

He lunged again, this time grabbing my arms and holding tight while Lam punched me.

Aided by the slick sweat on my naked body, I twisted from Massive's grasp and launched myself at Lam. He might have been the real deal but my Eskaalim frenzy was no-pain stuff.

I flung him across the room before he could put a hold on me.

I heard the crack. Saw the angle of his arm. His pupils went pinhead-size with shock.

Massive chopped me across the neck with one huge hand.

Down on my knees but I still couldn't feel the pain. *"Jales."*

I whirled, seeking out Lavish—the reason I was being denied.

But he was ready for me, a lion tamer with a stunwhip and an antidote spray.

As I collapsed to the floor, he doused Glorious as well.

She cried out at the sensory denial.

"Shut—the fuck—up!" Lavish screamed at her.

She jammed her fingers in her mouth and cowered

away from his rage, sobbing. "I—I didn't know this would happen, Delly. She's different. It shouldn't have been like this," she protested.

"You were indulging yourself, you little bitch."

As Massive dragged me from the room, I heard the sounds of Lavish slapping her.

"Merv," I screamed into the air. "Tell Lavish to leave her alone or I'll kill him."

"Calm down, Jales. You're in withdrawal. You're not rational." The calmness of the voyeur's voice enraged me further.

Massive threw me into my room and locked me in.

I paced, a brooding lunatic, slamming myself against the door for an hour or more until the very last of my energy was spent.

But it wasn't over.

Chapter Ten

The full withdrawal started sometime during the night.

Massive held me down while Lavish shot me full of sedatives. They tied me on my side in bed and shoved a dog chew in my mouth against the convulsions and peaks of rage.

I spat it out when the vomiting came.

And then the delirium.

. . . The Angel lounged on a sea of naked bodies. Legs and arms interchangeable, noises and damp skin smells.

This is far better, human. You can't fight this. . . .

I rocked and moaned in my restraint, gripped by thoughts of death. Then wishing for it. I hallucinated black whorls on my arms and legs.

The night passed in a hell of guilt and remorse and self-loathing. I'd never felt utter depravity before, or its flip side.

I'd put up no fight against the Eskaalim. Lust had become more dangerous to me than violence because I found it harder to resist. Then, when the lust had me, the violence returned.

By morning a residual headache, tremors and joint

pain were still with me. So was the bloating in my
groin and the mental scarring, leaving me exhausted
and depressed.

I had to get out of this place.

There was no pleasure in what I'd done. Pleasure
was conscious-choice stuff—*not* having the animal
ripped from inside you and put on parade.

I didn't need the restraints anymore. The self-
loathing was punishment enough.

Muscle Massive came to check on me. "You behave
now?" he asked hopefully, touching his steri-stripped
lip.

"Your mouth. Sorry . . ."

"I am Frederic from Ukraine. I understand how it
happened. I don't touch those girls—too dangerous.
You've got good . . . stamina."

He might look stupid but he was smarter than me.

And too damn forgiving.

My teeth chattered. "Thanks, Freddy Ukraine, but
I—I need t-to use the s-san."

He loosened the restraints and went to stand in
the doorway. "Hurry now. You must come."

"Where?"

"To the Fair. A good thing. Keep you away from
Glorious."

"What Fair?"

Freddy smiled and his eyes rolled into the folds of
his eyelids. "You'll see."

I showered, put the cheongsam over my leather
crop, and tucked a small derm of painkill into the
pocket with Ike's wetware. I'd lifted it from Lam
when they were doping me with sed and right now
I could feel another headache coming on.

Freddy walked me to a 'pede parked out on the
club's helipad.

Delly, Merv and Lam were waiting for us.

No one spoke. Lam's arms were both heavily
strapped.

As the 'pede climbed off down the side of the
building, I stared out at the ordinary cits going about
their biz and wished I was one of them.

"When's my interview with Monk?" I asked sul-
lenly.

Lavish looked over his shoulder. I barely recognized his face. One of the Fair rules—Freddy Ukraine
told me—was that all enhancements had to be
suppressed.

Without the insidious allure of dizzies, Lavish's
fine, athletic build seemed weedy, and his narrow
features twisted. I felt nauseous just looking at him.

"Not soon enough." He accessed his p-diary, a
wrist model. "Tomorrow."

I glanced anxiously at Merv but he was ignoring
me and petting Snout in the crook of his elbow.

We 'peded for an hour before Muscle Massive
Freddy settled us into a parking lot outside a
members-only lo-rise of shop fronts with clean windows and quality products.

I blinked over and over as I climbed out as if I was
waking from a faint, feeling the withdrawal finally
beginning to leave me.

"This is a *mall*?" I muttered tetchily.

Lavish smiled at Lam and led us to a door at one
end of the building; outside a lingerie shop. He then
marched us into a conveyor-lift that whizzed a klick
or more across to the other side of the complex.

I tried to count off the list of retailers on the display but the blur made my headache worse.

We stopped three-quarters of the way across and
exited straight into the back of another lift. A glance at
the display told me that it was between a patisserie and
a surf originals shop. I committed the spot to memory.

The next lift went down—sixteen floors. I felt the
weight of the ground above me as keenly as if I was
down in Gwynn's water pipes under the Viva–Tert
border.

This time the doors opened straight into something.

A club, I thought, only bigger.

Much bigger.

The floor stretched back farther than I could see in a glance.

Expensive noise. Exclusive clientele. Intimates serving free wine fizz and tailor-made smoke—dope, green leaf and thin cigars, beautifully rolled—filtered or nose-piped.

Lavish guzzled down a drink without ceremony and left Merv and me with Lam. He disappeared down a corridor of booths and siddowns clustered under a cute sign that read IMMORAL AISLES.

I refused the wine, shut my olfaugs down and wandered into another area designated BITERS. Even then I copped a headspin from the array of pheremonal scents and the heavy sublimmals. The advertising was rampant, aggressive, personalized—and the last thing I needed.

Unwittingly, I stumbled straight into a floating net of porn pics and for a full free-color minute I rushed on erections—the vreal so good that I could feel altering pressure between my legs as the sizing changed to find the right fit.

I tore the ephemeral off my face and flicked it to the floor. A gobbler scuttled up and digested the web, the space on its back offering me a free sample of a new enhanced Tao dizzie. I kicked it out of my way so I could move and got a perceptible jab from its sample probes.

Another free minute of jittery lust and a blast of marsala scents.

Sweat poured off me from the hyper-stimulation and a new kind of fear. The whole sex thing was like a bleeding wound that I wanted to cauterize. I staggered from one consumer trap to the next before I cottoned on to Lam's smirk.

He was keeping his distance from me, but it seemed to be out of respect rather than anger.

Who could figure people? If *he*'d broken *my* arms, I'd want to poison him.

"What's the trick?" I growled as a pair of hands grew out of a wall, slipped around my chest and began massaging my breasts. I chopped at the wrists. The wrists snapped off but the hands stuck to my cheongsam.

Lam's smirk turned to a guffaw.

"You're a newbie," Merv explained. "The products have a memory. They don't saturate you more than once unless you invite them to. It's the Fair etiquette. You're a target, though. First in, best hooked."

I wrestled with the hands, finally tearing the dress to get rid of them.

Lam obligingly bought a T-shirt from a nearby booth and passed it to me in his teeth. I didn't know whether he was rubbing it in that I'd broken both his arms, or if this was his kind of hero worship.

I took it anyway, ignoring the belly-dancing torso banging about on the front of it.

Soon as I put it on over the dress, the product clamor stopped seeking me out.

"You've bought something. The race is off now," Merv explained.

"Thanks." I nodded at Lam.

Taking some deep breaths to settle my shakes, I began to look around properly, sorting through the orgy of images, expressions and merchandise.

When I first saw Leesa Tulu, I thought I was hallucinating.

Or dreaming awake.

Only when she actually brushed past me to enter a mainlining booth did I react.

I recoiled at her touch but she didn't recognize me out of context, with my prettied-up face and city clothes.

A war of impulses flooded me. Merv, always watching, saw something in my face.

"Jales?"

"Do you know her?" I managed to get out.

He glanced carefully where I was looking and nodded. "Kind of. N-not good company, Jales. P-please don't stare."

I followed him a sufficient distance away so that my fixed attention wouldn't be as obvious.

"Quick," I ordered. "Tell me what you know."

"Her name is M-Madame Tulu. She's a s-spiritualist with a lot of influence in certain circles."

"Who does she work for?"

Merv got nervous, fidgeting.

I grabbed his arm and squeezed it.

He squirmed, uncomfortable with my touch and my insistence.

"Tell me what you know or . . ." I snatched Snout from him and put my hand around the toy's collar where its wireless sensors were.

He paled as if I had put a knife to his throat.

My friendly veneer had been stripped away. Only the slimmest thread of control and the security buzzards floating above my head were stopping me from going after Tulu right there, right then.

"I don't know if it's right, b-but they say she works for S-Slipstream."

"Who?" One hand had found its way to Merv's shirt, my fist clenching the material.

He began to sweating, glancing around. "They're f-finders—of a sort. B-but Slipstream are more specialized than the others."

"How?"

"S-Slipstream hunt out all the illegal genetics operations in the S-Southern Hem. They buy any worthwhile advancements and on-sell to whoever w-wants it."

"Who would want it?" My voice matched Merv's. Low and quivering.

"I don't know, Jales. T-truly. I can get Snout to s-sniff for you if you don't hurt her."

"Do it," I said. "Tonight. The other stuff as well. I need to know."

"Come and s-see me after the club closes," he said.

I gave Snout back and let him go. Lavish appeared out of the throng as if his antennae were wired to the intensity of our tête-à-tête.

"Secrets, Jales?"

"Sweet nothings, Lavish."

He squinted suspiciously. I couldn't have much longer before he pieced together who I really was and worked out what he would try to bargain for with that knowledge.

My time at Luxoria had nearly run out.

"I am waiting for an order to be filled and then we will leave."

As Lavish spoke Tulu left the booth behind us, swaying, wild-eyed. Stoned or possessed—it was hard to say.

Two bodyguards flanked her as she weaved along down toward the stage where spotlights roved and glitter motes spouted from the air plumes.

"What happens down there? Fashion show?" I asked.

Lavish threw me another suspicious look. One that told me I'd said something too stupid for my own good.

"In a way," he said carefully, and moved toward Tulu.

Muscle Massive came and pressed a hand against my back, herding Merv and me ahead of him without a word.

"What is it?" I hissed at Merv.

He drew away from me, silent and still unhappy about my threat to Snout.

Lavish found us seats a few rows behind Tulu. She was at the front, in an armchair, drinking Pernod straight from the bottle. A waiter appeared with a bidding slate for her. She slotted it into the armrest and tapped in some numbers. Another waiter came and offered her a glass. She cuffed him away.

Lavish curled his lip. "Vulgar bitch."

"Friend?"

"With Madam Prime-Evil?" He raised an eyebrow and sniffed, insulted.

The music pumped up, ending our conversation. The glitter motes changed color and a tall, unreasonably emaciated man took center stage.

"I am the Custodian," he whispered. "Welcome."

I was still thinking fashion right up until the moment when the first walker removed her coat and I saw a credit insignia tattooed on her thigh.

That—and the fact that the leather-clad Custodian used an instrument to expose her more secret attributes.

The catwalk was a slave market. Meat market. Call it what you like. This was flesh for sale.

I wanted to leap up there and shove the instrument down the Custodian's throat. I wanted to scream at the grrl to get some dignity. But I was pretty short of that myself.

Instead I sat rigid and silent.

Lavish sensed my distress and enjoyed it.

I included him in the list of things I wanted to damage.

The surge of anger fried away any remaining residue of dizzies and my head cleared properly for the first time in days.

I began to think.

Yet nothing . . . *nothing* could have prepared me for the next item in the meat sale.

He strolled down the catwalk, naked and glistening. Face impassive. Prosthetic arm gleaming with bandit appeal.

Loyl-me-Daac.

Chapter Eleven

I snatched Lavish's catalogue slate.

"What are you doing?" he demanded.

"I . . . er . . . fancy this one." I stumbled over the words. "How much is he?"

I knew I was acting strangely, that my shock was too palpable, but I couldn't contain it. In the front row, Tulu's reaction was similar. She scrolled frantically through the slate. Her name flagged instantly as a bidder.

As I requested a look at her price, the bidding chimes went psycho and the whole display dropped out to be replaced by the image of a half-naked couple sipping martinis on a secluded beach.

"What's happened?" I gasped.

Lavish prized the slate from me. "See over there, in the chair next to the voodoo bitch? An Intimate. I would guess that Monk or Laud's bidding for him." He pointed at an icon flashing on the slate. "Look. The bidding price is already withdrawn. Once an IO's bid high . . . the bidding goes off-line. No one can contest them." His fingernails raked across the skin on the back of my hand. "That's why I need him to be seen at Luxoria. You had better perform suitably tomorrow, or I'll hand you straight over to the Militia . . . Ms. Plessis.''

It had been so long since I'd heard my own name that it took a second to register. A flush of adrenaline followed. I was half out of my seat, ready to run or fight or some damn thing.

Lavish's fingernails hooked into me and Massive brought both his hands down on my shoulders.

"Sit down and behave," Lavish snarled.

My desire to damage him turned into something much more ominous. My fingers ached for a wire to whip across his sneering face. But I did what he said because a security buzzard had started recording right above us.

Like the rest of the audience my attention fell to the man on the stage. I wanted to look away when they made him stroke himself but I found it impossible to do so. I stared at his masculine perfection and listened to the voice-over reciting his pedigree. The women he'd "serviced" read like a media-star roll call.

Razz Retribution. Manatunga Right-Woman. Laidley Beaudesert.

A confusion of emotions beset me. Repulsion. Desire. Sadness. But mostly suspicion. What the freak was he up to?

He was sold quickly to James Monk for an undisclosed sum and the bidding display returned to normal after the sale was announced.

The Custodian drew him away from the spotlights, back to a dark wing of the stage, before loping back to introduce the next sale.

Daac scanned the crowd keenly from the shadows, his gaze abruptly halting on my section of the seating.

My body warmed. Had he recognized me?

Tulu noticed Daac's fixed stare, traced his line of sight and reached her senses into the crowd. The force of her energy curled around me. As I tried to repel it, something stronger reared. Tulu often channelled a powerful voodoo spirit who went by the name of Marinette. Marinette and I had met before. The creature got hot over human sacrifice and when she rode Tulu, the pair scared the Jeez out of me. Marinette knew me in a second and, like half the universe, we had some old scores to settle.

I gripped Lavish's arm.

"We need to leave."

He saw the commotion as Marinette jerked Tulu upright, overturning her seat, bottle smashing. "What's the problem?"

I gave him my most matter-of-fact Plessis stare. "If we go now, we'll all be alive for me to explain later."

He nodded, annoyed but not stupid enough to ignore me.

He quickly threaded a path for us down the Immoral Aisles to the lift. As we reached the doors, Tulu waded into the crowd in demolition mode. The Fair security swarmed in to defuse things. A security buzzard swooped.

The lift doors pinged open to reveal new buyers, an expensively dressed couple in matching suits, gloves and shades. Lavish jammed his foot in the door and I hauled one of them out by her velvet lapel. Massive launched the other into the air at the buzzard.

I had a second to be impressed. Sometimes there was no substitute for sheer grunt.

We made it up six floors before the lift shut down.

"Get the freaking thing open," Lavish snarled.

Lam was muttering in rusty Korean.

Prayers, I hoped.

Massive broke off a handrail and rammed it in between the doors. He wedged them open with force, sweat funneling from his face. I was beginning to love him more by the second.

We crawled out and onto the floor into complete darkness.

"Stay with me." I moved automatically to a wall and began feeling my way. The place smelled of dust and stale air.

No one had been in here for a while.

On the far side a crack of light suggested a fire escape. We tripped over each other until I issued another order, to grab the next person's shoulder. That worked better, despite Massive's anguished, "Delly, pliz, that's not my shoulder."

His labored breathing told me that the airless dark had made him jumpier than the rest of us.

"Easy, Freddy," I whispered to him. "There's a stairwell over the other side."

His huge hand tightened gratefully on my shoulder, crunching my bones. When we got within a few steps of the outlined door, he rushed past me, opening it.

I started after him, mouthing a warning, but the automatic burglar device detected him immediately. He pushed me back into the doorway, out of harm's way, and dived. The projectile splintered the wooden grip along the top of the rail and sprayed splinters into Freddy's shoulder and arm.

The impact of his recoil shook the railing all the way up and down the well. I grabbed him before he could topple over, my feet wedged against a step, knees locked, back straining.

"For chrissakes—help . . . ," I bellowed.

Lam danced around, useless with his broken arms, but Delly rallied, seeing his bodyguard about to tumble to his death.

"I've disabled it." Merv's voice came from behind the door panel.

Delly and I dragged Massive back from the edge. The huge man was ashen, trembling with pain and shock.

I whacked him up with the derm of painkill I'd been saving for myself. It barely touched his pain but his expression told me that now he could at least think a bit.

"Up and out," I said. *"Now."*

He nodded.

I climbed on to the step above him and hauled. From behind, Merv pushed and Delly swore ceaselessly.

Eventually the stairs came out behind the patisserie.

I steered Massive around to the front and down the gap between the surf-originals shop to the second lift, ignoring the terrified shoppers' stares. Delly and Lam and Merv trailed. Sweat streamed off all of us except Massive.

Blood streamed off him.

The atmosphere during the 'pede trip back to the Luxoria was sullen at best. Lavish hunched in the backseat, his face pinched with fury.

I wasn't much better. The whole withdrawal thing and then half-carrying Massive had drained all my energy. I managed to strap up his shoulder with strips from my cheongsam before I fell back exhausted.

Next to me Merv hugged Snout to his face, trying to block out Massive's moans.

Lavish leaned close to my ear. "Whatever you're up to here," he said, "your time is up."

I had the rest of the trip back to contemplate what that might mean.

Glorious came to me when I got to my room. "Lam said you saved Freddy's life."

"No," I said, too tired to be anything but short with her. "He saved mine."

"Oh."

"Monk's call is tomorrow. Keep away from me until then."

She flinched. "I'm sorry the withdrawal was so rough on you. You're different from anyone I've taught before. And for what it's worth, it probably happened because I was enjoying myself too much."

"I thought you *always* enjoyed yourself," I sneered.

"Not like that," she said, and left.

I kicked the door shut behind her and reminded myself that she was *Amorato*. They didn't care about anything but the next pleasurable sensation.

I had a shower and lay down fully clothed, asking the alarm to wake me before dawn when the club closed.

When it woke me I went down to the club and stood facing the dark mirrors. The smell of spilled spirits in the drip tray made me wet my lips and swallow hard—stale whiskey at dawn belonged with memories of Jamon.

"Merv?" I called.

He opened the mirror door, four-thirty–in-the-morning pale.

I went in and waited for him to speak.

He climbed tiredly up on the deck and twirled his charms in sequence.

"I've only f-found out one thing for sure. Brilliance has a s-snoop program out hunting information on Slipstream. Snout had to play dead to avoid being f-found."

"What's that mean?" I asked, impatient.

His voice dropped so low I found myself lip-reading. "It means that Slipstream must be working f-for the banks."

I didn't understand the nuance—wasn't able to make the right leaps. "Explain."

Merv rubbed a rabbit's foot for comfort as he gathered his thoughts. "Brilliance edits all the raw footage for the media s-so she s-sees everything that is c-cammed. If she has to s-snoop out information on Slipstream, then they must be working outside the normal c-c-corridors, otherwise sh-she wouldn't need to be watching them."

"You mean they're collecting information for Common Net and Out-World?"

Merv shook his head. "No . . . Common Net and Out-World are j-just Brilliance in a couple of her guises. She likes to m-masquerade as an independent s-source. You c-can't trust anything from them."

"So you're telling me *all* our viewing, *everything* we see is controlled by Brilliance."

"C-close. Enough to make you sleep b-bad, anyway."

"So where do the banks fit in?"

Merv frowned and interlocked his fingers to stop them shaking. I sensed that he was almost frightened to say what he was thinking. "Snout thinks . . . I—I think Slipstream is working for the banks."

My head hurt. Viva politics, beyond my understanding yet controlling my life.

"Clear as mud, Merv," I said tiredly. "Why would an organization that tracks illegal genetic operations be working for the banks?"

He shrugged. "I don't know w-why. M-maybe they are looking for s-something that will give them an edge against the m-media."

"Why do they need an edge?"

"W-when we had governments and p-political parties, they had a lot of p-power. N-now they don't have anything, except their royalty."

I thought about what he said. Information was everything in any war. Maybe Merv was right and something was brewing here in Viva.

"What about Code Noir, then?"

He rubbed his eyes. "Snout's searches t-tripped a

bunch of s-seekers. She had to bail out. The only thing I c-can tell you is that the s-seeker definitely came from one of the Jinberra p-portals."

I nodded. No surprises there. Only more reason for doing what I knew I had to do. "I have to get in there, Merv."

He shivered. "You c-can't. Not by y-yourself, anyway."

I slipped the mystic star over my head and placed it in his damp hand. "I'm all out of time, Merv. I have to do it now. I need your help. Please."

He trembled and kissed the charm as if it were his lover's flesh. Reverently, he laid it in its place and sighed. "You c-can ride with me."

His eyes got watery in a way that reminded me of Stolowski. Only it wasn't with trust. Merv was scared.

"I like Jales better than Parrish," he added.

I stiffened for a moment and then relaxed.

The only way that Lavish could have discovered my true identity would have been through Merv. Who had probably known who I really was from day one at the Luxoria.

"Sometimes, Merv," I replied softly, "so do I."

Chapter Twelve

Merv locked off access to his room and unfolded a jockey seat from the side of his chair/bed. The springs groaned with lack of use but he didn't seem to notice. His eyes and mind were flicking ahead to vrealspace like a dog scenting virgin territory down the road.

He handed me an opaline bracelet.

"What's this?"

"Put it on," he instructed automatically.

I turned it over in my hand, examining the sharp bumps on the inside of the band. "What do you mean? Is this the transceiver?"

He didn't answer.

"*Merv.*"

"Yes." His attention flicked back to me again. He looked slightly embarrassed. "It will link you to me."

I stared at the mound of cables and the wetware webs littering the room. "You mean this is all show?"

"Not exactly. Everything works. My backup, if you like. But it's best if Delly doesn't understand how I really do things."

I pointed to the wetware stains on his collar. "What about that?"

Merv's embarrassment turned downright sheepish. He pulled a little tube of dye from his pocket.

I laughed. Merv had seemed so incapable of deceit to me.

"Tighten the bracelet around your wrist. The connectors prick a little bit but then it's over. Your senses interpret the vreal first. You don't even have to close your eyes. You'll have to c-cadaver. It'd take too much time to configure a s-subtle enough avatar," he said apologetically.

Cadavers had no iconic representation or signature in vrealspace. They were worse than the ezy-rent ghosts.

That meant they had no rights. Voyeurs in vreal land.

"You've r-ridden before?"

I nodded.

"This vreal is called Chaos. It's Five-Gen s-sensory. Changeable and h-hard to read if you don't understand the p-patterns. The f-fringe areas are often olfactory," he warned. "Just don't lose me."

Hadn't Teece said the same thing?

I jacked down my augs as a precaution and tightened the bracelet.

The pinpricks were mild and the drop was smooth and seamless. One second I was tucking my legs under the jockey seat of Merv's bed/chair, the next I was floating down from the V-Net launch pad in neat spirals. None of the crazy head rush that I'd had with Teece.

Merv was slick. Only he wasn't Merv anymore—he was a tiny, faint light pixel, a firefly surfing an endlessly changing rainbow.

I was bodiless, weightless and his equal in shadow, all my hopes depending on staying with his almost indistinguishable flicker of light.

We sailed through the coils of data, changing streamers hundreds of times, darting in and out until everything blurred.

By the nature of his movement I figured that Merv's firefly was masquerading as part of the Vreal Net's internal spy system—a self-regulating program that monitored light organization and behavior. Snout probably did something similar.

Inside my invisible shadow body, my invisible shadow heart beat faster. If the system found an anomaly in Merv's disguise it would destroy us in a pica-second.

For the first time in a long time, I remembered a prayer.

Merv traversed the red spectrum, navigating on color subtleties and taste—amber to orange, sweet to fruity. Orange to sienna, fruity to scorched.

Five G—an almost unbearable sensory experience to the uninitiated. In realtime my mouth filled with saliva and my eyes streamed.

As we danced I began to discern energy clusters and finally shapes: light avatars forming exotic fractal creatures.

Decahedrons are the gateways. Merv thought-whispered. Data streams poured around them, creating whirlpools and lightfalls.

We swirled down them, attracting only a flicker of security.

The butterfly fractals are data miners, he thought-said.

We jumped aboard one that was trawling the violet spectrum. As we got closer to the edge of the range, we leaped from it into a dark worm-trail.

What's this?

A virus.

Somewhere, some part of me held its breath, watching as Chaos sent out its virus protection, shining helixes writhing like snakes.

Merv's firefly folded over me and we slid down the twirling killers.

His confidence and daring staggered me—a paradoxical contrast with the real person.

Momentum flung us into the wake of a fast-moving stream of indigo data heading right into the heart of a magenta cluster. I could taste strawberry syrup.

It was soon canceled out by the familiar smell of putrid meat that told me we'd passed right under the nose of the sifter and the odor firewall that had bounced me into mouth-to-mouth with Gigi.

Prison central.

When the indigo transfer was complete we dived into light quicksand.

Temp repository, thought-said Merv.

I wanted to reply but I'd forgotten how to do it, so I contented myself by watching light flickers.

A lifetime or many passed as we hid out in the shifting data pile.

When the swish of a new incoming transfer stirred the grains of our repository, Merv finally floated us upward.

An error alarm started as Chaos tried to work out what tiny thing was out of place.

Merv contorted his firefly avatar into a helix shape and the system passed over us. In a pica he'd branched back into the main data stream and we surfed the crest of a light wave right into the Jin-berra nexus.

It was an elegant move. Humble. Brilliant. With much less statement than most bio-hacks employed.

We sank straight into another quicksand data repository.

It was impossible to know how much time passed. Somewhere in my hindbrain I had a vague perception of discomfort—a twinge that all was not well.

I absorbed Merv's thought-speak. *Your realtime body is having circulatory problems. I'm going to move your limbs. This may cause you some disorientation.*

I thought-sent my agreement back to him.

Then vertigo took over.

The impression of the swirling grains of the repository disintegrated and I began to shoot upward into a curling viral blackness. Just like the nightmares I used to have of elevators exploding from the top of lift wells.

You're getting sick. Merv's thought-voice again, a tinge of annoyance in it. *I don't have suction so I'm going to derm you with an anti-spasmodic before you choke on it.*

His mind-voice disappeared and a malaise crept up on me, another bodily sensation that I shouldn't have been able to feel.

Panic.

What's happening, Merv?

A delay before he replied. *The node is defragging. We have to move ahead of it or we'll be sloughed. Your mind-body connection is messed up. You're going to feel things . . . they aren't real, but your body won't believe that. I've given you a second derm to counter it. It should work within a couple of real minutes; you just have to withstand the sensation of defrag until it does. . . . Good luck.*

His last two words were the quietest I'd ever heard.

He pulled us free from the repository and the torture began.

The system defrag tore me apart. I felt my muscle fibers being tweezed and shredded while they were still attached to me. My hair ripped out in tufts. The soft skin inside my mouth was carved with a knife and peeled back to flop about on my tongue. My tongue sliced into sections that were then pulled apart and down into my throat.

Pain with no endorphin rush to combat it.

A total rending so painful that I should have died from the shock. And yet I didn't.

I just lost everything.

My mind imploded. Only the pain stayed.

And stayed.

Some primal instinct took over.

I fled it, into a glacial darkness, dragging my memories with me.

I am Parrish. I am in vreal with a bio-hack. The pain is imagined. I am Jales. I am Roo. I am . . . no one. . . .

In the cold distance I saw a shape, a void at the end of it all. I labored toward it, the most wretched pilgrim, reaching it on determination alone.

This was the place I'd come to die.

Peace.

Finally. I deserved it. Mine.

But solitude, even there, was denied me. Something had taken my space, stolen my death's refuge.

"Who are you?"

The figure turned its shadowed Angel face to my impassioned insistence. Gone were the bloodied wings and statuesque body. Gone was the power of blood and lust.

It huddled in my last mindspace, as distressed and disarmed as I was.

"Why are you in my death?" I shouted.

Don't you know yet? it said. Wearily, it opened its eon-long memory to me.

With the wonder of a child I began to see . . .

A comet seeding—riding the tides of a galaxy. Parasites bred as agents of evolution. Spreading themselves. Catalysts of change.

Earth discovered and infected. What satisfaction and relief. The host is most suitable, the WE agree. Strong enough to withstand and not be destroyed. Strong enough to be pushed the next step.

But Homo erectus *had its own survival mechanism.*

The WE became trapped.

"You say we wouldn't have evolved without you," I say.

Yes. That is our single purpose. We have generated the higher evolution of many—those that can toler-

ate our needs. Some, of course, cannot. It is our hun-
ger, our lust, the nature of WE that has brought you
to where you are. See . . .

Thought-images ran past me then.

Mass suicide of species that could not withstand them.
Creatures so alien that they create only an impression.
There is no reference to build their appearance.

But the balance has been disturbed. You are in ex-
cess now. You are taking us over.

The WE cannot resist that which has happened.

"What if we try to destroy you? We will both die,
won't we? We will all die. . . ."

But the Angel withheld and began to dissolve into the
walls of my core.

What? Merv's mind-voice was back. *Jales, I mean . . .*
Parrish. Are you . . . can you still . . . think . . . ?

No more than usual, I managed after a time. Humor
not felt.

His relief enfolded me. And surprise. *You survived.*

I suppose. It didn't feel like survival. More like a
residue of what I had been.

I've found the place where the data is stored. But there's
one last hurdle, he thought-said.

Wasn't there always one last hurdle?

My thoughts drifted, still muddled by the thing I
had just seen, and by what the pain had cost. Slowly
the vreal began to reconstruct around me and my
bodily sensations distanced again.

Merv had set us down onto a crag above a crum-
pling data sea. Across it, the small, stolid light of an
infrared transceiver pulsed.

You want to know about Code Noir, Merv thought-
said, *you have to get yourself over there.*

Chapter Thirteen

*D*o I go on? the residue of me wondered.

It seems that is all there is, I answered myself.

And so . . .

How do I do that, Merv?

I've been watching. The impartial is periodically synchronized but I can't travel the light wave. My avatar can't be decoded in the infrared spectrum, and the impartial's got some old and ugly defences. You might be able to fly it, though. Nothing like you should have gotten this far into the Jinberra nexus. Your encoding is so simple, the most basic blip of information. It might not have a parameter to detect you as an intruder.

And if it does?

I imagined his shrug. *Your call.*

Momentum. That's all there is, the residue of me thought. *What do I attach to?*

A photon. I'll help boost you on to it. You'll have to flake off at the other end.

Coming back?

Silence from Merv.

Ah. I see.

The residue of me recognized irony. My whole life—the smallest dot of information. It seemed fair.

So why loiter?

I saw the shimmer of activity as a wall of data assembled, ready to convert and transmit across the connection.

Boost away, I thought-sent.

Good-bye . . . the whisper came back.

Riding the light wave was a roller coaster. Slamming and rising. Slamming and rising. Speed irrelevant and yet everything. Transparent and opaque at once.

Then . . .

Not anything.

I decoded after a delay into a temp reservoir that duplicated a watered-down version of the 5-gen vrealspace I'd just traveled.

I tried to recollect myself, to make some coherency, but bits seemed to be missing. I knew what I was doing here but I couldn't remember who I was.

Compelled only by the momentum of a half-remembered purpose, I sifted data quicksand until I found the shape of a name.

I imprinted the information in my shadow cadaver's infinitesimal storage and moved forward, searching for another shape.

I found it among other recognizable shapes but I ignored them.

As I imprinted, a hexagonal shape began swirling up and down the data streams, scanning for corruptions.

I finished imprinting and found a well to hide in.

But it vibrated on toward me. *Erasure. Erasure. Erasure.*

While my shadow cadaver stayed undetected by the ancient security, it picked me clean of the imprinted data and put it back.

Like an obedient robot on the assembly line I repeated what I'd done and squatted again.

The scan ran and re-sorted.

We continued the slow dance over and over. I stayed, trapped by my own lack of impetus and forgotten identity.

Get out now.

What?

Use smell to find your friend.

My friend?

I imprinted the information again and instead of finding my well, I began sniffing.

I followed a pale auburn stream of data, seeking out a familiar smell. It was there, behind the salty tangs of the data streams and the mustiness of the repositories—the faintest odor of life.

I set myself after it like a dog.

Chapter Fourteen

Merv booted me back to realtime with a derm of adrenaline.

I jerked out and struggled to get a handle. Everything seemed so dull and barren, even compared to the degraded vreal of the impartial.

The screens on the wall resembled bulging eyes.

I sorted smell and touch first because vomit had collected in the creases of my clothes and I was drooling.

The headache came next and was to die from.

I finally resolved the figure of Merv beside me. He looked tired and disturbed. Even more than usual.

I stumbled groggily out of the jockey seat, rubbing circulation into my legs. "Did you catch it?"

He nodded, his mouth ajar. "T-tell m-me, how did you get out of there?"

"Let's just say don't ever lose your sweet smell."

Merv grinned.

First time for everything.

"Give me the data I collected and then erase any trace of it off your systems," I said, too tired for niceties.

"Where do you want it?"

"Dump it into my p-diary. It'll give her something to think about."

A shower and some food brought me some humanity.

Or did it?

My references for that particular word had shifted. If my vreal hallucinations could be at all believed, I'd just found out that I was a product of a symbiosis with an alien parasite and without its presence I wouldn't survive another day. Not just me but all of us.

The entire human race.

It felt like the ground was shivering beneath my feet, so I sat on the edge of my bed and told Merry 3# to display the files.

"No audio," I instructed.

She primped and pranced about. "Euuch. What *is* this stuff?" she complained. "It's like my shoes are pinching."

"It's called work, Merry," I sniped. "You obviously weren't built for it. Life isn't just fashion bites and fake automatic-rifle noises."

She gave me the finger and changed into optical glasses and a cape, nipples peeping through.

Funny.

I read the first file. Then again, cross-checking with Merry's thesaurus for the meanings of some of the words.

It was a contract between the Prisons Corporation and a consortium named Stem. The prisons were to provide suitable inmates for the Code Noir project in exchange for a specified remuneration. ("That's money, Parrish," said Merry.)

"I know that."

I didn't even scowl at her.

Rage distracted me and there was too much of it to be provoked by something as banal as Merry's banter.

Voice trembling, I told her to show me the other file.

. . . aka Ike Del Morte. Jailed for a series of murders committed against media students. I read on impatiently. *Released to head the Code Noir project by the director of Stem corporation . . .*

I told Merry to shut the information down and purge it.

Then: "Cancel that," I said sharply. "And encrypt it."

"I should warn you," she said crossly, "my encryption is only factory-standard. Any halfwit could decode it."

I thought for a moment. Like all her generation of p-diaries, Merry was capable of making changes to her configuration and programs as long as she didn't ignore a direct command from whoever she was encoded to.

I tried to imagine the one thing she didn't want anyone to take away from her. Especially if that anyone was me.

"Hide it in your wardrobe files."

She poked her tongue out. "Is that a direct instruction?"

"Yes."

She gave a large, dramatic sigh and the information disappeared to the safest place she could put it.

"Access netspace and search on the company Stem."

It only took her a few minutes. "It's registered to a long string that comes back to James Monk."

Monk. "That was quick."

Merry gave me the smuggest of grins. "I've got friends."

"What do you mean, *friends*?"

She placed a finger on the side of her nose and tapped it.

I frowned. "You sure it's right?"

"*P-diaries* don't lie," she sniffed. "Why did you ask me if you weren't going to believe me?"

She had a point. So why on earth did the thought of Merry having a *friend* make me so damn uneasy?

I kept her working until I'd recorded everything I could think of. Then I got her to run Snout's pattern-recognition software. Merv had designed it for his seeker to be able to make sense of vrealspace.

Merry yawned and complained that she was too tired to think, so I minimized her and concentrated on the holo-schema from Snout's program.

Tulu worked for a broker who was selling information on illegal genetics to the banks. (If Merv was right.) This explained why she was hanging out with Ike back in Mo-Vay. She was poaching information about his practices and winging some of her own. If Slipstream had sold that info to the banks, then how were they planning to use it?

And why in the freaking Wombat had Daac sold himself at the meat market?

Thrown into that mix of questions were a few extra curiosities.

My media ally . . . who was she? And why had Monk accepted and responded to a call from an unknown *Amorato* named Jales Belliere?

Now that I knew he was the one behind the company called Stem, that question seemed to burn hotter than the others.

If I went ahead with Lavish's plan to try to persuade Monk to hire me, and succeeded, maybe I could find the answer.

But could I do that?

Could I play the *Amorato* game after my experience with Glorious? The experience was so fresh—a wound of sorts. Not something I ever wanted to repeat.

I'd started thinking about Glorious. I'd been harsh toward her. Unfair, maybe.

After I heard her come back from a client, I went and knocked on her door.

She'd already showered and was watching One-World.

"Jales, wait until you see this," she said.

I waited and watched until the five-second grab replayed—a live-to-air murder-suicide in the burbs with a house cam catching the moment for DramaNet.

"The effects are so clever. So *realistic*," she sighed.

As the bona fide images flashed by, my heart contracted. My hand fell away from her shoulder in disgust. She couldn't tell the difference.

Any lingering desire for her died a final, permanent death as she greedily watched the upcoming ads.

"I always wanted to go into acting," she said.

"I think you probably did," I said.

I left and walked slowly back to my room.

Why was I so surprised? Glorious was just one of us, a whole generation who couldn't tell reality from production. Didn't need to, really.

She came after me a few minutes later. "Did I say something?"

I didn't answer. A set of stiff lace underwear had appeared on my bed. We both stared at it as if it was a third person.

"Merv."

Merv answered straight away, as if he'd been waiting. "Delly said you've got half an hour to be ready for the call."

Glorious made a noise and disappeared to collect her array of sprays and makeup. She returned laden with lust makings and crooned over the underwear. "Delly has such good taste."

I poked the elaborate brocade and lace bodice with distaste. I hated being trussed up. Knife and pistol belts were one thing but this . . .

"It's all in how you take it off," she explained.

"You mean striptease?"

"We call it *unveil*. Certain repeated rhythms can enhance the release of pheromones."

I didn't want to shatter her illusions but I wasn't *unveiling* for anyone. I just needed to pass myself off as enticing enough to get hired by Monk—and get the hell out of here.

Glorious wiggled her hips and started to peel off her shirt to show me.

I was fidgeting-bored before she'd finished with her buttons.

Sensing my mood, she sighed and stopped. "Monk will be a veteran dizzies user. His tastes will be jaded. He will have a high tolerance for most of these things. You will need to find something inside you that will work with the chemicals . . . your unique signature." She looked at me almost wistfully. "For you it's probably violence."

Merv cut in before I could think of a reply. "Glori, tell Lam to bring Jales down to the sensorium. We're going to link sooner than we thought." He sounded nervous again.

"What's wrong?" I asked.

Lavish answered for him. "The Militia is out looking for you, Plessis. They know you're in Viva . . ."

"You bastard." I shouted. "We agreed—"

"Call it a performance enhancer. You get Monk here or I'm handing you over. I'm not having my club closed for harboring a media-murderer," said Lavish.

I opened my mouth to defend myself and shut it again.

Justification was a waste of breath. Lavish Deluxe was just the same as every other player in this players' world. Working an angle. Paddling his carcass up the river. He didn't care who'd been murdered or who'd done it. He just wanted the win.

I started shoving myself into the brocade bondage.

"*You*'re Parrish Plessis?" Glorious said.

"Yeah, well . . . sorry." I didn't usually apologize for being me either, but maybe I owed her that.

She grinned. "Don't be. It's kind of sexy."

Everything was *kind of sexy* to Glorious.

She held out her hand. In it was a plastic ring.

I raised an eyebrow.

"Take this as my apology. It's a truth-say. Only use it when you need to find out something important from someone. Slip it into their mouth. Their saliva will do the rest. It's my own blend."

"And we know what your blends are like."

She gave a rueful grin. "Sometimes you need an edge."

I slipped it on to my little finger and stared at her, feeling a kind of regret. I didn't love Glorious and without the help of dizzies I wasn't attracted to her, but you couldn't go to the places we'd been together without something sticking.

"You need anything, I can't promise I'll be around, but I'll help if I can."

Sucker, Parrish.

Glorious blinked back tears and set about daubing me with a freshly made concoction of lust. "I have a client coming, so I won't be there with you. I hope everything . . . works out."

I didn't know if she was sincere. How could you ever know with these people? But she'd helped me in her way.

I always kept track of those things.

Chapter Fifteen

Lavish was like a canrat with skinned-paws excitement, heightened libido and paranoid nervousness all clamoring to possess him.

I stepped wide of where he stood to combat my desire to throttle him.

Slapping a filter across his nose to nullify the effects of my dizzies, he waved me into the body sensorium.

"This model is top of the line. Profound senses reproduction. Monk will get the full benefit of your enhanced pheromones and he will trace the fluctuations in your body heat and pupil dilation. Believe in what you're doing or he'll know you're a fraud." Lavish's voice sounded soft through the filter.

I glanced around the room, looking for Merv.

He was in his chair, touching his charms in obsessive order.

"This is a live coded feed but some will still be able to trace and read it. Enough for me to affect the stock exchange. Get this right, Plessis, or I'm throwing you to the wolves. I saved you once. Not again." Lavish finished his homily and slammed the hatch shut.

I promised myself that once I'd hooked Monk I could be as pissed-off with Lavish Deluxe as I liked.

I was looking forward to it.

The sensorium activated and a thousand tiny sensors brushed my skin, taking readings. I closed my eyes for a second and tried to think of something that might turn me on.

Be authentic, Lavish had said.

Unique signature, Glorious had said.

The only things that felt authentic at that moment were fury, frustration and claustrophobia. I'd left a bunch of victims back in The Tert who were going to be wiped out if I didn't get my act together and stop whoever was pulling the strings in the immaculately rotten Viva.

And the damn sex coffin I was in stank of stale perfume.

I delved inside myself for something that would work—the way I had when I'd needed to get past the border guards.

I thought of Glorious—her hair, and the way she moved under me. A brief memory of desire stirred. I tried to build on it but it flickered and died out.

A voice filled the sensorium.

"You come highly recommended, Jales Belliere. But I need something a little *more* than that to risk the attention you are attracting. It's already cost me a most reliable Intimate."

Monk? Or someone in his employ?

I couldn't speak, too aware of the pinprick sensors under my eyelids, in my mouth and between my legs.

More meant going somewhere I tried hard not to visit.

Loyl-me-Daac.

I let the image of him standing naked under the lights of the meat-walk invade my mind. The oblivious concentration on his face as he stroked himself to arousal. What had he been thinking of so that he could get so hard in front of so many people? A soft sigh lifted my chest, and then, inevitably, I remembered his head between my thighs . . .

. . . Excepting that he had wings and was swimming in a river of blood. I dived headlong into the blood and swam toward him. The waves tossed me around, keeping him just out of reach.

He reached for me and dragged me to a red beach where he penetrated me without waiting. I orgasmed over and over until the sand between us rubbed me raw, and the crash of the waves turned into cries for help . . .

I came out of the hallucination gasping for air and disorientated.

"Interesting," the voice was saying. "Enough that we should meet in person."

I gathered my scrambled wits. "Yes. Now. But not here," I whispered.

A pause. "Transport will be on the pad of the Luxoria in around ten minutes to pick you up."

I fell out of the sensorium at Lavish's feet.

"You bitch," he squealed. "He's not coming *here.*"

I felt stale, pissed off and totally sick of this place. Lavish's declaration was pure histrionics. He'd get a mile of publicity out of the fact that Monk wanted to hire one of his girls, regardless of where it took place.

"You fucked the deal!" he ranted.

I stumbled to my feet and grabbed him by the throat.

"*You* fucked the deal, you piece of waste. Don't you ever try to blackmail me again."

His eyes bulged with a mixture of fury and fear. "Get out of here," he gasped.

I dropped him, surprised. What, no fond farewells? No seeing me to the door and into the arms of the Militia?

Something was wrong.

I turned to look at Merv. His face was strained and nervous, his stare flicking involuntarily to the bank of screens.

I scanned along them and spotted Glorious in one of the 'doirs. It didn't look like she was having fun. I knew that because Dazzle was unconscious in the corner.

"Where's Glorious, Merv?"

Lavish snarled a warning at me. "She is my business. *I* will deal with it if necessary. Now get out of here before someone damages my club trying to get at you."

I swiveled to examine the bank of units on the opposite wall. They cammed every exterior angle of the club and the commotion that was building outside. I saw on another viewer the two bodyguards who had shown an interest in me at the Globe on the orders of the red-haired woman and a rousty contingent.

I didn't know how much of it was actually to do with me and what was normal Viva security. But I was done with being conservative in my estimate of the trouble I could attract.

Something told me that I was about to be caught in cross fire.

Get smart, or get dead.

The smart thing would have been to cut and run while Monk was hot to have me. But there was the small matter of Glorious being tortured to death in a nearby room and Lavish not doing anything about it.

"OK." I nodded to him. "It was a pleasure."

I strode past him, hauling Merv with me. He squirmed to get away from me like a fish on a hook but I dragged him out into the bar and leaned him up against the door.

"Lock it," I said.

He stared.

"I know you can. *Lock it.*"

He tapped a combination on his p-diary. The lock cycled over.

Lavish's squealing penetrated the soundproofing.

I turned and found Lam waiting for me.

What now?

He gave me a small nod to let me know that he wouldn't interfere, and walked away.

Nothing like breaking a guy's arms to improve his disposition.

I nodded my appreciation to his back and turned to Merv.

"Where's Glorious?"

Merv pointed to one of the corridors that ran in the opposite direction to the helipad exit.

I gave him a gentle push. "Go and get my case from my room—and tell Monk's pilot to wait for me."

I ran off down the corridor to the 'doirs, pulling up short when Tae waved a warning hand at me. He obviously didn't share Lam's new devotion to me.

"Open the door," I told him.

He was panting in light, cat-sized breaths.

Stim.

I leaped forward, trapping him with my weight. Then I stepped back suddenly, flinging him against the opposite door. He bounced off without making a dent in it and collapsed.

I jumped to the door and pawed at its lock as an alarm started. But Tae jumped me and I fell backward, crunching him on to the floor. His fingers found my windpipe.

We rolled.

Unconsciousness swarmed.

Then Tae's fingers went slack around my throat. He slid off me.

Merv crouched behind us with a knife in one hand and my case in the other. "The copter is here, Parrish," he said—and then he fainted.

I stood up and kicked the door of the 'doir but the action was pointless.

The whole thing was freaking pointless.

Merv was out cold and I should have already been on the copter that was about to leave the helipad right now. Instead I was bashing at an immovable door, trying to rescue someone who was probably already dead.

I gave a frustrated howl.

It got the doors of 'doirs opening all along the corridor.

"Glori's in trouble," I bellowed at them. "What's the door code?"

No one answered—they were all paralyzed by mistrust. I grabbed the nearest person, a guy sheathed in plastic wrap.

"Help me."

He shrugged me off and teetered back.

I couldn't blame them.

How crazy must *I* seem? Brocade bondage was not my best look.

A tiny prepubescent girl who'd been entertaining a guy larger than Mama, Fishertown's sweet-tempered sumo, stepped forward.

"Tell me the code," I begged her.

She looked confused. "Where's Delly? Where's Dazzle?" she shouted over the alarm.

"Dazzle's dead. Glorious will be too if you don't get me in there."

The others called out warnings to her but she ignored them and darted across to the door to lay her print on it.

I knocked her down getting inside.

Glorious was naked and unconscious. Her beautiful hair had been torn out in handfuls and she slumped strapped into a chair.

Her spinner was gouging her teeth out with a barbed

fishing hook. The blood from her mouth drained to the floor, pooling around Dazzle's tiny feet.

I knocked the guy away from her with the most brutal head butt I'd ever delivered.

The skin on my forehead split but I had him by the throat on the floor before the blood even began to trickle into my eyes.

Things slowed.

I noticed a lot of things. The eyelash tattooed on the side of his neck. The smell of dizzies on his body, the flicker of a pulse at his temple, his fear and his arousal. Glori's literally tortured breaths.

Revulsion spun me into darkness. If I stayed and killed him slowly—like I wanted to—I'd spend the rest of my life in a Viva quod.

If I left now I still had a chance to do what I'd come here for.

But what he'd done· to Glorious was . . . animalistic.

Beautiful, seductive, dizzie-drenched Glorious.

Rationality threaded its way through surges of adrenaline pumping through me.

I snatched the rope off Dazzle's small body and, breathing deeply and raggedly, tied the spinner up. Then I dragged him to the window and shattered the seal.

I hoiked him up and out. At the very worst he might draw some attention away from me. At the very best the knots would slip.

I didn't look at Glorious. I couldn't. Instead I picked the kid-grrl up on my way out and stood her on her feet. "Get her a medic *now*."

She nodded and ran.

I stared at the rest of them.

Most of them looked at the floor; some looked at Glori.

I didn't need to say anything.

*   *   *

The helipad was retracting as I burst through the door. It paused, the safety protocol preventing it from pulling back totally while my weight was on it.

The copter pilot spotted me jumping around and signaling for him to come back.

He signaled back *No way*. Pointed down and then put up two fingers.

I had two minutes to sort it.

Below me a rousty crawler was heading up the side of the building.

Hugging my case to my chest, I edged back to the outside console and played with the protocols. But Lavish was monitoring me from Merv's room.

I activated the large all-weather wall viewer and roared at him. "Extend the pad, Lavish. It's the only way to get rid of me."

"You dropped one of my best clients out of a window on the one hundred and fiftieth floor. I can think of much better ways to get rid of you."

"He killed Dazzle. He might as well have killed Glorious. I didn't know you ran a slaughterhouse."

"A business, bitch. Not a slaughterhouse. He paid for the right. Besides, she needed a lesson."

My whole body quivered with rage. I wanted to storm back in there and strangle the life from him.

"Extend the pad and I won't tell Monk what's going on here. You'll still get your publicity." *And then I'll send you to hell.*

Lavish laughed. High-pitched. Crazy. "You really think he'd care? What primordial slime did you crawl out of? You don't have a clue."

"I understand this: You let me get on that copter or I'll have nothing to do but come back for you."

His laugh grew louder.

The copter's engine note changed as it began to drop away from the side of the building.

My desperation got desperate.

I waved frantically at the pilot, miming for him to

drop me a line to grab. He bobbed the copter back up level with the pad, a few meters shy of actually setting down, and began talking into his pick-up.

I dumped the contents of my case on the pad and grabbed my leather crop. I shrugged it over my shoulders, and in nothing but my brocade bondage and long hair, I made ready to take a run at it.

And there I'd been, just a short while back, worried about dying with no knickers on.

Half a dozen explosive steps and I pulled up at the last second, digging my toes into the edge.

Too far.

I couldn't make it.

I stood there trembling, besieged by a familiar thought.

I am not going to die here. I am not.

The pilot shrugged and started to lift away again.

The lights began to flash around the edge of the pad. I felt it lurch and begin to extend. The pilot saw it too and brought the copter back in.

I grabbed the struts as the machine touched down and lifted again immediately. I clawed my way up and inside.

Not exactly the elegance of an *Amorato*—apart from the naked bit.

I clambered in beside the pilot and stared into his viewer. The large wall screen showed Merv's room crowded with people.

Two in particular I recognized: Muscle Massive, heavily bandaged, and the kid-grrl giving me the thumbs-up.

Triumph unfurled in my gut and turned into hysterical glee.

A coup.

Chapter Sixteen

And a mistake.

The pilot was a woman. Big, broad, with a face that would stop Armageddon. Not in the good way, either.

"Thanks for hang—er . . . waiting." I stumbled over my usual speech and tried to drag some thought of my disguise back into being.

She gave me a sweaty sideways look and said nothing.

"You got something else I can wear?"

A shrug this time. "Try over the back."

I reached around and rummaged until I found a rainskin. Not exactly fashion but better than torn, bloody brocade.

I zipped my crop up and wriggled into the raincoat, finally calming down enough to look around the cabin.

The copter was big enough to be luxurious, small enough to be practical, and for the first time ever I was sitting in the passenger seat like a civilized human being. Not strapped to the tail, or trying to fly the freaking thing by myself.

It still didn't lessen my loathing at having my feet

off the ground. God wouldn't have just given us wings . . . he'd have given us motors as well.

God? Now there's a cute idea.

I hadn't reconsidered the notion of a higher being since my ill-chosen worshipping of the great freaking Wombat had turned out to be the venerating of a complete freaking maniac.

I really needed to work on improving my choices. *Starting now.*

For a second I relaxed back into the seat.

"Comfortable?" the pilot asked.

I nodded, eyelids barely open.

"Good."

The smallest of creaks and a restraint harness dropped over my head and shoulders, snapping tighter than one of Luxoria's bondage toys.

I squirmed and fought it. "What the—"

"Keep still or it will strangle you."

Sweet.

My few warm seconds of relief turned instantly to crap.

I struggled against the harness despite the pilot's warnings and it shrank until I could barely breathe, at which point I forced myself to calm down.

The city stretched out underneath us—the chrome-trimmed buildings and bright canal watercourses bleeding into one eye-hurting glare.

Viva might be huge, I thought, but it might as well have been the size of Torley's and the Stretch. Everyone seemed to know me. Everyone wanted a piece of me.

I closed my eyes again but they didn't stay that way long.

The copter took a sudden plummet and fell into some ragged ducking and weaving through the air traffic.

Sirens again. And some heated warnings over the comm from air traffic control.

The pilot ignored them.

"What . . . you . . . doing?" I panted.

She didn't answer but the sweat beading her upper lip told me that she had troubles of her own.

I craned every which way to see, catching glimpses of a media copter dogging us.

My square-jawed pilot took a risk and careered out of the orderly stream and low into controlled space.

A Militia bat appeared, its titanium and fiberglass blades dangerously close. Not shooting, but reeking of serious intimidation.

The ATC warnings got heavier. Two minutes longer, they said, and they'd blow us out of the sky.

I took it as bluff. Below us was the heart of Viva wealth. Mansions on mansions. Nobody would get away with sending copter bits to burn holes in the carefully electrolyzed lawns.

My pilot obviously agreed with me and stuck fast to her choice, even with a Militia bat posted hard on our shoulder.

The media copter, though, had other instructions and peeled away, losing itself back into the normal stream of traffic.

One down.

I was working on giving some advice to the pilot when she initiated a landing sequence.

Something in the protocol jogged my memory.

M'Grey Island. Shite.

I looked down. The floating bridge was locked into its daytime spot but we weren't headed toward it. The pilot's security clearance was high enough that she took us straight in, over Razz Retribution's ex-estate, into the heart of the canals, losing the bat at M'Grey's boundary.

I sucked as deep a breath as the restraint would allow.

We descended quickly, a flash of perimeter security disengaging, and we set down on a flat disk of land inside a palace.

Palace.

What did the freaking Royal Family want with me?

The pilot held a fancy snubbed Beretta at my chest as she unclipped the harness from the seat and shoved me out the door with one easy push.

I tried to run but the harness tripped me.

The pilot locked a hand onto the webbing and dragged me bodily across the pad to an open-topped 'pede. She shoved me in the backseat, ordering me with an ugly growl to keep still.

Panic replaced everything else in my head. Loyl Daac and Ibis weren't here to break me out this time. No one who cared knew where I was. Last time I'd been on M'Grey had been a setup, someone trying to pin me for Razz Retribution's murder. I wasn't cool with the place at all.

The Eskaalim ballooned like a fat tick. Its pincers hooked deep inside me. I found myself visiting that same dark place I'd lived in when Jamon had owned me.

Nothing got me crazier.

I kicked the pilot in the back of the head with both heels. The 'pede lurched and veered toward some small outbuildings. In a blind rush of madness I hoped it would crash into one of them and kill us both—denying their prize to whoever had gone to these lengths to kidnap me.

The pilot flung her arm around me to restrain me but I rolled out of reach as the 'pede smashed into the wall.

I waited for oblivion, but it didn't come.

Trapped upside down and alive—my mind skittered wildly.

Rough hands reached in. I bit at them.

Swearing. Then the pressure of a derm.

Not long enough.

The room I woke up in was in a basement and

disappointingly plain—almost empty. Just a sleeping mat, a walk-in cupboard and a comm viewer. No windows. No natural light.

The good news was that someone had draped me in a large coat.

Not her, I hope?

My friendly pilot stood, arms crossed, at the door. I took a better look at her. She had heavy doglike jowls and might have seemed motherly if you ignored the shok-stick tucked into her belt, the shoulder holster snug against her large breasts and the tree-thick diameter of her biceps.

I ran some far-fetched scenarios as to the identity of my kidnapper.

But when the truth came it was worse.

Or should I say . . . *her.*

"Hello, Parrish."

A young girl entered quietly, almost meekly. Pale-skinned, undersized, short hair and rich-tailored clothes but masculine. Cultured voice.

Most distinct were her eyes, huge brown irises and showing only a little white. And the fancy wireless graft made to look like jewelry around her ear.

Another person who knew me . . . but who was she?

"Sorry about the restraints but Mal—your pilot— thinks you should hear us out before we agree to remove them."

We agree?

I settled for a cross between a grunt and snort and a filthy look at Mal.

Her chin whiskers didn't even quiver.

The small girl circled me, clasping her arms to her body as though she didn't know where to start. There was something odd about the way she held them. Jerky. As if they belonged to someone else.

A suspicion began to weevil its way into my mind—a memory of a scrubber living off the scraps that the Muenos discarded underfoot. A kid who'd been stolen by a media 'Terro and had ended up being adopted by the banking Royals as a publicity stunt. I looked for any other similarity and came up short.

Can't be.

This grrl was educated and carried the air of someone much older. Still, the name fell out of my mouth.

"Bras?"

She paused, unsmiling. "Yes. Bras." She patted the silver-coated wireless connection. "Accelerated-learning deposit and a resocialization implant. But otherwise, right, Bras."

My heart pumped a bit harder, sending a woozy kind of warmth out to my limbs. "I wondered about you—w-what happened."

She frowned, rebuffing my sentiment. "I *knew* about you."

"*What* did you know?" I challenged her. "And how did you know where I was?" *And what will James Monk think happened to me?*

"We've been tracking you," she said simply, as if that was enough information.

Did the whole freaking world want to know what I was up to?

"Tell me why you changed your . . ." She paused as if she were searching for a word. Maybe she had the same dud language-infusion as me. "Appearance."

I wrinkled the split on my forehead. The blood had dried and it was already starting to knit. I grinned despite Bras's grave manner. "Necessity. My regular face had gotten way too popular."

She considered that for a while and then gave an agreeable nod.

I should have been steamed at that. The kid had me trussed up. But I felt relieved. Somehow it seemed important to pass her test.

"Sit," she ordered.

Mal materialized a chair and pushed me on to it with one broad finger. That was one woman I wasn't planning to get into an arm wrestle with. I reckoned Mal would have been able to match it with Mama.

I sagged into the chair, tiredness rolling over me as if someone had covered me with a blanket and turned out the lights. Through half-closed eyes I watched Bras muttering soft instructions into her pick-up. Soon the screen began streaming a montage of shots.

They woke me up with a jolt, sitting me upright as if I'd been stung.

The Tert again. Not just The Tert . . . Mo-Vay—wild-tek blisters and pus, dead bodies coated in Crawl.

The images stabbed into me as if they were the Cabal Coomera dagger. I think I even moaned. Seeing Mo-Vay unwound all my long-practiced sang-froid. My scaly beauty mark ached.

I'd lost Roo there. I'd nearly lost myself. Mo-Vay was my week in hell. A preview of what life would be if I didn't straighten things out. It lurked in my corner sight, a constant reminder.

Remember, human . . .

"Where did you get that?" I gasped.

"We paid a . . . collector to get it. Unfortunately, there is more. And we are not the only ones who have copies. This goes out on One-World over the holidays. Sera Bau's going to use it to cripple James Monk."

"What do you mean?" I shouted. Pieces of information flew around me and I couldn't catch them.

"Think about it," Bras said. "What gets prime air over holidays?" she asked.

Ker-clunk. "The Pan-Sats?"

She nodded. "Sera Bau owns over twelve hours of footage. It will rip gut out of Monk's sports programming."

Despite the cultured tone, her sentences weren't always quite right.

Bras replaced the paused montage with a head-and-shoulders of a man and woman. She focused on the man.

I squinted through watering eyes at the thick, heavy face.

"James Monk. Shareholder in Brilliance. Sports IO. That means Information Owner," she added as an aside.

She pointed to the smooth-skinned red-haired woman at his side. "Sera Bau. DramaNews IO. The other major shareholder in Brilliance."

I studied Bau's image. The woman from the foyer of the InterGlobe was also the woman who must have funded Ike in Mo-Vay. She'd given him his freedom so that he could create madness for her to film—something so horrible that it would take the viewing public away from the biggest-rating fortnight of each year—the Pan-Sats.

The calculation of such an act struck me like a body blow.

"My information tells me that James Monk was sponsoring this atrocity."

Bras gave me a look almost as disdainful as Lavish's.

"Then your information is wrong."

Something in her conviction convinced me too. Or was it the doubt that I already had about Merry 3#? *A reliable friend, eh?* I'd purge the stupid p-diary as soon as I got a minute.

Bras's eyes closed and she rocked forward on her toes, eyes rolling around under her lids. Saliva drooled out of one corner of her mouth.

Mal was beside Bras in a second, wiping the spit away, slipping a mask across her nose, patting her back with soothing strokes.

She turned on me like an accusing parent.

"You've stressed her."

I*'ve stressed* her?

I was on the point of telling Mal something to that effect when Bras opened her eyes again. Watching her slowly focus, I recognized something in her that made me want to run and hide.

"Did Razz Retribution work for Bau?" I asked.

"Mal—will—tell more," she managed, allowing the woman to lift her up and lay her gently on the mat.

Satisfied that Bras was comfortable, Mal turned her attention back to me.

"Sera Bau discovered that one of her Prier pilots, Razz Retribution, was the money behind some genetics research that interested her. She arranged for a criminal who called himself Dr. Del Morte to steal it and use it."

Mal spoke in a flat tone, as if the information to which she was privy was of only a passing interest. Her main interest lay pale and groggy on the mat before her.

I digested the information in little bits and, for the first time in a long while, pieces began to fit together for me.

Mal went on. "You were framed for Razz Retribution's murder and Bau got to make a film of something that will seal her ratings for the next year."

"Why me?"

Bras propped herself on a shaky elbow. "Convenience. Someone plausible. Someone with no redress. Someone who could die," she said.

I saw something in her as she spoke—like Daac and yet different. Bras had come from the worst of nothing to the best of everything. You couldn't do that and not suffer.

"So Sera Bau murdered Razz," I asked.

Bras nodded but Mal spoke.

"Not by her own hand, of course. You'll never

prove it, either. Which is why you must accept our offer."

"Our?"

"My family," whispered Bras.

Mal circled me, stopping near the door.

On cue, an auto life support wheeled in. The man it carried was bald and overweight. His scalp flaked onto a towel that covered his shoulders. His eyes were yellowed but keen. Behind him walked an identikit version of Mal, only somewhat older and larger.

"Parrish, meet Gerwent Ban. King of Viva and environs. Hereditary leader of the Electronic Transaction Polity."

The ETP. *Tigers without teeth* was how my stepdad Kevin described them. *The remnants of the old banking fraternity. As secretive as the Masons had once been. Now moneyed but powerless.* This *is Gerwent Ban?*

I felt ripped off. There was nothing exotic or special about him—apart from the pricey life support. Anyone else would be dead.

I considered doing something humble out of respect. *Nah.*

Gerwent looked to where Bras lay on the mat. "Are you unwell, child?"

"No, Father." She rolled away from us, eyes to the wall.

Father?

I stared in disbelief at Ban's decrepit flesh. Only a short time ago Bras had been forcibly taken from The Tert and adopted by the Royal Family as what I assumed was a publicity feat. What had really happened here, I wondered, that had got her calling this half-dead creature *Father?*

"Ms. Plessis. You've a talent for getting noticed." His voice was surprisingly strong. Amped and modulated by the chair, I figured—he didn't look like he had enough breath left to spit.

I crooked a finger—the only bit of me not

secured—and said the first thing that came into my head. "Is it normal behavior for the king to kidnap law-abiding citizens?"

He laughed—a cross between a wheeze and puff from the ventilator. The auto-chair moved him closer to me again, with Mal and her twin a step behind.

"Nothing is normal for a king. And it's been a long time since you were a law-abiding citizen, Parrish Plessis."

He had a point there.

I nodded at the cams on the ceiling and the two heavyweight guards. "Untie me. What's to be scared of?"

"The same thing that attracts people to you, I would guess. You're very unpredictable."

I laughed this time, at this gentle massaging of my ego. Maybe he wasn't as dead as he looked.

Moved by some unspoken command, Mal approached and freed me.

I rubbed circulation back into my arms and legs but made no move to get up. I was intrigued. King Gerwent Ban wanted me for something, and I wanted to hear what. This game I'd rolled my dice on had jumped to a scale way beyond my measuring. If I didn't learn . . .

I took a slow breath. "Bras tells me you're working up a revolution. How are you gonna do that?" I couldn't see any point in hedging. Blunt seemed to be everyone else's tactic.

"You are aware that our media communications are run by Brilliance, a constructed editing intelligence of supposedly infinite capacity to organize, select and edit information."

"Yeah, I'm familiar with it."

"I say *supposedly*. We believe that it is not an AI but has a biological component—somehow a real consciousness has become meshed with the editing processor."

I though about Merv's reaction when he talked about Brilliance. He knew something. "You mean it has a brain?"

"We think so."

I tapped my fingers on the chair leg. "Why don't you just shoot it in the head, then?"

Ban made a strange strangled noise at the suggestion. "Perhaps we might consider something so direct, *if we knew where it was.*"

"You've got no idea?"

He grimaced. "None."

"So what is your plan?

"We think that the meshed system has become unstable and that the constant editing choices are degrading its 'thought' processes."

"What are the IOs doing about it?"

"Nothing. With the complexity and volume of what is viewed, it is unprofitable and inefficient to use human labor to edit. Brilliance was . . . *is* a cost-effective and competent evolution in communication. She has developed her own editing technology that is swift and incomprehensible to us. To start again would cripple them."

"Which is what you want to do. Cause a media blackout."

"Crude but accurate. We want Monk and Sera Bau to vie so hard for ratings that the sheer volume and distress will cause Brilliance's new organic part to have a cerebral hemorrhage."

"What's that?" Was this the abridged version of perceived events suitable for dummies? I wondered. If so, then I deserved a freakin' medal for my new-found talent at playing along.

"We want her brain to bleed."

"If your self-destruct idea works, what happens then?"

"When Brilliance is incapacitated, we begin again with a more basic technology, including net-time with genuine free information. We will resurrect a political system in this country," said Gerwent Ban.

"Don't tell me . . . governed by the Polity?"

Bras sat up properly on the mat, drawing her knees to her chest. "I told him youse were smart."

" 'You,' " Ban corrected gently.

Bras colored.

"And that will make the world a better place," I asked, sounding innocent enough even to myself.

"Of course it will." Bras raised one of her small, newly crafted fists. "He promised me it would."

I caught a glimpse of what was left of the street kid behind the constructed crust of self-confidence. Bras had been saved from The Tert. But *had* she been saved? She was ill and I knew what ailed her.

I felt guilty—responsible. The Royals had fixed her arms, upgraded her speak, prettied her clothes, filled her head with propaganda and given her cred to wield. But they had no idea what was going on inside her.

I wished I hadn't, either.

"So what do you want from me?"

"We need you to light fires that will get Brilliance burning. Once she's damaged, we want to expose the extent of her control with a rogue broadcast," said Gerwent Ban. "We want you to anchor it when we do it." He paused a moment, switching his modulator over to a command tone. "But the timing is significant. Sera Bau plans to release her footage on the eve of the Pan-Sat transmission. We must have Brilliance primed for overload at that precise time."

"What resources do you have?" Maybe a silly question considering his wealth. Maybe not.

"We have a facility assembled. It contains all the communications technology we need. There is also a small collection of weapons there, should you need them. Once you agree we will take you there."

Bras stood and approached me, her face whiter

than the sheet on her sleeping mat. Mal sidestepped in behind her, ready to catch her should she fall.

"There's a condition to all this, Parrish," said Bras. *Truly?*

Gerwent Ban spoke. "Brasella feels that we need your old face back. When things change we will need to show an authentic figurehead. Someone wronged by the media."

You mean a reprieved criminal.

Well, the world was crazy. Officially. Someone was gonna give me weapons and a viewing audience to play with.

Hysteria would have been appropriate in the face of his announcement but a dam of unshed tears blocked its way. The impasse meant there was only room in me for calm.

Yet Bras, King Ban, Sera Bau, Monk, Daac, Tulu— every damn conniving person I could name in a breath—didn't understand one momentous thing.

The Eskaalim. The shape-shifter. The creature turning others into energy-driven sadists—violence junkies. The one turning me into a sex addict and a madwoman. The one, I'd recently learned, that we couldn't live with and couldn't live without.

I kept my tone very even. My words were clipped and clear.

"Do you actually know what was happening in the heart of the Tertiary Sector? In Dis?"

Bras shrugged. It turned into an odd kind of movement, even with the expensive prosthetics.

Ban spoke for her. "Our informant tells us that a man there was experimenting with hormones, prolonging puberty in young people. It turned their behavior animalistic."

"Your informant? You mean Leesa Tulu." The harshness of my voice was unmistakable. "Is that all she said?"

Ban's breather whirred louder for a second. "Yes.

Out of interest, how did you stumble over that connection?"

"Some information still comes free," I whispered. *Not really free, Parrish.* "Now listen. I'll be your anarchist. I'll be your anchor. I'll be anything you damn well want. But *I* have some conditions."

Gerwent Ban wheeled closer, energized with eagerness, until he was alongside Bras. She put her prosthetic hands on his shoulders. They looked so real that I could swear she felt his flesh. Maybe if I lived long enough I'd get Loyl Daac a new prosthetic like hers.

"Yes?" he said.

"First, I want Bau *and* Tulu."

"Afterward. Yes." The king's ventilator sucked in agreement. "You can *have* who you like."

"Second, I want you to find the best geneticist you can and analyze this." I reached into my crop and pulled out the neural spike that the Cabal had removed from Ike's head.

"And that would be?"

"You think you want to start a revolution. Actually, you need to stop one. A biological revolution. Something is changing people into beasts."

Ban blinked with unspoken scepticism. After all, someone like me had to be crazy.

"Why would you expect me to believe something so preposterous?"

"Ask Leesa Tulu what was really going on in the heart of The Tert. Better still: torture her. It's the only way you'll get the truth. Do it at least to help your . . . adopted daughter."

"Brasella?" His flaccid body quivered. Definitely not dead yet.

I felt Bras's stare on me too, intense and distressed.

Telling her like this was cruel. But I needed to make them understand—for me and for her.

"Because she is infected."

"What do you know?" Even the modulator couldn't keep the king's voice strong.

"Hallucinations, voices, violent urges. Sound familiar?"

Bras nodded, swallowing hard. "What is it?"

"It's a parasite that feeds off the epinephrine in your body."

"How do you acquire such a thing?"

"We all have it but it's dormant. Splicing of certain genes has released it. When Sera Bau found out what entertainment it could provide, she paid someone to spread the . . ." I stopped short of saying the word *alien*. I didn't really know what it was—only that it wasn't human. There didn't seem to be any other word in the human vocabulary to accommodate that idea, yet that one sounded so nuts. "Just get this analyzed. Quickly, if you want to help Bras."

Gerwent Ban nodded at Mal's near-double. "Melanie will see to it. Is there anything else?"

Mal and Mel. Cute.

For a few seconds I gave myself the luxury of considering a future. If I actually survived, what would be important to me afterward? I hadn't planned much past revenge.

Even if I didn't make it, maybe I could set some things in place.

But what? Clean up The Tert?

Sounded cool enough, but the reality was that the punters who lived there didn't want to be part of the supercities. They didn't want the interference and the regulations. And yet most of them didn't want the scum and deprivations of The Tert either.

"I want you to reinstate and maintain the public utilities in the Tertiary Sector. Running water and consistent power."

If Ban had had an eyebrow it would have cocked. "An interesting request. I can't guarantee that I can do it but while I have influence I will try. You'll have to believe that."

"And *you* need to believe that I will interfere with your plans in any way I can if you don't."

I didn't know how, but I would find a way. After all, messing up was my biggest talent.

"Right. I also need the help of a person I can trust." *Or trust more than you, anyway.*

He was prepared for this. "Give Melanie the name and whereabouts. I'll have them brought in."

"I'll need to make contact with them first," I said. "And one more thing." I opened the coat and flashed the torn brocade. The whine of his breather quickened. *Definitely not dead.* "I need some proper clothes."

The king nodded, rubbing the smooth fabric of his auto-chair, telling it to take him elsewhere. "We have a deal, then?"

"Yes."

For the first time since Jamon Mondo had come into my life a few years before, I felt light.

If this was power, I was hooked.

Chapter Seventeen

Mal and Bras took me to a lift that opened into a suite with a view.

"An Intimate will attend you here until tomorrow evening, when we travel to our hide," said Bras.

Hide?

I looked around. Another room of my own. Even better than the Luxoria. I should be enjoying all this. Instead, I prowled around. Restlessness plagued me as usual. Would I ever be rid of the feeling that time was running out?

I told myself that it was because I was used to acting quickly to solve things, and now I had to deliberate and plan. In truth, though, I couldn't shake the desperation inside myself. Real or imagined, it was with me in the same way that my lungs sucked oxygen. Since my overdose with dizzies, something had shaken loose. My grip had weakened.

I forced myself to change calmly into the jeans and shirt that Mal had brought me.

They both looked away.

"How secure is the hide?" I asked them.

Bras swung her arms as though they were uncomfortable or, now that I'd seen her own sparsely furnished room, I thought that perhaps she was as uneasy as I was with comforts.

The view, though, was worth it: east across hundreds of flowering bougainvilleas, white yachts. Picture-perfect and dangerously distracting. Enough to make anyone forget.

"Quite," Bras replied to my question.

"You got quality vreal there?"

"The best. Six-Gen."

I whistled. Five-Gen had just about cooked my goose. Only one person I knew could get me in and out of 6-Gen. Merv.

But how could I get him away from Lavish?

Glorious. Her name forced its way into my consciousness. *Is she alive? Can I bear to find out?*

I turned to Mal. "Do you know the Brightbeach bridge? I want to meet with someone there tomorrow morning, early. I'll need transport and some way to get past the ID scans."

"Yes, *miss.*"

Miss. The word me want to snap my teeth at her. But even I wasn't stupid enough to aggravate Mal. One swat from her fist and my brains would be paste. I settled for a grimace and a "Call me Parrish."

She grunted and left us, distrust knitted into the aggressive hunch of her shoulders. Mal didn't think I was suitable company for Bras.

Funny thought, considering.

I moved over to the window and tried to invent a plan. The Pan-Sats were due to air in a few days. What they wanted me to do was impossible.

Not that I was one to back out of a challenge. But pressure invariably got me acting crazy.

"I should thank you," said Bras.

"What for?" I didn't look at her. Whatever she was working up to had been long rehearsed. I could hear it in her measured tone.

"What you did in The Tert . . . those men would

have killed me. Or the next ones that came along. My death was certain."

Yeah, well, we all share that one. "What happened when the 'Terro took you?" I asked.

"They put me in a holding cell on Jinberra in the Midas section. I'd still be there if Gerwent hadn't been watching the LTA broadcast when I was taken. He made inquiries and bid for me."

I shot her a glance. "What do you mean, 'bid'?"

"It's the one remaining privilege the Royals share with the media. They have the right to buy anyone out of Militia custody for an agreed price."

"You were lucky."

Bras shrugged. "I'm not the only one who's been bought."

I nodded, encouraging her to go on. What had she heard?

"In Midas there are a lot of stories. A few of them are famous. One was about a witch doctor from Merika. I never knew her name because you only got told it when you paid for someone else to wind up dead. The other was about a man they called Wombat. It was the story that gave me hope."

My heart leaped up into my throat and made it hard to breathe. "What was that story about?"

"Somebody bought him out of a prolonged-life sentence. Then he kept coming back and getting others out. They say he was building a better, safer place. I used to dream about what it would be like there." She stopped staring out of the window. "I wound up here instead but I still wonder what that place is like."

I kept my shudder and the truth to myself. Let her keep her dream. "Why do you think Gerwent bought you?"

Bras's shortness of breath came back, and the wild, feral look. "Because he thought you would come after me. It's *you* he really wants. Not me."

I gaped at her in total disbelief. "You're winding me up."

"He's been planning this a long time but they needed the right person to be their focus. Someone convincing and . . ."

"Nuts?"

"That's you, Parrish." She trailed off into a whisper. "You didn't come for me. But he's patient. He waited for an opportunity. One of the Polity is a client of the Luxoria. We heard you were there, so he paid one of the employees to watch you."

"Who? Lam?"

"No. I think his name was Tae."

I stared at her, surprised in more than one way. "You expected . . . wanted me to come after you?"

"I told him you wouldn't." She shrugged.

I didn't know what to make of that. Had I somehow let Bras down? I'd barely known the kid.

"He gets what he wants," she added.

So I'm nuts and convincing, eh?

Then why were my knees trembling? Why could I picture a spider shutting its trapdoor?

And yet I couldn't run away from this opportunity.

"What will this parasite do to me?" Bras asked.

I sighed. "Nothing good. But if you fight, we might be able to find a way to stop it." I touched her lightly on the head. "Be strong *inside*, Bras. It's all you've got in the end."

The next morning at dawn Mal and an Intimate took me out in a baby Sikorsky that Mal called a Flash-Hawk.

I watched the rooftop advertibles as the Intimate logged into the flight queue heading south, and I contemplated how unfit I would be if I sat around much longer doing nothing.

I'd been past the limits of physical exhaustion in recent times. Now I was tired from inactivity.

And lack of sleep. I'd wrestled the entire night with my problems, till in the end I'd booted up Merry 3# and voiced in everything else I could think of. It was dangerous keeping a record like this but forgetting something might be just as lethal.

Merry had jigged as she looked around, acting like she'd made it first through the doors at an emporium sale. "Oooh, ooh. Nice. Ooh, gorgeous. Ooh. Gucci. No way, Henry Six."

"Yeah, well, don't get used to it."

"Oh? So what's next on our travel itinerary?" she sniped. "A pothole? No, let me guess again. A drain?"

"You wanna hear about what happens at p-diary rehab or are you just gonna run the patternware for me?"

She gave me the finger and disappeared. In her place a holo-schema of all the information that I'd collected shimmered.

As usual the overlaps and unmade connections gave me a headache. I didn't for a second think that Gerwent Ban's plan for a return to government was something that I really wanted or believed would make things better. But one thing I surely knew—*no one* was going to air what happened in Mo-Vay as a ratings ploy to be gawked at by dumb cits.

No one.

"Watch it."

Mal's curt order to the somber blue-liveried Intimate brought me back to the present. She sat next to it in the copilot's seat, possessively rechecking protocols. She didn't like it flying her baby.

Better it than me, I figured.

I transferred my attention to what the FlashHawk had in the way of extras that I could recognize. It was an impressive little beast, sporting a couple of 7.62mm miniguns hidden beneath the cabin windows, plus an external hoist, rappel, paradrop and fast rope. Seemed that Mal had done one or two quick extractions before.

A few minutes before we landed on the Bright-beach parking lot, Gerwent Ban commed. He sounded agitated and, when I craned over Mal to see, his face was slack with shock.

"I have seen the initial download from the bio-ware you gave me."

"Yes?" I tried not to hold my breath.

"There is veracity in your story and the implications are . . . extraordinary. But I'll discuss it with you on your return."

I didn't know if I felt relief. Or more fear.

"Don't run away on me, then," I said.

The link fizzed out before he could laugh.

We passed through security in the building adjacent to Cone Central and took the lift to Breeza's. I was already sipping tea and watching the 'pedes waddle around 150 floors below when Merv came in, head down, preoccupied.

"Hiya."

He jumped at the sound of my voice, recognizing it before he even saw me. Maybe he'd been having bad dreams too.

"Easy, Merv," I added, patting the chair next to me.

Mal sat at a nearby table and the Intimate wearing the royal insignia stood stolidly in the doorway of the café. More backup than I'd had in a long time.

I was starting to feel bulletproof.

Not good.

"I got a job offer for you," I said.

Merv sank into the chair, paler than normal and shaking. "W-what are you doing here? Delly said you were dead."

"No. But I *am* in a hurry." I lowered my voice. "Come and work for me. I've got Six-Gen vreal and I can't use it without you."

His eyelids fluttered. "Six-Gen. I m-mean . . . h-how are you going to p-pay me? You're a c-criminal."

Dead and a criminal? Nice. I winced and gestured to the Intimate taking up space in the doorway of the café. "Recognize the livery?"

He nodded, eyes widening.

"Well, I got a new boss. He's paying. Lavish won't be able to touch you and there'll be no more dead women to pack into the meat wagon."

The last bit hung in the air between us.

I wanted to ask about Glorious but I couldn't. If she was dead, which I was betting, I was afraid of what I might do. I had a lifetime of revenges stored up. The load was getting heavy.

Merv's stare darted to the royal insignia and the cuts and bruises on my face. "I d-don't know. Seems r-risky."

Too right. The hair on my body had begun to prickle. Something was wrong.

Mal must have had the same feeling because she pushed her seat back from the table.

"Decide," I hissed. "Quick."

Take him.

No.

I rejected the Eskaalim voice in my head. I needed Merv to trust me if this was going to work. Besides, I couldn't drag him out of here without attracting some major aggravation.

"OK," said Merv, a little too wild-eyed for my comfort. "B-but it's got to look like a k-kidnap."

I was about to argue the point when I heard the noise of too many unfriendly boots. Militia bearing the eyelash insignia on their helmets burst through the doors on the Luxoria side a second later. I caught the briefest glimpse of Lavish, dancing smug behind their riot shields.

I yanked Merv between Mal and me and shouted for the Intimate to help. But it had disappeared.

We hauled arse to the opposite entrance, knocking

diners off their chairs, but the lifts on that side were already opening for more Lashes.

"Get behind the cafébar and stay down," Mal ordered.

I didn't argue. I ran back there, hauling Merv with me, and vaulted the bench. Merv followed less easily, and then Mal, struggling, flashing her pylon-thick thighs. When she hit the floor the noise was deafening and the bridge shook.

No. Not Mal.

I peered up.

A hole had appeared in the top of the bridge, punched out by a neat laser stroke. When the smoke cleared the FlashHawk descended through the shattered glass, the Intimate calm behind the stick.

Who said it can't fly this thing?

The explosion had scattered the Militia Lashes entering from the Cone side but those approaching from the other side were waiting in safety.

"Move," I screamed in Merv's ear.

Mal catapulted us back over the counter and I scrambled over bodies and slammed a chair atop a table. It got me high enough to hook an arm around the FlashHawk's landing gear. I swung my feet up and climbed onto the strut.

Merv imitated me but fell back, unable to hold his own weight.

I cursed his weak body and jumped down after him.

Crouching, I ordered him onto my shoulders.

As he complied, the copter tilted dangerously, its rotor blades chopping the long chains of the hanging baskets. Ferns and dirt sprayed in all directions, blinding me.

The angle gave Merv some purchase, though, and he threw himself into the cockpit.

I dashed dirt from my eyes and scrambled up after

him. Mal climbed the chair to follow but it slipped
and the table collapsed.

The Militia Lashes were nearly on her when I
grabbed a minigun and started firing.

"Lower the hoist," I bellowed at Merv.

"I have the controls," the Intimate calmly in-
formed me.

"Then drop it."

I sprayed more bullets in an arc around Mal as the
cable unraveled. She saw it and grabbed it with one
giant fist.

We sailed up and out of the hole with Mal flashing
her softer bits at the soldiers.

I waited for them to pick her off but no shots came.

"They're not firing. They're too worried the bridge
will collapse." Merv sounded like he might cry.

"Get her in," I barked in relief.

The Intimate set the hoist to rewind. It groaned
under Mal's weight, reeling her in slowly until it
jammed just short of the cabin door.

She clung onto the FlashHawk's landing struts like
a heavyweight boxer trying to rock-climb. The copter
listed and Merv and I scrambled to the other side to
balance it.

"You will have to operate the manual controls on
the hoist," said the Intimate.

I climbed over the backseat to the winch mechanism and wound like a demon. Slowly the winch
turned over.

Mal felt the tug and let it lift her.

With Merv's help, I managed to haul her in.

For a few seconds we all lay on the floor, panting.

"Palace," Mal rasped at the pilot. And to me,
gratefully, "Thanks."

"Yeah, well. Likewise." *Some kinda icebreaker.*

The Intimate projected the royal insignia ahead of
us, making use of its priority rating to slipstream the
traffic and jump spots in the queue. A Militia bat

even escorted us part of the way until it peeled off
to an emergency.

"Why didn't they blow us out of the sky?"

"Running Man," Mal grunted.

"What the freak does that mean?"

She stared at me. Perspiration and plant food
weaved a muddy watercourse down her heavy face.
"Didn't you know? The Lashes work for Sera Bau.
Running Man works for Monk and Axes are S.K.
Laud. They only police on the same side or for the
same things when it suits them."

Mal wiped her brow with bleeding fingers. The
effect was like war paint.

I ripped the bottom off my T-shirt and passed it
to her. She wound it around her fingers.

"How do they enforce the law?" I said.

"However they damn well want."

Freak. Another thing I didn't know.

When we hit the approach exit for M'Grey, I was
actually relieved.

The feeling lasted a microsecond until I heard the
No-Fly Zone warnings blaring over our comm. More
Militia bats flew sweeping arcs over the island—slick
Lockheeds hovering like copters on fancy lift-fans.

"What's going on?"

"Access is denied," said the Intimate and peeled
us back toward the main traffic stream.

"What do you mean, 'access is denied'? What are
you doing?"

"The palace has been destroyed by a projectile. We
must go straight to the Burrow."

I craned to look behind me. A plume of smoke seemed
to be coming from about the right spot on M'Grey.

I couldn't take it in. "Destroyed? How badly was
it hit?"

"I have no way of knowing the true extent of the
damage."

"What about Bras and King Ban?" I demanded.

The Intimate didn't answer until it negotiated its place in-flow and consulted its data stream.

"The Militia reports are confirming that King Gerwent Ban and Ms. Brasella were in residence at the time of the explosion."

Bras dead? Ban's grandiose plans shattered?

Mal stared out of the window, her expression set.

We in-flowed north. The Intimate refused to be drawn on an exact destination and I had my hands full with Merv, who had gone into shock, his hands icy cold and shaking. I rummaged through the Flash-Hawk's medi-kit and found some glucose.

I dermed him up and the glaze began to leave his eyes. He drifted off to sleep.

I had to wake him when we landed.

We sat on a pad of a wheelport on the border between the burbs and the Medium Gyro. It was large without being dangerously busy like the Eastern Interchange.

"Transport will be waiting for you on the fifteenth spoke," said the Intimate.

"What about you?"

"My instructions are to hide this. It is easily recognized and not useful now that the king is dead."

The king is dead. "Instructed by who?"

It ignored me.

Mal flung the door open. "Hurry."

Merv scrambled down alongside me, groggy from the derm still, swaying a little. I helped him to catch Mal.

"Where are we going?" he asked.

I shook my head and stepped sideways to avoid a luggage drone. I was trusting Mal, and I wasn't sure why. "Nowhere fun, I suspect."

Chapter Eighteen

I was right for once.

We changed ped-ways and trains half a dozen times before Mal was satisfied that we were alone. Our evasion tactics had taken us in interlinked circles till we ended back close to the original wheelport.

We walked the last stretch through a maze of tunnels, until she keyed us into a service lift.

"We're back at the wheelport, aren't we?" I marveled at Gerwent Ban's audacity. A cell operating underneath a busy transport center.

Location, location, location, eh?

Mal's confirmed ID sent the lift shooting down at express speed. She braced herself in a corner and I crouched to keep my stomach intact. Lifts were creeping up the rankings on my phobia list. Merv didn't quite grasp this technique of travel and vomited over Mal's feet.

She picked him up by the scruff of the neck like a sick puppy and sat him down on his haunches, pointing in the other direction.

I watched fascinated while colorless cleaners appeared from a bottom panel and fell upon the mess

like tiny transparent crabs. Nanotek in Viva was subtle and invisible. This must be really old stuff.

By the time they'd headed back into their hidey-
hole, the lift slowed and bounced.

Merv vomited again while I prayed that someone
had bothered to maintain the cables.

The door finally opened but the lift had pulled up
too late. I could see a bunch of legs waiting for us.

"Wait," Mal ordered us. "They'll fix it but it could
take a while."

I started to shiver. Although crawling through the
opening seemed like a good way to get chopped in
half, I couldn't stand being trapped in here.

I had to get out.

Now.

Mal sank down onto the floor on her hands and
knees, her heavy face flushed and weary with effort.

I took one step over to her, avoiding the crab-
cleaners who were out and about again. Before she
could argue I climbed onto her shoulders and
launched myself through the gap.

"Don't be so stup—"

I got my torso out. Then the lift shifted a fraction,
trapping my thighs. Pain blocked out the sound of
Merv screaming on my behalf.

Stay conscious, human. I need you yet.

I was too tired to listen to the internal voice. Everything that kept me wanting to be alive faded.

I waited for the cavalry, the I-don't-want-to-die-
like-this rush that always gave me a last burst of
determination.

Nothing.

I laid my head in my hands and vaguely wondered
who was talking to me in a child's voice. Children
shouldn't have need to be members of a resistance.

"Parrish. Open your eyes." The voice didn't let up,
angry and insistent.

I tried to focus. Got a jaw outline and two huge shadowy hollows. Big, unnatural eyes.

"PARRISH."

Bras? Alive?

There. She had me. Adrenaline spiked and the world got sharper.

I watched her derm my arm three times like it belonged to someone else. "Stay awake until we get you to the pracdoc," she ordered.

I nodded, grateful that the pain had begun to recede.

"Ban?"

Tears spilled from her eyes. She didn't answer.

The lift shifted, releasing my legs, and with difficulty two sweating, sunlight-allergic hacks lifted me and staggered into a room humming with tek and then down a corridor leading to rows of bunks. At the end was a pracdoc like the one Anna Schaum had had at her compound.

They rolled me onto the slab.

I flashed back to how it had felt at Anna Schaum's—the lid sliding over me, the blast of recycled air—and I began flailing before they could activate the device.

"Keep her still." Bras came at me with a knife.

I grabbed the nerdy boy holding my head and flung him against the wall.

"Get that knife away from her," I screamed at the other one.

Instead, he let go of my hips and tried to push my shoulders down.

I head-butted him, reopening the wound on my forehead.

He fell down, holding his nose.

I flopped my body over to the edge of the slab, ready to throw myself off. Then the world fell on me.

Mal.

She heaved me back into place with a shovel-sized hand and held me down.

Someone snapped ties in place.

Bras ran the knife along the seam of my pants, cutting them off.

I screamed again as more old-fashioned nanos skittered up my nose and into my ear.

Memories. The spider thing in Mo-Vay—its abdomen exploding crawlers over me. Roo frozen with fear. My past came at me with waking fright.

Mal let go and the lid slid shut. I started to cry.

Something glanced against my cheek and sucked the salty fluid away. My claustrophobia expanded with each light touch. I battered my head against the lid.

Let me out.

Be still, moronic human. I'm working.

The Eskaalim's insult stopped me thrashing. Made me think.

It had healed me before. I just had to let it be and try to forget where I was. *Imagine Hein's after a feed and four beers. Or the glitter trails along the Stretch at night. Or the view over The Tert from Loyl Daac's tenements. Think about home. Think about what Loyl Daac is up to in Viva. Who is he balling?*

I took a deep breath and forced the air out of my nose.

Gradually I grew calmer.

No rush still, but a cold, calculating comprehension of what I wanted to do.

Another caress. This time from the sedation monitor—and I was gone.

Chapter Nineteen

"We're running out of time." Bras sat next to me in front of the screens, studying the different net news strands.

Nothing.

I was stunned. Nothing about the FlashHawk punching a hole in the bridge. Nothing about the attack on the palace. Nothing about the king being dead.

Common Net and Out-World had loose reportage of a disturbance on M'Grey that they put down to a religious sect. One-World had even less interesting Prier reports of floods up on the Cape and of Northern Hem terrorists being detained on the equatorial border.

Everything remained focused on the upcoming Pan-Sats.

How extensively the world was being filtered to me. My naïveté was pathetic. In its own strange, brutal way, The Tert was a way more honest place than Vivacity.

"How often do they do that? Not show things?"

She blinked. "Father always said that history is built on selective recall."

I thought about it for a while. "That's a pretty human thing, I guess. Every time we remember something it's only our side of it. But *this* . . ." I thumped the arm of my chair. "This is gross freaking manipulation. Why isn't the editing intelligence showing what happened on M'Grey?"

"Sera Bau's Priers are her feed for news. Maybe Bau ordered a blackout on the footage?"

Bras's eyes had seemed to get larger every day we'd been in there—four now—the hollows under them deeper. She'd blacked out twice. She ate little. Unprovoked anger attacks racked her thin body. We tied her to her bunk but even then her ranting filled our dreams.

Ban's hired teks deserted on day three. I didn't blame them. We were a hide of crazies.

My own healing was too slow. I could walk but the pain sucked. I kept the painblocks for sleeping, so they didn't muddle my daytime thinking.

That way they just muddled my dreams. And I'd been having plenty of them.

Sometimes it was Teece.

Last night it had been Billy Myora, the suited Cabal shaman. He seemed to be watching me mess up from a sullen, I-told-you-so distance.

Mainly, though, it was Leesa Tulu. I woke from those sweating, scared that in some way Marinette could reach me in my dreams.

This morning I'd woken with the heavy feeling that I was letting everyone down. I went straightaway and collared Merv.

He surfaced from his 6-Gen interface jerkily, as though he'd been speeding. We'd spent the last few days vrealing together, working up some rumor chaos on the news bays and boards until exhaustion claimed me.

Merv's vreal stamina was humbling.

"Merv, tell me what you really know. What happened to the AI?"

Fear filled his tired eyes. I hadn't seen that look in them since he'd left the Luxoria.

"M-my job when I worked for S-Sera Bau was Five-Gen on the Prier feeds. One t-time I got s-stuck in vreal during a sh-shiver. I heard whispering, s-saw sh-shadows. When I came out I had this damn s-s-stutter. I don't know what h-happened . . . and v-vreal is so c-crowded with shit I thought maybe I imagined it. But after that the anomalies s-started. The shadows are there n-now, every time I go in."

"Is that why you call Brilliance 'she'?"

He nodded. "It's like she got a personality then. I-I mean she had one before but it was j-juvenile and p-pedantic like m-most AIs." After the sh-shiver she s-seemed older. Almost c-canny." He gave me a look. "B-bit like Jales and P-Parrish."

I ignored the last. "King Ban believes she has a bio component now. What do you think?"

Merv's eyes widened. "Th-that makes sense. But how?"

"How should I know?" I snapped at him. Then I pulled myself up. Merv was doing everything he could. It wasn't his fault that it wasn't enough. "How's Snout?"

"She's still lighting hot spots but Brilliance is getting s-suspicious," he said.

Merv had wormed Snout a channel into Monk's and Sera Bau's raw-material streams thanks to his knowledge. By falsifying Priers' reports, Snout was force-feeding Brilliance news. It added to the list of sensational reports we'd generated: child abduction, abused children, a celebrity baby, celebrity chemo-death, sports-star injuries—everything that might register high on DramaNews and Sport—competing stories vying for attention.

"She's g-got her own veracity markers and not all my s-sims are good enough."

"How suspicious?"

"I'm going to have to take Snout out of the l-loop for a couple of days."

Days? The Pan-Sats screened in less than that.

"It's not working," I said.

"It is. The newsfeeds are backing up. There have already been a few blackouts in Tasmania and the Interior, so her p-processing capacity must be under stress, but it's t-taking time."

I could see only one way to hurry things up.

Start a real fire. My idea had been brewing. I just didn't know how I could pull it off. "Does James Monk celebrate the opening of the Pan-Sats?"

Merv nodded.

"Who goes to that?"

"Traditionally, all the m-media heavies."

"Including Laud and Sera Bau?"

Another nod. "I worked the p-pyrotek sequences on it a few years ago. They were all there. And their s-security."

"What are you thinking?" asked Mal.

"I'm thinking of a little extra aggravation. Something that Brilliance won't be able to ignore. Something that will really tangle her wireless. How do I get to that party?"

The room fell silent at my ridiculous question.

Only Merv seemed to give it serious consideration.

"You could p-put yourself up for auction at the m-meathouse," he said. "Monk entertains a lot of people at that party. He'll be hiring for it, and he wanted you b-before."

No.

The thought of playing the *Amorato* again frightened me more than my dreams of Marinette. More than meeting all my phobias on a dark night in a small space.

I twisted the ring that Glorious had given me. I didn't want to have to use it. I didn't want to go back to the place where she'd taken me.

There was nothing good there.

"When's the next one?" I forced myself to ask.

Merv dipped into his data stream. He resurfaced tugging his ear and wiping his nose nervously. "T-tonight."

I stood up and looked at Mal. "Looks like we'd better go clothes shopping."

Bras followed me out of the main room to my bunk.

"This is not in our plan, Parrish. Even if you get there the place will be so saturated with security that you won't be able to do anything."

I'd been waiting for her. In as few words as I could, I told her about Wombebe. "Someone working for Monk is jerking my strings. It's a safe enough punt that Monk will bid for me at the auction, whatever the reason behind it," I said.

"What about our plans?"

"I didn't come after you when you were taken from The Tert. Maybe I can make up for that by finding Wombebe."

Bras flushed with anger. "You're going to ruin everything on a whim."

I rounded on her. "There won't be an *everything* if we don't melt Brilliance's wires by the time the Pan-Sats screen. We've got one chance. That's all. If what I'm planning comes off, then great. If it doesn't, find yourself another leader. And another cause."

She wanted to hurt me then, for not seeing things her way. I could see it in the way her fingers clawed the palms of her hands. The way her eyes darkened. She fought it by turning away from me.

I waited for her to swap shifts with Merv.

He staggered wearily to his bunk.

I sat down alongside him before he could lie down.

"Thanks," I said.

He rubbed his forehead. "W-what for?"

"You took a chance coming with me."

"N-not really," he corrected me. "Delly would probably have killed me s-soon enough. He knew I'd helped you. And you blackmailed m-me anyway."

I grinned. "I need one last favor. I'll probably have to go into vreal again sometime. Even if it's just in a LAN. I need a portable connection."

Merv sighed. "You'll f-fry if you go on your own, Parrish. You're not very good at it, y-you know."

"I'm already fried."

He shrugged his agreement.

Merv and I weren't all that different. He had his sinister shadows following him. I had mine.

He took off the mystic star and handed it to me. "I can send Snout sniffing around the p-portals. She should be safe doing that. If you make enough waves she'll c-come—if she can."

I took the charm and slipped it around my neck, knowing what it meant for him to part with it. "I was kinda hoping you'd say that."

In return I handed him a pistol from the cell's stash. His eyes wide, he handled it like it had a disease.

"This is how you use it," I said.

I showed him how to load and point and fire.

Merv listened obediently. Only when I was finished did he ask the question. "W-what's it f-for?"

I lowered my voice and jabbed the barrel in his abdomen, near the adrenal glands. "If Bras turns werewolf before I get back, shoot her right here. If I don't come back, shoot her. Go to The Tert. Find a guy named Teece. Tell him I said I owe you. He's a good man. He'll help you out."

"You m-mean you're not going to hold me t-to this?"

"Keep Snout in the system until just before the

party—no longer. Then get the hell out of here and get a life."

"You s-said the s-same thing to Glori."

I stared at Merv, trying to remember when I'd said that to her. Did that mean she was still alive? I dared not let myself hope but I couldn't bring myself to ask him outright.

Some things are best not known.

I climbed up to the top bunk and went to sleep.

Mal and I left the hide at dusk and trudged for two hours up and down transit tunnels before Mal reckoned that it was safe to surface. My still-healing legs ached so hard that I winced with every step.

I found myself getting angry with the Eskaalim. *Can't you do something useful—like fix it?*

It didn't respond, lurking somewhere underneath the pain and frustration. It had been so dormant since the bridge that I wondered whether I'd imagined its presence over the past few weeks.

Maybe the voices in my head were my own.

But then Gerwent had said I was right in the things I'd said.

And how did I explain Bras? Her symptoms had worsened. I watched her constantly for signs of the dark whorls that came before the change.

"We must avoid public transport. Sera Bau records everything," said Mal. "That's how she gets her Priers out so quickly."

"What about the FlashHawk?"

Mal shook her head. "The Intimate has instructions to hide it and remain with it for an emergency."

"How do I contact it?"

She gave me a Mal look. "You don't."

"Well, you'd better stay alive. Because I'll be betting that we need it. What about the Polity he talked about? Can they help us?"

She puffed and I winced as we walked out of one wheelport spoke into the 'pede park.

"An organized polity was just Gerwent's dream and is the reason why the Royals have become so powerless. There isn't a backbone among them. Only Gerwent. That's why Mel and I stayed even when his ideas got so wild. At least he has some. I've grown to believe that his is the way to start again. Only we don't have him driving it anymore. We've only got you."

Great.

The grimace that Mal gave me was deprecating. So far she'd saved my life twice. She was telling me that I hadn't done enough to impress her in return.

I changed the subject.

"Was Mel related to you?" I didn't show any sympathy for the other woman's death in the destruction of the palace because I didn't know that Mal needed it.

She sighed. "I am her genetic copy—the younger version. I've—we've—been royal servants for a long time. My genes condemned me to loyalty. I've been cloned to ensure their reproduction from someone who already had that character trait." She rumbled a loud, derogatory laugh. "We're like the eunuchs of old, only you didn't have to emasculate us. Our genes did it for us."

I wasn't going to argue with her on that.

I watched a group of athletes boarding a private 'pede.

"Can Sera Bau tap into the private 'pedes?"

Mal saw where I was looking. "Not that one. See the Running Man emblem? Those athletes are sponsored by James Monk."

"Even better."

Mal strode in front of the transport as it crawled toward the channel for the downtown traffic stream.

Somehow she bluffed us a ride with a story that I
was an athlete and we'd missed our own ride.

The driver checked me out. I tried to look flexible
and toned and chokked on whatever the latest en-
hancers were.

"ID?"

Mal gripped the window frame like it could be
his neck.

"You're jerking me, right? This is Jales Wyzconkski."

I bit my lip at her retro-hip lingo and the absurd
made-up name, and scowled at him.

Athletes were always pissed off about something.

"See if there's room," he grumbled and released
the door lock.

I wedged in among some cricketers heading in for
a night out on Brightbeach.

Stoned and excited, they ribbed each other over
which *Amorato* they'd end up with and who among
them had the most staying power.

A week ago their chatter wouldn't have bothered
me but tonight I found it depressing. Glorious could
have been one of their jokes.

And Glorious was probably dead.

A sunburned guy whose receding hair circled a
pink scalp and who had the beginnings of a soft belly
ran his hand along my thigh.

I dropped my fist down hard between his legs.

The others roared with laughter as he yelled. He
threw me sulky glances for the rest of the trip.

Stupid, Parrish. Casual enemies I did not need.

Mal and I parted from the cricketers at an intersec-
tion a couple of blocks away from the Fair.

I worked my way back into a Jales Belliere persona
as we walked. Merv had registered me ahead of time
for the meat tray. By now my forged pedigree would
be bouncing all over the auction bid-bay for pre-buyers.

The shopping trip, without Gerwent Ban's credit,

had fielded only a cheap, ill-fitting, short flared skirt, a loud satin tank top and some slightly wonky heels. All I had to do now was walk out on the dais and act like meat.

With luck, James Monk would do the rest.

The risk, of course, was someone else taking a fancy to a badly dressed *Amorato* from the Interior. If you believed the flesh merchants, there was always a market for exotic meat.

Merv said he'd attempt to keep out the wrong sort of bids from his end by pushing the price. But nothing was certain.

The other risk was Lavish. Merv hadn't been able to find out if he'd survived the bridge episode. The Luxoria wasn't taking calls.

And Leesa Tulu. If she was there . . .

My registration numbers got us into the lift, which stopped automatically a floor short of the Fair. We walked down a short corridor to another registration check. Behind it was a crowded body shop.

That's what it reminded me of, anyway.

Meat being molded, primped and corseted. Pubic-hair exfoliations. Cosmetic sculpting like the sort I'd had in Plastique. All shapes and all sizes of genitalia and physique. Air thick with pheromones.

As soon as I scented the dizzies, the Eskaalim swelled.

"I thought the Fair's rules said no pheromones?" I gasped.

"The produce can use them. Not the buyers."

I found myself automatically seeking out a primp station, right next to a pair quietly fucking.

Mal followed me and grabbed my shoulders, giving me a shake, her nostrils flaring. I hadn't noticed before how smooth her skin was, almost grrlish.

She slapped my ear and shoved a mask over my nose and mouth. I fell off the chair and came up cocked and ready to fight her.

She blocked my fist with one hand and held me still.

"Save the sex for the stage."

My face got hot with all kinds of emotions. Mainly humiliation.

I grappled for some semblance of self-control and let a primper come and look me over.

"Who dressed this bitch?" he said to no one in particular. Like the rest of the workers he wore a mask that sucked in every time he breathed. He got busy programming the beauty nanos to rouge my face and eat any dry skin and unwanted body odors. They skittled over me while the primper squeezed my breasts into something impossibly narrow and high.

Boy, was I getting tolerant. In fact, it felt kinda . . .

"My—er—luggage was stolen by the border Militia. I think they liked what they saw in it," I said, forcing myself to think.

"Typical. Those border boys are such grrlie wannabes." The tight suspicion around his mouth eased a little.

His touch was tantalizing. The dizzies leaked in around the edges of my mask and set my skin afire with sensations.

I tried to think about Leesa Tulu.

Bitch-doctor. Enough bad karma to dampen anyone's ardor.

Instead, my thoughts strayed off-track to Loyl. If Monk bought me, I might wind up seeing him. I planned to kick his arse for lying to me about the fact that I'd shape-changed.

"OK?" Mal brought me back to the present.

I nodded. A high-pitched ring told us that the market was in interval, and an exotically tall, thin man in a full-length leather coat wove among the meat and the primpers. He flexed an electric probe in his hands as if it was a whip.

"Custodian," Mal said.

"How come you know so much?" I asked.

"Underestimating people is dangerous," she replied, refusing to be drawn further.

The couple in the next station heard the ring and pulled up sharp on their antics, smoothing down their clothes.

I felt simultaneously relieved and disappointed that they'd stopped.

"Is he a big deal?" I asked the room at large.

"Don't stare or he'll come over here," said the grrl next to me as she shoved her breasts back into her corset. "If he thinks you won't raise a high enough bid, he'll on-sell you to the quods. You earn squat in quod."

Quod. Was this the thing Gerwent Ban had talked about—the way Ike got all that meat to experiment on: buying criminals? "He can do that?"

She gave a quick, fearful nod and turned her back on me.

As if he'd heard us, the Custodian stopped and swiveled.

As the primper bitched on about the size and state of my skin pores, I let my gaze casually slide in another direction until the Custodian had disappeared into his own booth.

I checked the wall screen for my number. I was first up after the interval.

How the freak was I going to walk out there and keep my 'froid? To my mind meat markets were on a par with rape and murder. Yet I was still horny.

I noticed that Mal had left my side. Then I heard a commotion.

I located Mal's broad back to the left of the main door. Above the entrance a ceiling-mounted semiauto had descended and begun a whirring scan of the room.

The meat and primpers saw the hardware out and started screaming and running around.

I pushed my primper off me and hit the floor, crawling behind the line of chairs to get a better view.

From between a whole lotta legs it looked like security had some non-meat baled up in the corridor.

The leather-coated Custodian stepped from his booth, bearing his own spectacular piece of hardware: a twelve-gauge shotgun with a modified-choke barrel. Old but immaculate—ultimate close-range stopping power.

The place went into hush mode.

"I want to pre-buy her," a voice demanded.

I recognized the deep guttural.

Bitch-doctor.

I had more than a few scores to settle with Leesa Tulu, but if she got in my face before the parade I might not live to see my plan out.

I kept my head down and prayed that the bouncers didn't like her attitude.

"Mad-dame Tulu, as a frequent buyer you know that the regulations of the Fair are quite clear. No one may procure stock from the green room before the parade. *No matter who they are.* Otherwise we would cease to be able to operate a fair system," said the Custodian. "The rules of bidding are immutable."

"If I lose her because of this, Listrata—"

"If you lose her it will be the result of equitable bidding," the Custodian interjected. "Happy Pan-Sats, Mad-dame Tulu."

I could see the relief in Mal's profile. She backed away from the corner of the door and returned to where she'd left me.

I made sure that the door had closed in Tulu's face before I stood up.

"Why did she want you?" Mal asked.

"Long story," I said. "And grisly."

"*Jales Belliere?*" My *Amorato* name pinged off the walls of the green room like gunshot. I adjusted my expression to innocent and approached the Custodian, my head lowered.

"We don't like troublemakers at our Fair. If you cause the slightest problem during bidding I will sell you privately." He slapped the shotgun painfully against my ear. "*Comprends?*"

I didn't doubt him at all. He had no respect for the people he sold off like cuts of meat. Not surprising, really. Most of them didn't have respect for themselves.

But then they were here for practical reasons. If you could get a regular income and better working conditions, who'd be stupid enough not to take them?

Me, probably.

I stood mute in front of him, fighting down the anger. The Custodian took my reaction as fear and moved off, satisfied.

My number chimed and another primper hustled me straight to the service lift. I didn't get to speak to Mal. There was only time enough to snatch the mask from my face.

In the lift the primper squirted a vial of diz up my nostrils. I stared at his bare shoulders and hairless, overpainted face, wondering what he might look like naked.

Thankfully the partitions lifted before lust overpowered sense.

Showtime.

Chapter Twenty

The spotlights warped my view of everything except Listrata, the Custodian, who stood center stage, his stance provocative and arrogant.

The man surely dug what he did.

His honeyed voice was a lure that he used to maximum effect as he talked up the success of the markets.

I made three trips up and down without generating a single bid.

I felt naked under the lights. Not the bare-skinned kind of naked. The unsafe kind.

Blind and weaponless.

Disadvantaged.

I was turned on by the dizzies and worried by the knowledge that Tulu was in the crowd and gunning for me and I couldn't see a damn thing.

The sensations warred inside me.

To make it worse the Custodian had left his position at center stage to stalk me with his probe.

"Perform, bitch," he murmured as he rubbed it up against me.

The voice-over recited the ridiculous made-up personal history that Ibis had created for me. Transparent lies.

And yet the wall screen to my right flicked up a bid.

Guess who! My favorite voodoo mama.

Maybe it was the effect of Marinette so close, but the dizzie began to wear off abruptly. Cheap house shit.

Its withdrawal left me dangerously pissed off with the whole charade. Make that the whole world.

Oh, oh. Comedown.

I suddenly stopped parading and strode right to the end of the dais, where I stood belligerently, hands on hips.

The indifferent background buzz instantly dropped a few decibels. *Meat* didn't eyeball the buyers. *Meat* simpered and pirouetted and coquetted to attract the highest prices.

I felt the probe sting my buttocks and begin to prod between my thighs.

I spun on instinct and booted it right out of Listrata's hands. He swore softly and drew a shok from his coat pocket, smiling at the crowd as if my reaction had been choreographed.

"I should have picked you," he said under his breath. "Faux bitch."

"Pick this." I head-butted him in his cadaverous stomach. He folded like a shawarma wrapper and we catapulted off the stage, taking out most of the front row.

I recovered before him, tearing my cheap high heels off to use as weapons. Behind me the wall screen started flickering, going crazy with bids.

Seems the buyers liked a grrl with attitude.

Suckers.

Knowing that I'd blown my chance with Monk, the least I could do was salvage some dignity . . . and run.

I clocked the exit just as Tulu's two bodyguards plowed through the upended chairs and buyers toward me.

I evaded them as far as a vreal-sex booth.

Muscled and fit, they jumped me together. One pinned my legs while the other punched me hard. I felt my nose crack.

Pain and then welcome numbness.

I kicked out hard and furious. The strength in my still-sore legs bounced one of them back on to an advertiser's sensor pad. A cloud of happy granules pumped into the air around him. He gobbed a mouthful, slowing him down to a giggle.

I spat blood and roundhoused the other guy. He collapsed back on top of his partner. The two of them wallowed about in slow motion, caught in a fug of free powdered bliss.

I climbed unsteadily to my feet, breathing blood bubbles out through the split in my nose.

Compound fracture. Crap.

Tulu approached me from one side, Listrata from the other.

I wondered if Marinette would show herself again. She seemed to have a bit of a thing for me.

I really had to do something about the caliber of the people I attracted.

Security materialized, wearing uniforms and jewelry. They formed a ring around me. I looked for a sign of their allegiances but couldn't see a Lash or an Axe, or Monk's Running Man.

Mercs. That was a good thing.

I took Listrata low and dirty, grabbing for his genitals. At first I thought that he was padded well but then I suddenly knew the reason for his hatred of meat. Someone else had beaten me to the mutilation.

"Eunuch," I spat and reached for his throat.

He pinged me with the probe on full charge and I collapsed into convulsions.

As he untangled himself from my twitching and salivating, Mal burst out of the lift, taking a line of pretty security with her. She waded toward me with a determination that warmed my shuddering body.

I watched her go down an arm's length from me under a paralysis net.

Our stares met.

Nice thought, Mal, mine tried to say.

Stupid, hers replied.

Me or her?

Security closed in for the cleanup while Listrata stood astride me with the arrogance of a slave trader.

I couldn't stop shaking and dribbling to do anything about it.

The Custodian lifted the probe to jab me again when the bidding chimes pealed and stopped him.

He froze mid-probe, glancing around at the screens. The one above me on the ceiling had blanked, pumping out Caribbean music to entertain the crowd.

Someone was engaged in an off-line negotiation.

Someone with money was buying.

Me? Please.

I craned my neck back to look at Mal. Hope lit her eyes, the only part of her able to move.

A voice-over announced the end of bidding for me and a closing of the deal.

Security shoved Tulu aside to come and get me.

Listrata knelt down close to my ear, a hand up to shield himself from my spit.

"I'll be watching for you," he whispered.

Then he was up and striding back to the stage to quiet his dissatisfied crowd.

I dragged myself over to Mal and flopped my arm over her.

"M-mine," was all I could make my lips say.

Security tried to drag me off her and roll me onto

an inflatable stretcher. I concentrated everything to make my fingers grasp her.

"They're together," someone in the audience called out. "I saw them in the lift."

"You'd better take them both," another called out.

Security hesitated while they conferred quietly. After a few moments one of them ordered in another stretcher.

The crowd gave a little cheer, too busy with the conclusion to my drama to engage with the newest selection from Listrata's meat tray.

My appreciation of their intervention was silent but intense.

Security floated us to the lift. In a minute or so we were on the roof. I sucked in a lungful of clear air, thankful to be out of the markets.

A copter landed within the hour. With relief I saw the Running Man emblem on the side.

The pilot folded the seats back and security laid Mal and me side by side behind him.

The trip took longer than any other copter flight I'd been on, the pilot finally bringing us in steep and quick, landing on a promise.

Beside me, Mal was still immobilized by the paralysis net. The pilot refused to disable it before arrival.

"Y-you leave her too l-long, she'll g-go b-berserker," I pointed out when I regained some power over my tongue.

He didn't care.

Nor did he care about the blood still bubbling from my broken nose onto the plush carpet on the floor of the copter.

So much for the cosmetic surgery. A whack on the cheekbone, a few new scars and a change of clothes and I'd be back to my old self.

Sometime during the flight I stopped twitching but parts of me still felt numb and heavy. I'd swallowed so much blood that it felt as though my tongue and throat wore a coating of warm metal.

The abruptness of the landing got me vomiting.

I managed to sit up and peer out of the window. My misery vanished for a few seconds as I absorbed the vista.

Where had I been expecting James Monk to live? In Hi-tel luxury?

I stared in naive wonder. This was luxury, yes, but not the high-rise sort. Or the antique-obsessive Gerwent Ban sort.

This was something else.

A mountainside of sweeping lawns and flat-roofed white buildings dotted in between waterfalls and ponds. Tropical landscaping bursting with frangipani and passionvine that made Viva seem bare and ugly.

Nobody could afford this much space on the coast. It just didn't exist.

But it did. Monk owned a flat-topped mountain and a whole coastal plain in Northern Viva, complete with pollution sweepers kiting about in the sky and giant water filters rolling about in the waves breaking on the beach.

I thought of Fishertown and the slick, oily gray of the water there. It was impossible that this could be the same ocean.

Tears smarted in my eyes at the sheer beauty of it—and at the sheer selfish greed. No one should have that much.

I hated Monk already.

North and south of where I stood, neighboring mountains repeated the pattern.

Not just Monk but others.

I'd heard talk of a place where the mountains jutted up from the ground like teeth. As I watched the cable car speeding up the mountain toward us, I tried to think of the name.

Chalice?

I'd learned about it in net-school, a national park in another era when such things existed. That meant that I was at the northern tip of Viva, over five hundred klicks from The Tert.

The thought alone gave me vertigo.

As we landed an Intimate appeared on the pad and opened the door. The pilot disabled the web spread over Mal and the Intimate began plucking off the tendrils.

"Be careful—" I warned.

The big woman regained feeling in and control of her muscles in an uncontrollable rush.

I scrambled for the door but she swiped at me with one hand, shoving me out so hard that I somersaulted across the tarmac. Dissatisfied with that, she turned on the Intimate and kicked its abdomen so hard that the bio-plas skin covering split.

The pilot panicked and lifted the copter up a few meters, tipping Mal out. She landed on the pad with a sickening *whump.*

It didn't seem to have any ill effect. She stood up like a beast shaking off flies.

"Mal. You know me?"

She had a think about it. After a moment she nodded.

"Your senses are freaked. It's how everyone feels if they've been webbed for too long. It passes."

She grunted, whirling her huge arms as if she was getting the circulation back in them.

I hopped back, wary.

The Intimate righted itself and, holding its stomach together, politely invited us into the waiting cable car.

I stumbled straight in. Mal might be the best backup I'd ever had, but right now I figured that she was Monk's problem.

I shouted at the Intimate, "Move before she pulverizes us."

It had enough smarts to see my point and back-tracked quickly, leaping into the cable car as Mal came after us.

I slammed the door and the Intimate hit the button to get us moving. We rattled downward, leaving Mal to vent her aggravation on the oleander bushes around the edge of the landing pad.

Still holding its innards, the Intimate introduced itself and welcomed me to Chalice Two.

"Where's Chalice One?"

It pointed north to the next mountain.

"Who owns that?"

"Sera Bau."

Figures.

I leaned against the cable car window and took in the Intimate's denims, shiny shoes and clean white long-sleeved shirt with the buttons missing where its guts hung out. Despite the injury it launched into its programmed tourist blurb.

"Monk House extends over many levels. Your accommodation is situated on the twenty-fifth terrace. Terraces twenty to thirty are reserved for employees. You are permitted to visit certain areas of the beach, the dais and the gymnasium. The rest of the estate is restricted."

"What's that?" I pointed at a huge structure midway down the mountain.

"The Orchid Cage is a restricted area. The plants are easily disturbed. The gardeners will choose flowers for display in your cabin on a daily basis should you wish. A mellifluous version of the *Oncidium's* cultivation is available to you on Channel Sunshine of your in-house entertainment. A medic has been requested to attend to your wounds."

I cleared my throat. It still tasted like blood. "No medic." I said. "Just painkillers."

"Painkillers will be available to you via the service chute located near the bathing pavilion. Perhaps when you have had time to reflect on your appearance you may wish to request further assistance. In that case, please call the housekeeper."

I glared at the Intimate, searching for signs of intended insult, and found only a bland expression. If it was trash-talking me, it was very subtle.

"Mr. Monk's personal assistant will contact you in due course. Please feel free to make use of all the accoutrements and services provided in your cabin."

Whew. I'd never been spoken to like that. It was downright freaky. And what the hell did *mell-if-luous* mean? I delved into my language infusion and inhaled a snort of laughter.

Well, *mell-if-luous* orchid song probably beat the hell out of Tert homebake.

The cable car trip was nearly as bad as flying—the car flapped about on its cable like washing in a cyclone. It took all my powers of self-control not to jump ship and climb.

That and the sealed, bulletproof safety doors. Maybe I wasn't the first person to have that urge.

I stumbled out of the door and felt the *woosh* of air as the Intimate rattled away. It seemed an archaic way to get up and down a mountain but there was no accounting for a rich boy's tastes.

The doors to the cabin were all open and I wandered around inside like a burglar in the wrong house. Lavish's club had been luxurious but it was still a club. Gerwent Ban's palace had been a showpiece—a mausoleum of useless antiques. The sort of thing you'd expect from a king.

This was something else altogether. All the little touches of wealth: the telescope and viewing lounge on the deck, the translucent walls shimmering with high-density art, the crisp white sheets, the crackle of the bug net safely collecting and delivering stray insects back into the world unharmed.

Why would Monk care about keeping bugs alive? I wondered.

I wandered through, searching for the chute with the painkillers. It was between the san and the bedroom. I sucked down twice the recommended dose, then continued taking a tour as though the cabin was the dark side of the moon.

"San" was hardly the word to describe—what had the Intimate called it?—the bathing pavilion. I stood, torn between wanting to wash and get the blood off my face and the need to check the place out.

The recce option won.

I couldn't lie naked in the bath until I'd checked out what might be looking back at me through the untinted windows.

From the balcony the gardens dropped away steeply into jungled terraces, each with its own white-topped cabin. No telltale goat tracks for hikers. James Monk's guests weren't encouraged to wander.

Not convinced that everyone on the mountain couldn't see me, I climbed into the viewing lounge and peered through the telescope.

Maybe I could see them too.

I swung the telescope through several full arcs until I felt satisfied that I was currently unobserved.

Fatigue began to take over. I forced myself into the bath (Teece's tub was never gonna feel the same), thinking that the water offered some privacy at least, and was almost asleep when Monk's PA contacted me on the wall screen.

It told me it would come in a short time and that, in view of my hurried departure from the markets, I should avail myself of the wardrobe provided for guests and of the light refreshments that were also supplied.

A tray of unrecognizable food was waiting in the bedroom. I roamed around it, stuffing the strange tastes in my mouth and pondering a whole range of things.

In between mouthfuls I tried on clothes and stripped them off again. I spared a moment to look in the reflect. My nose had stopped bleeding but was more than a mess. Gaping skin and chipped cartilage.

Not exactly a good appearance for an *Amorato*.

The why-had-Monk-hired-me question surfaced again and bobbed about.

I climbed into a pair of tight pants and, despite the warm temperature, a high-collared silk coat. I'd had more than enough public nudity for one lifetime. Monk was out of luck.

As promised, another Intimate arrived to escort me to the boss's pad somewhere in the middle gradient of Chalice Two. I saw figures in their transparent cabins all the way there. Monk was obviously keen on entertaining—and on voyeurism.

Must be a media thing, I mused.

For what it was worth I'd tried to reassume the mantle of the haughty *Amorato* again, twirling Glorious's dizzie ring on my finger. As the Intimate gave me a *mell-if-luous* travelogue, Glorious occupied my thoughts, until the car wobbled to a stop outside a pagoda. The outside reminded me of Lavish's club. A stern mixture of opulence and extreme cleanliness. Or maybe I was too accustomed to filth and poverty.

After Mo-Vay most things were hard to digest.

The Intimate walked me through a detector and into a sparsely furnished room with doors and solid walls and banks of screens. In fact, all the walls in the boss's pad were opaque.

Seemed that he liked to look, not be looked at. Even the view over the sparkling beach was through tinted shutters.

"Jales Belliere? I'm James Monk."

• *Finally. Let's get this over.*

He stared at my nose and for a moment I thought he was going to laugh.

Then I thought I was going to.

Monk was actually not much older than me. I stifled my reaction immediately. One thing that living with my stepdad Kevin had taught me: never let age or physical appearance deceive you. People who blew your expectations were dangerous because they nearly always had a point to prove.

Hell, I should have known that—I was one of them.

"Your public fotos are fake," I said.

"Wouldn't do for everyone to know what the most powerful man in the Southern Hem looked like."

"Are you?"

He stared moodily out to sea while I appreciated his deep tan, sprinkling of freckles, and thick brown hair. If Loyl Daac had cornered the 'zine-centerfold-only-barely-tainted-with-the-slums appeal, Monk *owned* the sophisticated-gangster look.

Even the flat metallic plug behind his ear glinted style. I figured the guy was getting live sport while we talked.

"Man? Yes. Person—soon enough. You don't appreciate what comes to you too quickly," he said.

This time I couldn't hold back my laugh or its derogatory edge.

Monk stared back at me, his shaped eyebrows drawn into a frown. "And why, Jales Belliere, do you strike me as *not* the person you say you are? Could it be that unfortunate mess you've made of yourself *brawling*?"

My hand moved automatically to partially cover my face. "Wouldn't do for everyone to know the real me," I drawled softly. And waited.

Intuition told me that even though I'd piqued his curiosity I stood on the edge of an abyss. If his interest turned to annoyance—or, worse, suspicion—I'd be in a quod somewhere quicker than Raul Minoj could close a weapons deal.

Monk knitted his fingers together, the gesture of an older person.

"Aside from your injuries, you *look* like an *Amorato*. And a review of your earlier communication with my factotum suggests that you have the talents of one. But you are rough and your language is rented. *Amoratos* also don't usually come complete with battle scars."

Rough? Rented? I paid a fortune for that infusion.

For half a cred I'd snot him. How did the world get to be filled with so many conceited, arrogant people? It felt like I was sizing up against a Loyl-me-Daac with money.

But I gave a little subservient bow instead—the hardest thing I'd ever done in my life.

"I'm from the Interior, sir. My manners may be coarse, but my talents are considerable. May I ask . . . why did you choose me if you thought as you seem to about me?"

I kept my head bent as Monk circled me, prodding and squeezing me like I was a side of meat on a butcher's hook.

"Let's us just say . . . a good friend recommended you." He touched the skin of my neck. Then he lifted my coat to look at my figure.

"And what's this?" He touched Glorious's ring.

I kept my head down, hoping that he wouldn't spot how rigid my jaw had become.

"An *Amorato* is never without some tools in"—I drew on my infusion for a word—"company."

He pried the ring off my finger, then walked to a small diagnostic module in an alcove. When he'd finished examining it he brought it back to me, satisfied that it was harmless.

"I've scheduled you for an exhibition this evening.

Tomorrow I am having guests and I am short on entertainers. If you impress me tonight you can work tomorrow and I shall be happy to recommend your services." Monk's voice dropped lower. "I hope you're as good as you imply you are, Jales Belliere. I risked a considerable amount bringing you here— a favor to a friend. In fact, let's make the situation quite clear. Perform well, or I shall consider the investment a bad debt." His face lit up with a brilliant, handsome smile and he made an expansive gesture. "In the meantime, get your face fixed."

Interview over.

Chapter Twenty-one

I told myself that I was letting the medic attend me because the painkillers weren't working, not because Monk had told me to. I had no desire to make myself attractive for my evening *exhibition* but the fact was that I *had* to get to Monk's party.

"This mess needs proper reconstruction," the skinny medic grumbled through her body film. She was taking no risks with my body fluids on principle. "I really can't spare the nanomeds for employees. Do you know how many people are staying here? The skin peels alone are stretching my limits."

"Just give me something strong and straighten it."

Her eyes brightened. "You mean . . . the old-fashioned way?"

I pulled a face.

Like a kid given a gun to play with, the medic dermed me up and stuck a thin straightening probe up each nostril.

My eyes watered as the cartilage crunched like gravel trodden underfoot.

She was whistling by the time she glued the skin flap flat and heal-creamed the splits there—those and on my forehead—and gave me something for the bruising.

I stood up groggily.

She tossed me another derm. "Take this for later. You look like you know what to do with it."

I prepared for my evening appointment as if I was going to war—dread and determination mingling to keep me in an unsteady state.

Could I keep this together?

I'd thought I'd made some hard choices recently. But now I realized I hadn't. All those decisions had been made under threat, under the pressure to survive.

Simple stuff. I hadn't really had to think about them.

But this I could run away from.

No one but me was looking over my shoulder telling me that I had to go through with it. It all came down to how much I truly cared about what was happening to The Tert now that I was no longer mired in the stench of it all.

I stared morosely up the mountain at Monk's prized Orchid Cage and then at the darkening sky. Although the air was clear of pollution, I still couldn't see the stars for cloud.

My resolve was slipping. All of a sudden I wanted to talk to Teece and eat shawarmas at Lu Chow's. I wanted Larry to pour me a beer and tell me that Riko was planning to ambush me at the next full moon.

I could handle those things. I knew what to do about them.

But this was a foreign place. Wealth so unmerited. So wrong. Yet, from inside, so . . . seductive. So liberating.

Losing myself would be too easy.

Yes . . . yes . . . lose yourself. . . .

The Eskaalim urged me toward surrender of a dif-

ferent kind. A new trick: Parrish without anger was
Parrish without purpose.

I pushed away the languor by recalling images of
Roo as he drowned in the poison canal—victim of
Ike's post-human lunacy, funded by Sera Bau.

When the memory was fresh enough in my mind
to bleed, I ordered some innocuous provisions from
housekeeping and inquired after Mal.

"Your companion will be released when the medi-
cal staff deem her free of symptoms," the housekeeper boomed.

"How long will that be?"

The housekeeper consulted her data stream. "On
current available prognosis . . . tomorrow afternoon.
In the meantime you may visit her at the Terrace
Seventy-two infirmary."

Satisfied, I switched the screen to music-feed and
dressed for battle.

First came the heels. So high that the air got thin.
I practiced on them a bit as I ate some more squirm-
ing things delivered to the cabin by a white-suited
Intimate.

Next I chose a sheer top with a high neckline, taking care to wipe the food crumbs off my fingers and
onto the sheets of my bed before I buttoned the
skimpy item.

The House Rules waw-wawed at me until I
thumped the speaker. What the freak was wrong
with wiping your fingers on a sheet?

I chose another skirt. Black and short.

Restless then, I asked the housekeeper to read me its
boss's public biography. Monk's image sprang to life
on every wall as the housekeeper drawled through the
details of his education and media ownership.

I half-listened to most of it until it moved on to
Monk's ancestry. Like all natives, I was fascinated by
my country's royalty.

James Monk is a descendant of an original Australian media dynasty from whom he inherited his entrepreneurial skills. Such pure lineage is almost impossible to trace in the Southern Hem today. James is an icon. One of a kind . . .

I grinned to myself. Loyl might have some argument with that.

. . . Among his many hobbies and philanthropic pastimes, James Monk is renowned for owning the most extensive and valuable collection of orchids in the world. Once a year botanists are invited in to view his advances in species hybridization. . . .

"Enough," I told the housekeeper.

The bio shut down and I practiced reruns of my plan until an Intimate came for me.

Outside, shouts punctuated the air.

"Mr. Monk prefers his guests to sleep during the day and revel at nighttime," the Intimate observed as we climbed into the cable car.

Revel? I stared out at the glowing lines, invisible during the day, which snaked all over the mountain. Intermingled with the fairy lights, they gave the impression that every level had a party going on.

"What are those lines?"

It paused for a few seconds as though it was checking its protocol for the correct answer. "Mr. Monk has a separate mode of transport around the estate."

On cue a sleek, bullet-shaped luge shot ahead down the line from the top of the mountain, running parallel with the cable car for an instant.

Don't tell me my date is late!

When the cable car stopped it wasn't at the palm-surrounded pagoda but at another functionally shaped building. The Intimate ushered me to the front door and told me in clear terms that I should wait.

But waiting got on my nerves. And I had plenty

of those. I flung the doors open and wobbled right on in.

High heels suck.

The first room was empty apart from a collection of beds and cushioned benches set at various heights. The wall space overflowed with close-up, weirdly erotic multi-D representations of orchids, each one exuding a faint scent.

A door at the other end led through to a bathroom of sorts with a rough-tiled floor and a hundred and one different spouts, nozzles and other ways of getting wet. In one corner, a narrow two-directional elevator slipped noiselessly into the floor.

I rode it down in the absence of any other ideas what to do.

The low light at the bottom sent me flashing back to memories of the Pain Parlor with Big Hands and Stellar. Down here was a place of torture. Some instruments were crude and unimaginative, others exquisite and subtle.

Some I had no clue about.

I shot back up the elevator before Monk found me there and got the idea that I might like to use some of the apparatus.

I wandered among the water fountains of the tiled wet-room and wondered what the hell they were for.

"Water can be very erotic. And I like my guests to be clean." Monk stepped from the room of beds and ran a gauge over me. "You had high skin toxicity when you arrived. The purifiers in your bathing water have sufficiently decontaminated you. You've been exposed to heavy metals. Can you explain that?"

A shiver of fear trickled through me. How should I answer him?

I settled for vague indifference. "I never said my origins were quality. Just my talents."

He laughed outright. "Your sense of humor is

keeping you alive, Jales Belliere. Let's hope you can find something . . . less tenuous."

Monk held out his hand to usher me forward.

I felt another tremor of fear. Who the freak was I about to play marbles with? My stupid disguise had trapped me in this insane game.

We walked from the wet-room back to where the orchid images hung.

Someone was waiting there, dressed in a loose robe and anointed with heavily scented oil.

Someone I knew all too well.

"Jales, meet Loyl. He will be your partner in this audition. He too has been recommended to me. Let's hope that you are both worth what you cost me."

I choked so completely that the world darkened— and I welcomed it.

But my new partner wasn't letting me off so easily. He squeezed my arm until my eyes popped open again with the pain.

"Hello, *Jales.*" He spoke the words grudgingly, as if he'd rather have ground them into a paste.

I nodded, still unable to speak.

Monk sat down in an armchair and waved us toward the only large bed. "Commence."

I circled Daac like a wary animal rather than a professional lovemaker. My heart thumped painfully. *How the freak did I get myself into this?*

With *him.*

Daac's expression didn't mirror my panic. I saw only fury and a cold satisfaction in his eyes. I'd lied to him and run away. I was going to pay. Right here. In front of one of the world's richest men.

He stretched his flesh hand out and stroked my neck with fake tenderness, trailing his fingers down to the front of my sheer top. His prosthetic hand rested on my waist, clenching as he dragged me close.

"Ruin this audition and I *will* kill you," he whispered in my ear.

My heart stopped thumping.

In fact it just stopped.

Daac put his lips to my throat, trailing his tongue along the skin. Before I could force a breath he'd torn the top away from its high collar, leaving me with a silk choker and naked breasts.

"Then kill me," I whispered back.

He caught me, using his weight to force me down on to the bed.

I raked my fingernails down his oiled side and rolled out from under him as he flinched.

"Afterward," he replied. "Gladly."

He grabbed for me and we fell to the marble floor. The cold bit my flesh. My head banged down hard as we wrestled in earnest.

With an exclamation Monk reached for his comm. One word spoken into it and Daac and I would be locked away somewhere that no one even knew existed.

I had the longest moment of my life. . . .

But I couldn't give in to Loyl. I couldn't go to those places with him. Or with anyone. The parasite was too strong in me now. If I succumbed, I would never rein it back.

I clenched my fists for a knockout punch.

Daac spotted my movement and then the ring on my finger.

His eyes told me that he knew what it was. He grabbed my hand and forced my finger into my mouth.

I fought him but his prosthetic hand was an invincible clamp and in a few seconds my saliva turned my resistance into passion.

And the Eskaalim got free.

Daac kissed me, his tongue exploring every part of my mouth as it sought the chemicals.

I felt him shudder as Glorious's dizzies went to work in his system.

This time I rolled away from him to strip my skirt off. The cruel satisfaction in his smile should have made me feel murderous but I was in the grips of something stronger. Darker.

"Lie on your back," I ordered.

Surprisingly, he complied.

To one side of us Monk settled back and stroked his crotch, his gaze flitting back and forth to the walls.

I moved to straddle Daac but without warning he rolled me and trapped my arms. He entered me slowly—and an explosion of sensations stole my mind.

This was not like Glorious. Never with her had I felt the same fierce burst of happiness. I couldn't keep it from my face and the look Daac gave back to me stopped my breath.

Before he had been full of a desire for revenge. Now there was something else—a craving. He wanted me—no, he wanted *my approval.*

I swore.

Glorious's cocktail wasn't merely an aphrodisiac. It was a truth drug, ripping us back to the bare bones of honesty. "I never changed. Why did you lie to me?" I was compelled to ask.

"How else could I keep you near me?"

The happiness grew. "By asking."

He gave me a rueful grin and drove hard into me. "I tried that."

The beginnings of an orgasm trembled through me.

He sensed it as well, his own face contorting with passion as he quickened the pace of his thrusts. "Parrish, you idiot, can't you see how much—"

A spray of antidote drenched us, the moment denied and lost.

My fingernails hooked deep into the flesh of Daac's shoulders.

To one side of us Monk put the spray back in his pocket, wiped himself down with a towel and threw it on the floor. Then he closed his pants.

"Enough. I'm not employing either of you to enjoy yourself with the other staff. You're both hired," he said, and left.

Loyl lay still, bewildered by the sudden sensory deprivation.

I would have laughed if I'd had any control over my feelings. But I didn't.

The antidote hadn't worked on me.

And this time there was no going back.

Sera Bau will be here soon. I almost had sex with Loyl Daac.

The two thoughts ran laps in my mind well into the night.

I gave up pretending that I was normal, and that I might sleep, around 2 a.m. I got up and dressed in track pants and a T-shirt.

I collected the things I'd ordered from housekeeping at separate times and assembled them in the moonlight.

When I was finished, I stepped outside and thought it was hard to believe that a place like The Tert existed. Out here the night was warm and clear, the only noise drifting laughter and the muted grumble of the cable car. Out here I could pretend I was still Parrish Plessis in a way that I couldn't when I was lying down alone with my thoughts.

The cable lines lit the night, dividing the mountain in half.

I followed them upward, clinging to the shadows, climbing my way to the helipad.

Though the pad lights were on, nothing was happening. I crept past a line of four copters and into the fuel shed. I found the hydraulic fluid in stacked containers behind an in-flight refueling snake.

I siphoned off enough to fill the resealable gel pack that had contained my complimentary bubble bath.

Slipping it inside my T-shirt, I began the trek downward.

The night lighting showed only one guard at the entrance of the Orchid Cage. I waited until he stood, stretched and took a bored lap of the building. Then I slipped inside.

The cage was climate controlled, and humidity sweat ran off me like dirty water. I wandered around the rows of plants, using my language infusion's auditory supplement to help me pronounce the names on the labels.

Bulbophyllum, Vanda, Dendrobium, Cymbidium, Thelymitra, Calochilus—thousands of orchids exuding exotic scents, some of them beautiful, some ugly. Unlike most plants their roots climbed free from their pots like antennae seeking radio waves.

A couple of basic robot units worked methodically between rows, fertilizing and checking moisture content in the bark chips. I crouched, ready to disable them, but they took no notice of me, so I stepped through a vine-twisted arch and into a side cage.

According to the signage these orchids were Monk's exotica, each with its individual climate requirement. An electrified barrier separated off each delicate native hybrid.

With steady fingers I mixed the hydraulic fluid in the gel pack with the chemicals I'd obtained from housekeeping. Then I buried it, together with a complimentary p-diary, deep into a pile of something labeled sphagnum moss.

As I straightened up, the scale on my cheekbone began to ache.

Then sting.

It felt hot to the touch, like a recent burn.

I stood for a moment, confused, thinking of Wombebe.

It was as though the little feral thing hung around my neck, picking at the edges of my scale to get my attention.

Stupid fancy, Parrish. Get moving before someone sees you.

With a final look around, I made my way back to the entrance. The guard was back at his post wearing a portable vreal mask and picking his teeth. Not a lot of entertainment up here after dark.

As I slipped behind him I silently promised him a show tomorrow night.

The climb down to the party dais took the rest of the night—and most of the skin off my knees.

Crouched behind the cover of Monk's manicured bushes, I checked the layout for the party by the light glancing across from the nearby cabins.

The roof was a cathedral-high imitation thatch with roll-down sides and a circulating bar. The nanos were at work, polishing the floor and gobbling specks of dust from it. I could see them spark and burst every now and then. The faintest translucent glow from the open sides of the dais warned me against walking straight in. Security was on and humming.

I crept through the landscaped bushes and rockeries until I found the sleek lines of Monk's private transport. Then I traced the path back to the dais, counting the steps and memorizing the curves several times over. The last time I walked it backward with my eyes closed, hands out like a blind person.

A few meters short of the line I heard a new noise.

My skin prickled. Someone was watching me. I turned and forced myself to walk slowly back to the main line, where I rang for the cable car. I waited while it descended from a few stations above, feeling my watcher's stare right between my shoulder blades.

I pressed the panel for my cabin and sank low into the seat, out of sight. As the car moved off, I crawled along the floor and jumped out on the other side into the dark.

I slid down the embankment until I reached the dais station again. On a hunch and with painful care I crept to Monk's private transport lines, where I lay on one side of the track in the darkness to wait.

After a time a figure emerged from the path, stooping into the shadows.

Monk's private luge slid silently alongside me with a warm rush of air. The watcher walked toward it, stepping over me. A boot scraped my face.

I felt rather than saw the person pause and peer back into the dark as they sensed a wrongness.

I held my breath and clenched my fists, ready to use them.

Then a voice resonated from the comm inside the luge.

"Where are you?"

My watcher sank into the seat. "I couldn't sleep." *Velvety voice. Female.*

"Get back here. Now." *Monk.*

A sigh. "Yes," she said softly and closed the hatch. The luge slid away.

I lay for a long time staring at the stars and wondering why the velvet voice sent echoes across my memory.

The climb back to my cabin took forever. I didn't dare use the cable car and the terraces seemed steeper and slipperier than earlier.

In spite of that, my inner rage welcomed the real strain. Too little exertion always made me stale and jumpier than usual.

Leaving the lights in the cabin off, I bathed again

and put some healing skins on my hands and knees. Then I threw away the lid of a bottle of something green and covered with warnings. I settled in front of the big screen in the living room.

"Show me a map of Monk House."

I swigged from the bottle and got a rush. The map wavered for a second, then came back into focus. I studied the detail closely, working out the distances from the dais to the helipad.

"Which cabin is Mr. Monk in?"

The map stubbornly refused to answer anything about its owner or the other guests.

I went over the layout again and made some guesses.

"Now a map of Viva." It enlarged. "Now the greater environs." I avoided saying Tertiary Sector. It enlarged again.

I told it to download the maps into the cabin's complimentary palm-pad.

When I'd learned what I wanted, I took another few swigs until the absinthe numbed my nerves enough for me to wireless in.

I slipped Merv's mystic star from its chain and held it against the base of my neck. The sensors reacted to my body heat and I felt the uncomfortable prickling of the polymer interface budding.

Monk House's local vrealspace was conventional and image based. A sunny island of blue skies, salt breeze and beachcombers. The launch pad was a yacht moored just off a long jetty. I borrowed a bikini-clad avatar from the guest register and dived straight into water that was the same color as the absinthe.

I swam inexpertly to the jetty and climbed the steps. At the top of the steps the housekeeper presented itself. It looked uncannily like Mal— monstrous biceps, face like a rampaging bull.

While it verified my ID, I ran the gamut of the

menu and blew a hole into Monk's armament inventory. The alarms tripped and all the virus breakers swarmed the hole. While they patched madly, I slipped unnoticed into the transportation section and preprogrammed the luge. I was in and out without a ripple and back in my avatar just as security caught up with me.

The jetty dissolved under my feet and dumped me in a tidal rip. In a flicker of net-time I was swept out to sea. I struggled to stay afloat, telling myself that this was just high-definition vreal. But my brain couldn't cog the difference.

Panic took over and I began to sink. Under the water I could see dark virus shapes pursuing me. Sharks and rays.

I kicked out at them.

They wouldn't have to worry about eating me, I thought: I was going to drown in a figment of my own perception.

Too stupid. Too vreal.

Teece.

Help.

But Teece wouldn't hear me in this little corner of paradise.

Water forced its way into my lungs and everything began to drift away.

I only vaguely noticed being shot from the water and caught on a broad hard back. On the third bump I snorted seawater out of my nose.

Air rushed in and I collapsed, clinging to the slippery creature underneath me. My vision cleared a little.

Snout.

She bobbed her head as if to say, *It wasn't my idea*, and started cutting through the waves back toward the island.

Sharks converged, biting chunks from her skin. She

raced them and I clung on, helpless as her blood streamed behind us like a veil.

Save her, Merv.

Her avatar began to disintegrate underneath me, lasting just long enough to dump me in the shallows. I struggled to the beach and looked back. Snout had fragmented under bloody froth and dark moving shapes.

I found the exit under the beach umbrella and crawled underneath it, surfacing into realspace.

The absinthe bottle beside my ankles was smashed and my skin prickled in the air conditioning, wet with booze and sweat and real blood. The gashes were small but messy.

Back in there, Snout was bleeding to death. Savaged.

I started to cry.

Stupid Parrish. Stupid vreal world. Stupid life.

I sat and watched the glass and its potent liquid absorbed by the nanos and wondered whether, if I died right here on the expensive mat, they'd do the same thing to me.

Chapter Twenty-two

Glorious would know what to wear.

I'd palmed forward and back through the catalogue until my eyes watered. Monk House's range didn't account for my fashion taste. Could I wear a dress as the house protocol required?

No. I don't think so.

In desperation I closed my eyes and stabbed my finger on an image. Without looking at my choice I gave my size and shut the page. The housekeeper told me it would be delivered in an hour.

Problem solved.

I called for the cable car and asked to visit Mal.

She was still in the clinic up near the helipad. I found her sitting in front of One-World, unseeing. One side of her face was still unresponsive.

I walked her out into the garden and started throwing rocks into the water feature to upset Monk's listening bugs. I didn't need to tell Mal to keep the conversation cryptic. She still couldn't talk much.

"You OK?"

She nodded. She'd lost weight, and the blackness

under her eyes told me she wasn't sleeping due to the paralysis withdrawal.

"Can you fly?"

Mal thought about it for a few seconds and nodded. The good side of her mouth crinked and a spark lit her eyes.

"Can you deal with trouble?"

She flexed her good arm and wiped the saliva away from her lips. "Wh-en?"

"You'll hear the commotion."

"Whe-re?"

I handed her the palm-pad in which I'd flagged the coordinates. "Tourist route."

She looked at the map and wiped her chin. "Fu-n."

I went back to my cabin and got ready. The suit I'd ordered had arrived. Halter necked, emerald glitter sequins, gaudy and revealing. I felt like one of the babes on the Shadoville strip. The only extra I wore was Merry 3# on my wrist.

I took the cable car down to the dais and let security scan me.

By midnight the night sky was alight with copters. Most of them were queuing for the helipad on the dais terrace. The cable car worked furiously up and down the lines, ferrying those who chose the scenic route from the top.

I recognized some of the famous faces as they arrived. Manatunga Right-Woman, Laidley Beaudesert, Chaos Left: the media's most famous anchors—Prier pilots like Razz Retribution had been. I realized now how Daac had met his patron.

What struck me, though, was the uniformly healthy color of their skin and their easy laughter. In The Tert laughter was both rare and dangerous. In the burbs it was a kind of watered-down response.

Yet these people spent it so carelessly.

The circulating bar became crowded with them—extravagantly attractive galahs riding above each other's noise. Intimates lined the shadows' edges, silently waiting on the whims of their owners.

It should have been glamorous to me. I should have been awed or impressed. Something.

Instead I felt hollow and grim.

The gulf between the haves and the have-nots was no new stain on life's fabric but I'd never had my nose rubbed in it like this before. I understood more clearly why Loyl had become such a zealot, so obsessed with making a better life for his own. He'd spent time among these people as paid meat. He'd also spent time in the inland mines.

To him the economic divisions in life were raw wounds.

Suddenly I wanted to see him, overwhelmed by a need to be with someone who knew my life. Knew me.

The memory of his scent lingered on me still.

"What *are* you wearing?"

I jumped as the subject of my thoughts spoke in my ear. I felt myself flush. He was damn near perfect at bursting my bubble.

When I didn't answer, he cut to the chase.

"And what are you doing here?" Loyl persisted. "Why did you run out on me in The Tert?"

"You lied to me."

He stiffened. "What do you mean?"

"I didn't change." I kept my tone flat and measured as if we were swapping directions to the nearest drinks waiter. "You thought that if you told me what you did then I'd toe the line. . . . You thought I would . . . need you."

Now I turned to him, heat radiating from my skin. "Let's get one thing straight, Loyl. I will never need you. I will *never* toe your line."

We eyeballed until a waiter broke the tension with a tray of drugs.

I gulped a fizzy yellow liquid that bubbled in the back of my throat. Loyl reached into a bowl labeled 'Phets.

"They're bad for performance," I remarked.

He didn't attempt to hide his sneer. "Performance, Parrish, is one thing I never have a problem with." He buttoned his suit coat to hide the patches of sweat on his shirt.

I'd upset him and the thought gave me powerful satisfaction.

Loyl glanced into the crowd, smiling his best at someone. "I don't know what you're planning. But it had better wait until after this party. I've got business riding on this. Understand?"

"You're chasing an investor to replace Razz, aren't you?" I accused.

"You didn't think I would just stop, did you?" he said softly. "Now that you've seen what they have, surely you understand?"

Someone in the crowd signaled to him and he stepped in among the crush of elegant shoulders. A hand gripped my elbow before I could follow him.

Monk stood at my side, suited and handsome enough.

Boy, was I over handsome men.

"I told you to get your face fixed," he said, furious.

I touched my still-swollen nose. "Your medic didn't have enough beauty gobblers to go around."

"Fortunately for you, I have no alternatives. You're about to meet Lat Lindstrom, a Northern Hem business associate here for the Pan-Sat screenings. You will entertain him to his satisfaction or I shall find you a very quiet place to live."

The threat was delivered with his trademark boyish smile.

He steered me into the crush of bodies yet nobody

brushed against him. The crowd melted back as if his personal space was sacred.

Or contagious.

We made our way to the raised dais at the edge of the dance floor where he touched lightly on the shoulder of a tall, athletically built man in an expensive evening suit.

I felt a sliver of relief. If I had to pretend to entertain someone, at least they weren't shaped like a toad. The man stepped back to accommodate us into his circle. Behind him stood a short, round guy wearing a floral suit and snappy heels.

It took only an eye-blink to realize that I'd made a mistake. The athletic suited body belonged to a woman. As she turned my back stiffened and a chill pimpled every last piece of my skin.

Kat. Little sister?

I automatically put my hand out to touch her. She took it, her grip stronger than mine. Unsurprised to see me, she turned my reaction into a handshake.

"Good evening . . . Jales, is it? Your services were recommended."

I returned her handshake, "And you are?" *Tell me, Kat. For chrissakes. What are you doing here?*

"I'm a convalescing athlete—"

"You *were* an athlete," interrupted Monk. "Katrilla is now my best hound-in-training."

I looked between them, confused.

Kat dropped her head. I saw her fingers curl into her palm. "James means I am noviced to him as a Prier pilot. A temporary change of profession."

Monk snorted with derision. "Your running days are over, Kat, face it."

You. You took Wombebe to get me here.

She saw my expression, my sudden comprehension, and swiftly changed the subject. "I'd like you to meet a dear friend of James's and mine, Lat Lindstrom."

James's and mine. Three little words that continued to burn into me. A warning and a crucial item of information all at once.

Don't let them know about us, Parrish, they told me. *Don't for a second let them know.*

I let go of Kat's hand. She looked amazing. Lean and magnificent, skin sheen courtesy of the best nutrient supplements and the perfect muscle tone of the physically elite—how easy to believe she could leap tall buildings and outrun a fire.

And sexy, her breasts swelling in the vee of her suit coat. She wore nothing underneath it, the material so fine that you could see the sculpting of her muscles, the curve of her back.

Only the slightest telltale yellowing of her eyes told me that her liver was under stress. The tightness around her mouth indicated duress of a different type.

In one choreographed movement Kat tore her hair free of its tight braid and let it spill down over her shoulders. The highlights glinted with obscene health.

I suddenly knew why I hated narcissism.

It had come between us always—beauty and self-interest before sisterhood.

Just look where those different values had gotten us.

I *definitely* had it wrong.

Kat interrupted my silent musings with a sharp nudge to indicate I should make room for Monk.

I glanced across at Lindstrom.

He eyed me greedily and I wondered what he'd been told I could—or would—do.

"Lat, I must apologize for Jales's appearance. She had a most unfortunate accident, tripping and falling from the cable car. It hasn't, of course, dampened her spirits. Jales?"

I nodded, still incapable of getting my tongue to play the seductress. My mind was too busy making sense of events, accepting that *Kat* must have recommended my 'services' to Monk and that it was *Kat* who had stepped over me last night. Kat with the new silky, cultured voice. What had she been doing these last few years? And why was she with Monk?

I had to talk to her.

"I like it. It's so butch. Come stand next to me, Jales. Tall women always make me feel so safe." Lindstrom gurgled like a baby.

Kat and I exchanged glances, brief, innocent enough: a collusion of tall women—not sisters.

Before I could reply, our happy tête-à-tête grew by two.

"Laud." Monk's voice had a tighter edge. "I hope you are content."

The ex-musician of the media-famous ménage à trois stepped into the circle, bringing his dance partner along.

Loyl.

If this got any more ridiculous I'd laugh till I died. It did.

The band started up: Garter Thin and the VBs.

I kept my back to them . . . just in case.

Introductions led to more talk. More drugs. Around us the crowd loosened, lubricated by whatever they needed to lower their inhibitions. But wherever our circle drifted on the dais, the invisible barrier kept them at bay.

"You kidnapped the kid to get me here," I said quietly to Kat when I got the chance.

"Yes." Her eyes were sharp despite the amount of alcohol she'd drunk.

"Why?"

She slipped open her coat and showed me a brief

glimpse of the scarring on her ribs. "The organ re-juves won't take. I can't play anymore. I got this . . . job and I saw what was happening. I wanted you to have a chance to prove that you didn't kill Razz. You didn't, did you?" she whispered.

I wanted to believe her—that she had my best interests at heart. But I didn't know her anymore. "Where's Wombebe?" I said urgently.

Kat leaned closer to whisper but Esky Laud interrupted us, complaining to me about the quality of the band.

I agreed heartily even though I wanted a gorge to open and swallow him for his bad timing. "Yes, they suck."

On my other side, Monk was back in Kat's face. "Go and flirt with the male whore. It will annoy Laud. If you are good, I might watch you both later," he told her loud enough for me to hear.

Kat's Intimate brought her a tiny box. Obediently she selected a patch from it and slid it under her tongue. She kept her gaze averted from mine as she crossed the circle and slipped her arm through Loyl's.

Kat and Daac flirting.

He seemed captivated by her.

Laud got petulant. Monk seemed entertained by it as he kept up a quiet monologue into his comm.

Inside me emotions welled that I hadn't felt since living at home, and all the while Lindstrom's sweaty hand roamed my back.

Only a bit longer, I told myself. *Just put up with this crap a bit longer.*

Sera Bau made her entrance around 1 a.m. as I drank straight from the champagne bottle.

Lindstrom had wedged his crotch against my thigh, rubbing against me like a tomcat happy to find a tree that his competitor had urinated on.

Possession. I hated it.

And soon it would be over.

I felt the wash of Eskaalim adrenaline purge me of all the deceptions and the pretence. In a few moments I could be Parrish again.

Without regret.

Whatever the consequences.

Finally.

I idled in those minutes like a prizefighter preparing for the ring, a runner for the race. From a distance and without emotion I watched everything being played out in front of me. Daac and Kat dancing close, Monk working, Lindstrom pawing me, the sharp tone of Garter Thin's voice pack, the whiteness of the fish against the silver tray the waiter brandished, the security drone.

Sera Bau making her way toward her host. Gracious, powerful and dirty with death.

At another level I ran a check of the things I had planned, right up to my feelings when the creator came face to face with what she had created.

I didn't contemplate failure. What would be the point?

Win or die was how I would play it.

Now, here I go . . .

I keyed into Merry 3# the numbers of the complimentary diary I'd planted in the Orchid House and pushed CONNECT.

As I took the first step, Daac let go of Kat and whirled toward me as if he'd been waiting. My name formed on his lips.

I faltered for the briefest of seconds, testament to the feelings I had for him, and gave him a smile. No apologies. Not angry. Not smug.

Just me. Parrish.

His face was stripped of artifice. He reached out for me but it was too late for that.

Way too late.

The explosion rained unique orchids and shredded bark chips down the mountainside and on to the roof of the pavilion. I catapulted Lindstrom straight into Sera Bau's closest bodyguard and broke the champagne bottle on the bar. I put the jagged edge to Bau's throat and the whole party went crazy.

Chapter Twenty-three

Sera Bau was pretty calm on the face of it.
More so than me. I was on an adrenaline rocket. I tried to look everywhere at once. Behind and above at the security drones, at Monk, Loyl and Kat. At the partygoers running for the cable cars and scrambling to hide under tables. Everyone was going somewhere.

"What do you want?" she breathed.

"I want to show you something."

"Couldn't you have just asked?"

Her perfume was so subtle and pervasive that I guessed it was manufactured in the pores of her skin. I wondered what other personal accoutrements she had. What weapons were concealed under the folds of her evening wear?

"Strip."

Her composure slipped. "No."

I raised my voice to the knot of security that had gathered around us. "If anyone bothers me I will cut her head off. Even this expensive body won't recover from that."

Their expressions showed disbelief and expectation. Disbelief that this was real. Expectation that the hoax drama would end.

The moment stretched against a backdrop of confusion and panic.

"Believe her. She'll do it." Daac's voice came loud and hoarse from the back of the group. I heard the emotion in his tone. I'd just signed a death sentence for myself. It bothered him and that made me glad.

Now he was risking himself by adding weight to my threat—a sacrifice. I forgave him a lot for that.

Laud's bodyguards were straight on him. I couldn't do anything to help.

His choice.

Instead I sought Monk. His mouth moved, issuing instructions to his security.

When he howled I figured that he'd worked out what the explosion had brought crashing down the side of his hill. Yet he didn't look at me. His stare was fixed on Kat. The woman who had convinced him to let me inside his sanctum.

What my actions meant for her, and for Loyl, and for Mal waiting for me on the top of the mountain— I didn't know. But the thing had gone too far now. I couldn't worry about their fates. They had to fight their own battles.

"Strip now or I will cut out your comm implant with this." I held the broken bottle against Bau's neck and nicked the skin on the side of the transceiver. From the confusion on her face I reckoned it was enough to interrupt her data flow.

She gagged and swallowed, then began to peel off her dress. The silk dropped to the floor like a puddle of tequila. I kicked it out of the way.

She stood there in her underwear, her flesh pimpling and Monk's cams recording it all. How long before he went LTA on what was happening? Or was he already? A real hostage drama of this importance from his raw feed.

Would it be enough?

"You're going to bend down now and unstrap your shoes. Slowly," I said.

She jerked her head in agreement and leaned away from me.

I was watching the crowd so hard I almost missed her ambush.

Only my olfaugs saved me. I detected the scent of poison as soon as it was released from her sweat glands. My vision started to swim.

Glancing down, I saw that she was holding her breath and I thumped her on the back. She took an involuntary breath and inhaled.

"Switch it off," I gasped.

She coughed several times and the scent abated.

"Try that again and I *will* skin you."

I felt her first tremor of fear—an acknowledgment that I was serious and crazy, not just crazy.

"What do you really want?" she hissed.

"Come. I'll show you." I wrenched her upright and addressed the crowd around us, particularly Monk. "We're going to walk out of here. I'm going to take Sera Bau for a ride. Then I'm going to bring her back. Nothing will happen to her. Clear?"

Monk stood frozen, desire for revenge radiating from his skin. I wondered what he would convince the Militia to give me for blowing up his precious plants. Prolonged life in quod with augmented memory?

To one side of him, Kat smiled and nodded. The faintest of movements. I was doing what she'd hoped.

Whatever that was.

We backed slowly off the dais. I held Bau by the neck, feeling her fury and embarrassment at her near-nakedness.

I walked us backward to Monk's luge, counting the steps and the kinks in the path.

Not one stumble, until one of my feet twisted on the luge rail.

I fell sideways, dragging Bau down with me.

It was all any decent sniper needed. He took a shot, grazing my arm, but I was so jacked that I barely felt the burning.

Another from behind. This one in my shoulder.

I dragged us upright again and sliced into the gel coating Bau's comm transceiver. She screamed with the pain of an information junkie denied her juice.

"Stop," she begged. "Not that."

With relief I heard the luge slide in behind us as I'd programmed it to. I leaned back to spring the hatch but as I did I copped a rifle muzzle in the face. A guard started to lever himself out.

"Give me the bottle," he ordered.

Bau relaxed in my grip, thinking she'd been saved.

The guards who had followed me from the dais surged toward us, then stopped again as the guard in the luge exploded.

Deafened in one ear, I ran a check of my body parts. Still in one piece but decorated with blood and bits of flesh.

Bau screamed in my good ear. Those who hadn't run to the cable car joined in—all the frightened, bright galahs screeching together.

Who had done that?

Kat. She was kneeling down near a bush, a pistol in her hand. She hadn't used one before much. I could tell by the way she held it. It had been a lucky shot.

"I'm coming with you," she shouted and threw the pistol to me.

I caught it with one hand as she ran toward me. Quicker than any of them. Quicker than me.

I fired two shots to cover her but then the ammo

ran out. A bullet hit her while she was still a few body lengths away from me.

She fell heavily and Monk's guards swarmed toward her.

"Parrish—" she gasped.

"Get over here," I bellowed, caught between conflicting impulses. "Get over here—I can't help you from there."

She ignored me, collecting her breath to finish her sentence. "I'm sorry about the kid. . . . Thought she'd be safe in the cage. . . . Had no idea you would—"

Monk was on her then, strangling her unconscious. *Wombebe.*

The fist that had closed over my heart when Roo died tore it clean out of my chest. *In the cage . . .* I wanted to scream but I was on a road and traveling at speed—that didn't allow pulling over to indulge in histrionics.

I scooped what was left of the guard out of the luge and pushed Sera Bau into the small compartment, wedging myself alongside.

She was still screaming at me.

I punched her in the mouth as we shot to the top of the mountain.

Monk tried to override the controls all the way up but my patch held and we made it to the top.

Mal was waiting, guarded by another knot of agitated security.

I pressed the bottle into the pounding pulse in Bau's neck.

"Tell them to get back."

In seconds they'd withdrawn without her moving a muscle. Either her comm implant was still working or she had a backup set.

I ran my stare over her. *Where is it?*

I dragged her across the tarmac, making sure that her body shielded my most vulnerable parts. The

wound in my arm had nearly stopped bleeding but
blood and the leftover bits of the guard were pasted
all over both of us.

For once I wasn't concerned about what I might
be spreading with my body fluids.

To my mind the Eskaalim symbiote hiding in Bau's
genes was already out of control. Why else would
she fund a place like Mo-Vay for ratings?

I pushed her into the copter behind the pilot's seat,
climbed in and slammed the door.

Mal lifted off on her pre-planned course without a
word. I was growing real fond of the woman. She
didn't know the meaning of the word *flinch.*

I clipped Bau on the side of the head. As she reeled
from the blow, I locked her head in the crook of my
arm. With a few quick jabs I gouged out her implant.
She salivated and frothed at the sensory dep, so I
dermed her with the medic's painkill to keep her
conscious.

A mass of airborne lights followed us. Priers, Militia with one of the three insignia pulsing a warning
and some private voyeurs jostled for position.

We flew fast and straight into the dawn on the
bearing that I'd given Mal. When we passed over the
edge of the Viva environs, some of the private light
aeros dropped away but most of the convoy stayed
up close and personal.

I studied Bau's twitches carefully to see if she was
communicating on a backup. Chances were that it
was hardwired to something vital. I didn't want anything to happen to her until she saw what she'd
created.

Our flight path took us along the coastline between
Viva and Jinberra Island. When we left the city, Mal
veered slightly southwest, in over the wasteland and
Torley's. Every punter on the north side would have
neckache from watching the air convoy.

I imagined the rumors and the dread. If the Priers were giving live feed on something approaching the truth, Teece would be crazy with worry.

Me, I'd gone past worry the moment I put a broken bottle to Bau's throat.

Was this how Loyl felt? Not bulletproof—judgment-proof.

"What are they showing on LTA?" I asked.

Mal flicked around the frequencies. "The whole net is on us. The Pan-Sat telecast has been delayed." She gave the shortest, driest laugh. "You think you were famous before . . ."

"What about you?"

"Nobody remembers the pilot. Anyway, there's other things for them to think about."

She pointed east and west. Behind us a trail of ULs flew like the frill of a bridal veil. Every punter who could get into the ether was up there.

I suddenly had an idea that might save our lives. Mal's, anyway.

"Take us as low and slow as you can. I want everyone in The Tert to see this. And I want all the smaller craft to be able to keep up."

Bau twitched as if she could read my mind.

I ignored her and pressed my nose to the window. In the soft pink smog-streaks of daybreak, the familiar sickness of Mo-Vay began to unfold. First the sparkling blue strip of copper-poisoned canal. Then the bright colors of the rampant wild-tek as it mingled exotically with the jungle strip.

"Lower."

The fiber-optic towers had grown, soaring into the sky like bleeding glass fingers. We wove through them and I saw lumps of flesh dotted along their lengths—humans sucked dry of moisture.

"What is *that*?" Mal gasped.

I didn't answer but hauled Bau upright and shook

her to consciousness. Her eyes took seconds to focus. Then they showed only confusion.

I put my mouth to her ear and told her a story.

"Once upon a time a rich and famous woman decided that she needed to destroy her competitors. She hired a bad man named Ike Del Morte and told him to go forth and engineer the devolution of the human race. Experiment on the criminals and the poor. Do any number of things to them. Make them as grotesque and as terrifying as you can because *I need better ratings.*"

Bau's eyes cleared slowly with understanding.

I tightened my grip on her and slammed her face against the window.

"See the ring of buildings?" I told Mal. "Get as low as you can without setting us down."

Mal nodded. We slowed and descended farther, the mass of the airborne flotilla piling around and above us.

I wrenched the door back. Rotor-blade noise and the sweet pungent decay-reek of Mo-Vay air rushed in. Ike's shop of horrors, set in the center of the old fuel farm, rippled with a life of its own. Crawl had smothered all the building surfaces like dust sheets covering an abandoned furnished room. Only these sheets writhed and stank and ate at themselves.

As if it could sense the nearness of fresh, untainted material, it began to froth, spurting Crawl into the air.

Was it only Crawl?

Maybe my imagination had gotten beyond wild but I thought I saw human shapes swimming in it.

The shock on Bau's face told me that maybe she was seeing something as well.

"Take us just out of the ring of the buildings. I want you to find anything that's alive and moving down there. When I tell you to, I want you to take me in as close as you can," I shouted. "And pass me the transceiver jig."

The Priers owned by Monk and Laud hovered in close, camming everything. They were getting in the way of Bau's Lash Militia, who were getting in the way of Bau's Priers, who were dodging the ULs.

Chaos.

They couldn't help themselves.

I'd hoped that would happen. Needed it to, in fact.

"Mal. What are you tuned into?"

"Common-Net and One-World instream. Say the word and everything else will stop. Half the world is watching you already," she shouted back.

I slipped the jig on and pushed Bau to the edge, forcing her to put her legs out. I crawled next to her. We sat side by side like two kids swinging their legs over climbing bars. Except that I was holding jagged glass at her throat and Priers were hanging dangerously close to each other to film us.

"For the record . . ." I waited a few seconds before I continued, long enough for online word to silence, to catch up. "For the record . . . I am Parrish Plessis and this is Sera Bau, Information Owner of Drama-Net. I wanted her to see, and you to see, something she is responsible for. This is the Tertiary Sector. . . ."

And I told my story. The whole thing, beginning to end, in hoarse, desperate tones.

I finished quietly.

"Two things worry me now . . . that's all. One of them is that you won't know if this is real or staged. The other is . . . will you care? I guess I can't do anything about whether you care but I *can* do something to let you know it is real."

I motioned to Mal and she took us down within meters of the ruined Mo-Vay rooftops. We flew along the diseased alleyways, alongside bleeding villas until we flushed out some of the remains of life, beastlike and no longer human.

Shape-changers.

I saw again the horror of what I would become, of what we all would. It renewed my absolute conviction.

"Swing us around."

Mal managed the maneuver, bringing us into a direct line of sight with the peeping Priers.

Without conscience or warning I scrambled back inside and booted Bau squarely in the back.

She fell, grabbing desperately at the copter's struts.

"Fuck you!" she screamed.

I stamped at her grasping, frantic fingers but she resisted me.

Tearing the jig off, I lay flat on the floor with my head and shoulders hanging down. I stared down into her face. "No," I bellowed, "I think it's *you* who's fucked." Then I began slashing her hands with the bottle.

She fell, but her final words whipped back at me in the rotor wind. "Killing . . . me . . . won't stop it. . . ."

Right about then hell opened its gates and welcomed me in.

Chapter Twenty-four

I slammed the copter's door and we lifted away a little. Priers converged into the airspace above Bau's fallen body, a plague of them as busy as wasps around a nest intruder.

"What now?" said Mal.

"Over to you." I gave her the grimmest of smiles and went back to staring fixedly out of the window at Bau's body.

She was alive, her back broken, I guessed.

The shape-changers crept up on her, driven by their hunger despite the cacophony above.

Mal grunted. "The Priers aren't even trying to help her."

"They never do," I said dully.

"I can keep us alive while they're camming, if I stay down here among them. But when they've finished, her Militia will most likely incinerate us."

"I knew that."

I crawled into the seat next to Mal. I didn't say sorry. She'd signed on for this bit, so I guessed she was ready.

"My story . . . Do you think anyone listened?" I asked.

Mal pulled a face.

We laughed and continued to hover, Mal with her thoughts and me turning Bau's last words inside out, over and over, until . . .

"Shit, Mal," I said softly. "We have to get out of this. There's something I still have to do."

Her jaw dropped at my demented optimism. "Well, I think you've left it too late."

I looked around desperately for some reason for hope to materialize.

For once, just for once, it did.

ULs thronged in around us as cover—and as an escort.

Bau's Militia buzzed and roared above them like leashed guard dogs straining to get at a prowler. Even they couldn't risk the LTA coverage of a massacre of innocent spectators.

I switched the screen to Common Net. It was crazy with cheering and wild rumor. A book was already running on whether the banks would adopt me as royalty. The Tert had claimed me as its own sort of hero. I flicked back to One-World. The reportage was somber, unable to deny the horror of Dis. Already links to Sera Bau were being unearthed.

I let it flow over me, drinking in the power of rumor and scandal.

Mal kept us hovering tight among the ULs like a queen bee at the center of her swarm.

The UL armada worked on my psyche in the same way as the bikes powering across the waste had—the thrill of being in a pack. But this was better. This pack was working for me.

They shepherded us toward the gray beach of Fishertown while Bau's Militia paced us overhead, waiting for a chance, and the net traffic went into a frenzy of accusations.

Then it stopped.

Just like that.

All nets.

All frequencies.

Mal gave a shout of triumph.

I felt a smile trying to crease my face. The first real one in so long that my jaw wouldn't cooperate. *You wanted a revolution, Gerwent.* I sent my thought silently to the dead man. *Well, maybe you got one.*

Mal came to her senses first. "We need to get down. Quick. Before the Militia decide to take a chance at wasting us."

She dumped us hard and fast on a patch of beach where Mama was waiting, shaven head looming above the crowd, fat belly pushing folk aside.

I fell out of the copter into his arms. "I've got to talk to Teece."

"You look like dog meat." The ex-sumo was not impressed despite the cheering on every side. "Didn't I say you had it coming?"

I burst into tears.

He held me at arm's length, relenting. "You take a bike later, after dark. Those bastards be gone by then."

I squinted into the sky as three Militia bats swept low over the beach. "How do you know that?"

" 'Cos tonight the city be going to the shit."

Mama was right: the bats kept us guessing until sunset. Then they disappeared, leaving the skies eerily quiet.

From the entrance of his tent I watched them go.

Outside, his women were cooking fish and damper and shouting at their children. Despite the evening noises and rowdy celebrations something was missing. Net flicker. As if the noisiest person had just left the party.

Even somewhere as poor as Fishertown, the disappearance of the energy of a continual flow of information had left the place feeling hollow.

"You did this, Plessis?" Mama stared mournfully at the blank, lifeless screen under the canopy of his tent.

"I—I guess so."

He sighed. "You better get moving on soon, then. Some of these people gonna hate you."

I watched those people drinking and laughing, not sure what he was talking about.

Later on, after the wrestling and skulling matches had finished, I saw what he meant. As though by reflex each person drifted to a nearby screen, stopping to stare, willing something to show.

"You think it will be that bad?" I asked.

One of Mama's wives handed me the hot bread and some greasy fish.

I thanked her and watched him fiddle with a small flat box.

"What's that?"

"Wireless. Hobby." He puffed between each word as he scraped corrosion off a flat metal plate inside it.

"Listen," he hissed, punching the frequency finder.

After a while we caught something. A young voice, frightened.

"*. . . couldn't get any net. Dad went to find out what's happening. He hasn't come back. He told me to keep the doors locked. I can see someone lighting fires but I can't . . . What's happening out . . .*"

The reception floated away into the night. Mama kept punching the frequency finder but the other signals were too weak.

I finished the plate of food and tipped the fish bones into the hot ash. A fight had broken out at the next campfire. Sand kicked into the breeze sprayed over us.

Mama roared a warning at the brawlers and then rounded on me.

"We've had this stuff in our life so long now. You take it away and it's like someone cut your eyes out."

I got a cold feeling that told me it was time to move. "You said I could have a bike?"

He wasn't letting me go without a lecture. "What about all them wetheads? What happens when they can't do their thing?"

I thought about Merv, the Prince of Vreal. How was he faring?

"You think you've fixed things, Parrish Plessis? Well, you fixed them all right. The whole world's gonna go to shit now. Not just this place."

The panic in my throat was making it hard to breathe. "Gimme a bike, Mama."

He held out a key card for the lock on the compound. "You go get one. Leave the key inside. I got another. Then you go sort out this mess. I want my wrestling channel back."

He bellowed threats at another fight that had started up on the edge of the water and turned back to his wireless.

I convinced Mal that she should stay behind. She argued for a while but there was nowhere else for her to go and I think she'd taken a shine to Mama. That, or she fancied beating him in a wrestle.

"I have to sort some things out."

"Yes, Plessis. You're good at that." Her heavy sarcasm bore no malice.

I rode the waste slowly, without headlights, thankful for some moonlight. Thankful—more or less—to still be alive.

I got to the other side, woke Teece's new man and left the bike with him. The first one that I'd left intact.

I walked through the night to Torley's. No one stopped me. No one noticed me.

But I noticed them. The restlessness on the pavements. The absence of screen flicker and drone.

*   *   *

Muenos were playing cards outside my door. When I turned up they crossed themselves as if I was a spirit from the dead.

I went inside and checked all the rooms.

They stood in the doorway, watching me awkwardly.

"Where's Teece?"

"He has a place with his woman now," one of them said.

My heart dropped.

"Go get him. Tell him I'm back. Tell him it's not over," I said and shut the door, feeling the rush of relief that came with being home.

I stripped off and showered. My closet didn't have much in it. But what it did contain was mine. I climbed into some well-worn fatigues and spare boots. They felt better than armor.

Teece didn't take long.

I guessed that, like everyone else in The Tert, he was having trouble sleeping.

I waited for—wanted—a hug, a slap on the back, *some* physical contact to confirm to myself that I was alive and home.

But he closed the door behind him and stood back from me.

"It's you?"

It seemed like a stupid thing to say, but I understood what he meant.

"For the moment," I said slowly. "I have something else I need to do."

There was a knock at the door. Teece opened it and took a tray from someone I couldn't see. Shawarmas and beer.

I got a lump in my throat.

He put the tray down on the table near the couch. "Lu's not open yet. No sweet dough. Sorry."

I laughed and wiped a tear on my T-shirt.

He waited while I ate, studying me.

I noticed now how pale he was. "How much did you see on the net?"

"We saw you take the Bau woman at the celebration. Then the copter flight. What has happened in Dis? We saw you push her out. She got eaten, Parrish." Teece's voice was hoarse and brimming with revulsion. "You told me about it, I know. But I didn't . . . couldn't . . . understand."

I nodded, swallowing the last of the meat.

"What's happened to the net now? People are scared," he said.

I told him about Gerwent Ban's plan. And about Monk. And about what we suspected Brilliance had become. Then I drank the beer and told him about Merv and Glorious and Mal.

Teece whistled low. "I've heard talk of shadows and things but I thought it was all spook stuff. Wetheads are crazy superstitious bastards. And the shiver—I figured it was just a rogue program.

"Maybe not."

"The king's plan worked, then. You've shut her down."

"For the moment. I thought that would be a good thing. Now I'm not so sure."

"Why?"

"I have to find Brilliance. At least her biological part."

He raised an eyebrow.

"Teece." I watched him to see his reaction. "Bau said something to me at the end. I'm not sure that I did the right thing."

He drew a sharp breath. "If you want a confessional, Parrish, you've come to see the wrong guy. We've seen now how they live in Viva. And what's happened in Dis."

"What do you mean?"

"I mean that the Cabal and the Muenos want to change things now."

"The Cabal? But what about Loyl?"

"Daac is somewhere in Viva chasing dreams—and women, no doubt. The Cabal has had enough of his antics. Pas and the Muenos are sick of waiting for you. They want to meet to discuss a war with the city."

No.

Yes.

"You can't," I said.

"We can. Especially now that the net is down. There'll be chaos in Viva. We can use the underground pipes you came through to get there unnoticed. Once we're in the city they won't know us from the rest. It's the right moment to change things—while there's panic and no communication."

"It's suicide. Do you know how many people there are in Viva?"

"Millions. But they don't know the sharp end of a knife from the blunt. We'll target the public utilities. After that, the rest will be easy pickings."

"What happened to you while I was away?" I demanded. "What happened to 'anything for the quiet life and a view of the waste'?"

Teece gave a short, dry laugh. "I musta been hanging with the wrong crowd. Loyl was right about one thing, you know. We shouldn't have to live like this. Not when *they*'ve got so much."

I saw stubbornness in his eyes. And something new—a conviction that hadn't been there before.

Could he raise an army?

What had I done?

"Just give me a little time," I said.

"What's time got to do with it?"

"I need to find out if the bio component really exists. Maybe *it* was behind Mo-Vay."

Teece folded his arms. "So now it's about you getting it right?"

"Yeah." I searched his face for understanding and couldn't find it.

He picked my last beer up off the tray and opened it, handing it to me. "You said no one knew where her bio part is—or even if it exists."

I swallowed a few mouthfuls, savoring my next thought as much as the beer swirling around in my mouth. "Actually, I think I do."

He grabbed back the beer and took a deep swig. "Well?"

"I think she's hiding *here*, Teece. In The Tert."

Chapter Twenty-five

"Ridiculous."

"Why? Why shouldn't she pick the place where no one wants to live?"

Teece glanced at his wrist p-diary. "I have to go. I'm meeting with Billy Myora and Pas soon."

"Billy Myora?"

"The Cabal has been divided over who should give guidance. The younger ones support Loyl. The elders say that Billy Myora has right of way. When Loyl ran off to Viva this time, Billy convinced them to back him."

"Where are you meeting them?"

"At Hein's. Lu Chow's bringing breakfast across. You still hungry?"

I grinned. "What sort of a question is that?"

Pas and a horde of Muenos were already there. He welcomed me with a low, forehead-scraping bow.

"Oya. You live and you have opened our eyes. It is time to stake our claim for a better life."

I bit my tongue. Pas's florid dramatics usually hid another agenda. What actually scared me, though, was the presence of his wife, Minna. Mueno custom did not include wives at a war council. She stood at his shoulder, her eyes downcast yet her whole bearing radiating staunch resolution.

"This is craziness, Pas."

He puffed out his fat cheeks. "There comes a time when everyone must face judgment. When I face mine I wish to have enough credits."

From anyone else it would have been funny, but Pas did not joke about honor.

Behind me the door swung open. Thirty or more Cabal members entered, painted in ceremonial colors, each carrying explosive spears. More waited outside.

They must have scared the jeez out of anyone out and about on the pavements.

Billy Myora entered last, dressed in a faded pinstripe, his face streaked in thick layers of ocher and white. He didn't seem surprised to see me.

"Plessis, this is not woman's stuff."

I lifted my chin, ready to argue, but Pas intervened.

"Muenos do not hold with women at war council yet I have brought my own woman to listen and to speak. Our numbers are too few. We cannot do this without them."

Billy glowered in my direction but let it pass, looking to Teece.

"We will plan a strategy but we must move quickly. While there are no comms the time is right."

He projected a map of Viva into the center of the circle.

"You can't expect to win a war against such sophistication," I said.

Billy froze me with a stare. "Their sophistication is nothing when they have no eyes. Anyone can seize a blind man."

"Teece," I pleaded, "why are you doing this?"

He stared me straight in the eye. "Because, Parrish, I have my child's future to make better."

His words were a body blow.

I took a long, slow breath in an effort to absorb them, aware that everyone was waiting for my reaction.

"Then," I said slowly, "I'd better make sure that you have a chance."

I walked out of the meeting.

Teece and Honey were going to have a child. The shock of it ripped through me, leaving me feeling nauseous and weak. But at least I understood the new determination in Teece's eyes.

Everyone needed a reason.

Maybe I couldn't stop this slaughter from happening, but I could make sure that they stood a chance.

Brilliance has to stay out of action, I thought.

A pain in my feet was making it hard to walk, spiking up my legs with each step. Whatever the cause, it was worsening.

"Oya?"

Link and Glida. Shadowing me. Twin masks slung around their necks.

"Did you find Wombebe?"

I nodded slowly and touched the scale along my cheekbone. It was shrinking. "She's safe now."

Glida read my face and my gesture and didn't ask any more.

"I need your help." My voice was hoarse with too many emotions.

"We've pledged all our bioweapons to the Cabal. Anything else, Oya, is yours," said Link.

Oh, my God. "I'm searching for something. Some bio-ware. Very powerful bio-ware that doesn't want to be found."

They looked at each other—a silent consultation between friends that eased some of the pain and guilt I felt over Roo's death.

"For that you need Ness. She is the oldest now that Vayu has gone. She has the most power."

I nodded.

They followed me as I limped back to my room. "You are hurt?" Link said.

I shook my head. "No."

They looked puzzled but stood guard by my door as I hobbled to my gun safe and unlocked it. I selected my new Colt SMG with the 9 mm conversion, my last magazine of ammo and the Cabal dagger. Then I dermed the strongest painkillers I could find in my drawer. It dulled the pain in my feet enough for me to walk without a limp.

I threw together a kitbag. The rest of my derms, some pro-subs for energy—some tastes die hard—the knife and my wires. I strapped the SMG to the back.

"You know where she is?"

"In the Home of Spirits."

I flashed on the place where Vayu and the others had died. The place where Jamon had tied me up like a pig on a spit.

For me, no place in The Tert was more haunted.

Like parents chaperoning their child, Link and Glida walked me to the edge of Torley's.

The Spirit Home squatted on the border, different from the rest of the detritus architecture. For one thing, a breeze always seemed to be blowing there.

Ness was waiting for us, the way Vayu had waited for me before—cross-legged on the floor among a litter of candles, her waist-long hair tied in elaborate coils.

The similarities sent a shiver through me.

Stix sat next to her, using a tiny comb to clean the feathers implanted into his skull. He didn't look up from his task.

Ness smiled at me but there was pity in her expression. "Your time has finally come, Parrish. How can I help you get through it?"

I sat down and didn't ask what she meant. Why would I?

"I'm looking for some powerful bio-ware that is hiding itself here somewhere. It owns the net and now it is injured. I don't know how to find it."

"What would you do with this powerful thing you seek?"

"Frankly, I'm not sure," I said. "I've started a whole lot of trouble. The Cabal are talking about war with the city. Maybe if I find the bio-ware I can help them or end it." Ness, like Vayu, was not a person you bothered to lie to.

She laughed outright at that. "Always so simple, Parrish. Always the direct line and with a well-intentioned heart."

I didn't like her summation of me but I didn't take offense either. "Can you . . . *will* you help me?"

"Of course. Sometimes it is of no use to see too many options."

Stix dropped the comb and put a hand on her arm. I felt his disapproval like a slap against my face. "You endanger her," he said to me.

Ness shook his hand off gently. "Choice is a gift. Do not take my gift from me, love."

He blushed. Both at the endearment and the rebuke.

"Come here, Parrish," she said.

I crawled over to her uncertainly. What was she risking?

"Our mind bond still holds. There is no need to drink the juice. You will have to work harder, though, without the hallucinatory aid."

She took my hand in hers and a tingling warmth seeped into every corner of my mind and body.

For the first time I could remember I felt loved and safe. I curled into it like a child.

A small gift for you. But we cannot linger.

Gently the warmth unfurled and we were flying high above The Tert.

I sighed as the warm feeling seeped from me and the clear chill of spirit travel replaced it.

"What do I look for?" I asked her.

"Look for what you can't see."

"Jeez, Ness, less of the cryptic—"

I squinted against the whiteness of the sunlight and into the thousands of dwellings. Gradually I began to pick out landmarks. The border of Dis. The Slag Piles. The long silver snake of the Trans heading for Plastique.

"I see zip."

"Don't try so hard."

Trying again, I took what felt like a breath and let my eyes defocus.

A different Tert revealed itself; a maze of colors, some pulsing, others static—much like the spirit circle that Leesa Tulu had drawn me into. Auras. A welter of browns in most of the villas—people energy.

In other places—bars and dens—the colors bled together. Then some stood out fiery red or sparkling white.

"Shamans," said Ness.

One bright golden arc, beating strong and steady.

"Mei Sheong. I know her."

"And she knows you. The bond is still strong there."

"Mei?" I called.

"What you up to this time, Parrish? Where's my man?"

"Daac is still in Viva, Mei. I need your help."

Sneer. "Got any sort of good reason?"

"The Cabal and Muenos are going to war on the city. I have to find bio-ware to help them." Not strictly true but I had no compunction lying to Mei.

"War. Loyl's gonna be pissed off with the Cabal doing this."

"Billy Myora drives it."

"We should have left him behind in Dis."

"Maybe . . . Will you help?"

"What you looking for?"

"A color . . . different from the rest."

"You'll owe me."

A statement. "OK. What?"

"You stay away from my man."

I thought of Loyl and knew my answer. "Yes. Deal."

Ill-concealed relief. "Let's fly, grrl."

Her mind slid over mine and Ness's like crude oil on seawater and we flew the spirit winds in layers. Viscous hunters.

With the strength of the triple mind The Tert unfolded to us. A map of information energy, its flow marred by tiny whorls of black.

The parasite was spreading.

"Hurry," I told them.

We left the main energy throngs and began to roam the life-empty corridors outside.

Then, finally, the waste.

It was there, buried in swirling shadows of ironstone, the smallest glint of fire in a hostile darkness.

"Are you sure?" Ness said doubtfully.

"I can't see anything," said Mei.

Like an opal best viewed wet and in the sunlight, I tilted our mind-view this way and that until they saw with me. The aquamarine, cobalt and sienna of hidden intelligence.

"Clever," said Mei.

"A jewel." Ness pondered. "Shall we speak with it?"

"Can we?" asked Mei.

"I sense so," she said.

"No." I was curt. "The rest is for me to do."

"Yes," said Ness.

Her tiredness engulfed me—and her wish to be back with Stix. "Perhaps that is best."

"Just don't go messing up this time, Parrish. Remember our deal." Mei peeled off and slid away.

*   *   *

I came out of it to find myself with my head in Ness's lap. Embarrassed, I rolled away and sat up.

She watched me, amused and weary. Stix was already giving her a warm drink and massaging her neck.

His chlorine-colored eyes flashed a clear message. *You have what you want. Now get out.*

I didn't go back to my rooms in case something or someone got in my way. Ness's warning that my time had come had me more than a bit fevered. But then I figured that I had a sufficient supply of painkillers and enough of an arsenal to see this out.

I said good-bye to Glida and Link and hired a strong-looking Pet to take me through the Slag to Plastique. Going back via the Fishertown Trans station wasn't really an option.

As we labored through the myriad of gaudy Mueno alleyways, I went over my mind-map. The bio-ware was somewhere out past the edge of Plastique, across the river, deep into the waste.

When we reached the Plastique border, I told the Pet to stop while I paid toll and purchased a double layer of boot protectors and a dust mask. Wouldn't do for my boots to disintegrate on me before I kicked some bio-ware butt.

The Pet refused to go past the border. I didn't blame it. I didn't like the look that the Plastique toll boys were giving me either.

Plastique punters were a different breed to the rest of The Tert: they didn't care about the world. They cared about the success of their skin cosmetics and their profit margin. No one was singing Parrish Plessis's praises down this way.

I hiked alone toward the edge of the habitable villas, stopping only to derm some of my painkill.

My feet burned now and daggers stabbed my ankles.

My fingers tingled as if they might go numb. My body was doing some weird stuff and it hadn't bothered to share the reason with me. I don't think I really wanted to know, anyway.

Dust, dark mold and cobwebs decorated everything. I checked my compass implant and kept a steady course west toward the waste.

A few minutes from the Plastique bank of the Filder River, the alley I was in suddenly got crowded.

"Parrish. How nice of you to visit."

I tried really hard not to look bothered. "Road. Small world."

"Only when you're on my turf." Road Tedder sucked his smoke like it might give his cadaverous body some energy.

Road figured he had a score to settle with me over the finer details of drug distribution.

I could cop that.

But not now.

Any time but now.

"I'm a bit busy," I said and moved past him down the alley. He followed me to the end, where a dozen pumped-up Plastique types were waiting, spread in a semicircle.

"Bit of overkill, don'cha think, Road?"

"Not for a dangerous media-killer like Parrish Plessis."

I sighed. "The Muenos and the Cabal are planning to go to war against the city, Road. I'm here to do something that will make sure that they stand a chance."

He frowned and lit another smoke from his dogend. His hands and forearms looked jaundiced. "And?"

"Can we settle this later?"

Road laughed then. And coughed some. "They tell me Teece Davey is the one running your affairs. They say you're just the . . . pretty face. I asked them if they'd actually seen what you look like."

I resisted smashing his tobacco-stained teeth. Road Tedder might be the King Provocateur but I was the Queen of "I'm over it." He could even call me grrlie if he got the freak out of my face.

Something of my lack of interest must have penetrated his awareness.

"I'm sure Teece will agree to much more prudent business terms after you are dead," Road said and turned, making his way out through the circle of buff flesh.

The buffs waited obediently for his dramatic exit, but I wasn't so respectful. I jerked the Colt free and pumped out a stream of hot lead. Half of them went down before the magazine jammed.

I dumped the gun and took the closest buff left standing with a wire.

No niceties. Jugular through to vertebrae and twist.

Then I had a second wire out and looping around a hand of the next one, who was fumbling with a pistol.

Good thing about buffs. Too much time spent *building* the bod—not enough time *using* the bod.

I accounted for nearly all of them before the last one got it together to shoot me. I threw a knife at him after I went down.

He fell dead on top of me.

I lay under his warm, bleeding body and wondered how alive I was. I didn't have the energy to move or feel.

Just to wonder.

I wondered lots of things. . . .

What would happen now? Where was Loyl? What would Teece and Honey's baby look like? What was that scraping noise in my ear?

It registered louder than the Apocalypse in the dead-buff quiet.

I inched my head sideways from under the corpse's armpit. Something was moving nearby, sampling flesh with a probe.

I strained to see, intrigued in a detached sort of way.

It capered right up to the dead buff on top of me and scraped mucus samples from inside his mouth.

I held my breath. Could it sense that I was alive?

No. I didn't think so.

But what would a robot like that be doing out here?

Wonder became a trickle of hope.

I began to squirm, trying to shift the dead buff's weight. I rocked and groaned until I got an arm out. Then a leg. The effort hurt my chest and I rested for a while. I still wasn't sure where I'd been shot because so much of me was numb.

The robot scavenger busied itself around the other bodies, taking bits of hair and sticking its probe up their nostrils and in their ears.

When it got to the last one I knew that I had to move or lose sight of it. As it trundled down the alley toward the river, I used whatever strength I had left to heave the stiff off me.

I sat up and stared at the hole in my shirt. Most of the blood was on my shoulder. It seeped blood slowly, not gushing like it should have.

I *should* have bled to death by now.

But I hadn't. Bonus.

Spitting the buff's armpit hair and blood from my mouth, I decided, as before, that it was better not to know why.

With laborious care I unwound the garroting wire from the throat of the first cadaver I'd felled in that way. His head came away from his shoulders, draining fluids all over my boots.

I shuddered and spat some more.

One thing at a time.

The scavenger was disappearing.

I got to my feet and lurched after it.

. The only pain I felt was the burning in my feet and the stabbing in my ankles. My shoulder felt . . . nothing. I just couldn't use it.

Keep going.

I'd clung to that mantra before. Sometimes movement was the only way to keep death at bay.

I made a clumsy job of tailing it but the robot didn't seem to notice me. Designed for only one thing, it scuttled home across a walk-bridge and out onto the wasteland on the other side.

I stopped to rest for a few seconds, and to convince myself that I had enough strength left to manage the climb. The river wavered in my vision, a ripple of dull, noxious water lapping the pylons of the old bridge.

Oxygen had become a priority. I couldn't get enough of it to clear the dots that came and went in front of my eyes.

It seemed safer to crawl, so I set to it. *Hands first, then knees. Hands first, then knees.*

Every so often my hands, wet with blood, slipped out from underneath me and I banged my chin. The water hurt my eyes as well, reflecting a blinding new-summer sun up at me. The heat rose from the waste, warm with smells of decay.

It's just plant rot, I told myself. *Not people.*

But I couldn't get Roo out of my mind. He called to me from the water.

I might have slept for a while on the bridge. It was hard to say.

Consciousness returned only as I began to roll down the other side, my feet sliding over the edge.

I grabbed the railing on instinct, remembering where I was.

Who I was.

Check shoe guards. Get upright. Walk.

I staggered and lurched out onto the waste, direc-
tionless under the sun.

Thirsty now. So thirsty.

Over there. Cool rocks. A place to sit.

I staggered a long way toward the low granite out-
crop, delirious. A crunching noise underfoot.

Roo walked next to me, scratching his head and
arguing.

"Wash your hair, Roo," I told him.

"I said I don't get involved with older women,
boss."

"Wassat got to do with it?" I was mad at him for
not listening. "Wash your damn hair."

"Aww, ease off, boss. Why don'cha ever worry
about the important things? Like that guy."

"What guy?"

"There."

Roo pointed, then walked back toward the water.

"Don't go. Don't." I was crying, wasting water.
"Come back, Roo. I won't hassle you."

"Gahhh."

I glared at the sound. Not Roo. That damn kid had
run off.

Someone else?

Someone else, over there, standing in the shade of
a rock overhang, in front of a dark hole. A small cave
and a small . . . man, hunched shoulders, eyes under
heavy brows, sloping skull, grizzled hair.

Shock jerked me out of the realities that I'd slipped
between. Skeletons littered the dirt around the out-
crop. The crunching underfoot . . . I looked behind
me at what I'd walked across.

A burial ground.

"Who are you?" I whispered.

Squatting down, he beckoned me inside, his yellow
teeth bared and broken.

I shook my head as if to clear it and stepped forward onto sun-hot ironstone.

I had to bend double to enter the cave. He was smaller than me. Much.

I rested again. My eyes slow to adjust, seeing spirals in the dark. Spirals and ghosts. Roo, Wombebe, Jamon. *Dead people never leave you. Never. They hang out, all melancholy, in your mind-corners.*

"Gahhh."

The noise again.

I followed the sound, crawling forward and downward, fingers clawing into the packed-down dirt. The dark was welcome. I shivered in it and began to see shapes other than those in my conscience.

It leveled off into a larger, brighter cave, and another. Joined together by a low passage.

I recognized crude furnishings and worship poles. Food scrapings and the smell of waste. Enough light to see. But coming from where?

The short figure poured water on my head and into my mouth from a muddy puddle that had collected against the wall. The cold bitterness of it stung me and constricted the back of my throat. I coughed and coughed.

Then the man pushed and chivvied me on, into the more distant cave. I felt his sinew and muscle and hair and smelled the scent of a different animal. The smell made me gag again.

He dropped me on the packed dirt in the middle of the smaller cave.

A woman reclined there against the wall, her outsized skull hooked into and supported by a tangle of mismatched mekware that lay scattered around her like offerings to a god. Some of it was older than me; some as spanking new as the gear in King Ban's hide.

Organic tendrils fed back into the ironstone of the cave from her withered brown-skinned body. Around her the rock radiated warmth. Smooth furrows existed where her hands rubbed restlessly.

I couldn't speak—my throat was too dry and sore—only wonder.

"I'm the one you have come to kill."

Brilliance? This clumsy bio-atrocity is Brilliance?

And yet her presence was strong, shimmering around me, sinister and aged.

Amusement crinkled her thick, dark lips.

"Not what you was thinkin', eh, darlin'? See, I'm from the old tribes. *Homo erectus,* you lot called us."

I strained to remember my conversation with the Angel in vreal land. Its story of its origins.

. . . Earth discovered and infected. What satisfaction and relief. The host is most suitable, the WE agree. Strong enough to withstand and not be destroyed. Strong enough to be pushed the next step.

But Homo erectus *had its own survival mechanism. The WE became trapped. . . .*

"That can't be," I finally managed, swallowing between each word.

"Ho, ho—yes, it can. *Anything* can be. I am an original. Survivor of the bloodsucker when it first come here. One of the higher evolved." A rattling laugh. "Like you, I was a freak—one who survived out of balance. That's how I live so long. Mebbe the same will be for you." She rambled on. "Mebbe you're one of my tribe. Come closer. Lemme check your gene code."

I backed away instead.

"How can you be Brilliance?"

"That kid not me."

"I don't understand," I said.

Silence for a bit and then another chuckle. "See, grrl, this is how it goes. Them local tribes bring me all this tek. Works real good in this place." Her broad, slippery hand patted the rocks. "Ironstone. So I go muck in that place—what youse all call it—vreal. I'm not so bored when I there. Met me some hard-working kid—the one youse keep calling Brilliance. I say roll over, kiddo. Let me have a bit o' fun."

Her laugh this time was genuine and rusty. *Big joke.*

The short man wiped a thick, sulfur-stinking paste onto my palm and squashed something that squirmed into it. A worm, long and thin.

"Eat, so you can listen better," the woman ordered. "I don't get to talk with this old throat much."

I swallowed obediently, like a kid, and got a small surge of energy followed by spasming pains in my arms and throat.

"Cabal, youse call them local boys," she said.

"The Cabal *help* you?"

She giggled. "They think me Biami's child. Think I'm dreaming in here. I tell 'em, yeah, I need big tek to dream."

"You've been living in vreal?"

The old female ignored me, rambling on. "My god's a damn grub—a parasite from out there in them dark frozen places."

"It's not a god," I protested.

"You gone broke me and my fun, grrl. Given me one big headache. I gotta regrow all this stuff. Takes time."

I stared at the rock under her skull. The tendrils writhed, growing as I watched. The cave was one large transceiver and she would be back online soon.

"Someone's started spreading the parasite again not far from here in a place called Mo-Vay."

She gave a sniff through broad, crusty nostrils. "That one damn bad place. That woman you dropped in the shit there—Bau? Good job, I say. She knew I was roundabouts here. She set all that stuff goin'. Wanted to stop me havin' fun."

I finally exhaled the breath that I'd been holding. I *hadn't* killed the wrong person—it was just more complicated than that.

And now I had to stop this creature broadcasting—having her fun. If she went back online, then Teece and everyone I knew would perish.

I raised my hand to send my wire slicing through her brain.

That was when I saw it—a dark whorl on my fingers where they gripped the wire.

She rolled her eyes slyly. "Kill me and the net stuff stays dead all right but then you got no clue how to beat the grub. You got the change comin' *now* and I know how to stop it. You can be like me, living on forever." The giggle. "Say, grrlie, what you gonna choose?" she asked.

Roo was back again, hat pulled low. Wombebe hung around his neck.

I wasn't going to let them down again.

I coiled the wire. "You're wrong. See, this time there is no choice."

Marianne de Pierres was born in Western Australia and now lives in Queensland with her husband and three sons. She has a BA in Film and Television and is currently completing a Graduate Certificate of Arts (Writing, Editing and Publishing) at the University of Queensland. Her passions are basketball, books and avocados. She has been actively involved in promoting speculative fiction in Australia and is the co-founder of the Vision Writers Group in Brisbane, and ROR—Writers on the Rise, a critiquing group for professional writers. She was involved in the early planning stages of Clarion South and is a tutor at Envision. You can find out more about her at www.orbitbooks.co.uk and on her Web site: www.mariannedepierres.com.